MW00873702

BOOKS BY KEELY BROOKE KEITH

UNCHARTED
The Land Uncharted
Uncharted Redemption
Uncharted Inheritance
Christmas with the Colburns
Uncharted Hope
Uncharted Journey
Uncharted Destiny
Uncharted Promises
Uncharted Freedom
Uncharted Courage
Uncharted Christmas
Uncharted Grace

UNCHARTED BEGINNINGS
Aboard Providence
Above Rubies
All Things Beautiful

Want to be notified when Keely's next book is available?
Add your name to her list at keelykeith.com/sign-up

Uncharted Grace

KEELY BROOKE KEITH

Edenbrooke
Press

"And on this road to righteousness
Sometimes the climb can be so steep
I may falter in my steps
But never beyond Your reach"

—Rich Mullins, Sometimes by Step, 1993

CHAPTER ONE

January 2031
Summer in the Land

The azure sky spread above the thriving orchard like an unending wealth of promises only Caroline could see. She had never beheld such a limitless sky, at least not since before the haze. That bane was gone from the Land now, and so were the scales from her mind's eye.

She could imagine it all so clearly—the possibilities awaiting her here in Good Springs. The past and the pain and the lies hadn't followed her here. She had denied them passage on the journey, and now anything, everything, was possible.

Even the coastal breeze that rustled the orchard's trees hinted at dreams to come true. In this new village she had a future and the potential of making friends, maybe even finding a soulmate. Glee filled her heart at the thought of a lifelong companion she could trust to the core—even with her family's long-held secret.

Morning sunbeams sparkled on the daylilies' dew, reflecting a thousand glints of hope in the perennial garden bed that bowed before the recently inherited farmhouse—Noah's recently inherited house, to be exact, but he graciously referred to it as *theirs*. Caroline's elder brother wasn't one to claim any possession as his alone, despite the influence of the Land's patriarchal traditions. This inheritance was for *them*, he often said, meaning himself, Caroline, and their younger sister.

Caroline clipped a select few of the golden daylily blossoms, mixed them with purple coneflowers, added wisps of waxy fern, and held the fresh bouquet up to the crisp blue sky to admire the color contrast.

Perfect!

Not only would the perky flowers add much-needed cheer to the drab old house, they would also brighten Lena's day. Though the quiet girl would never admit it to Caroline, she was surely missing the intriguing man she'd met on their journey here, Philip Roberts, the overseer of Falls Creek.

No matter the reason, Caroline found it her duty to nurture her little sister. Lena had never been thrust into a new life before—not to her conscious memory, anyhow. Caroline had spent the two decades since the tragedy protecting her shy sibling from knowing about it, just as she'd been instructed. Those instructions were probably for the best.

After all, the past was called the past because that was where it belonged.

Besides, this relocation differed from what happened to them twenty years ago. This blessed move to Good Springs, this new-to-them house and orchard, this gift of a livelihood was for them—all three of them—to keep for a lifetime. What grace beyond measure!

Noah finally had his own farm to manage, and Caroline and Lena had their own home to maintain. And they wouldn't simply maintain it, if Caroline had anything to say about it—and she certainly did! They would transform it, maybe not into the opulent estate home Mom and Dad had built outside Boston or the tech-heavy condo the family owned in Palm Beach yet only visited once every winter. But it would be something that would have made Mom smile, of that she was determined.

She wiped her dewy fingertips on her muslin apron as she meandered to the back porch with the cheery bouquet. One of the tabby cats that lived on the property rubbed his face against her ankles before she climbed the steps.

"And good morning to you too, sir." She knelt to pass a hand over the tomcat's gray furry spine.

He spun and swatted at the freshly cut flowers.

She chuckled at the frisky cat and lifted the bouquet out of harm's way. "You're going to be easy to name if you keep behaving that way."

Of all the animals that lived on the property, only the dog's name was known. That left them with two well-trained horses, a grouchy milk cow, and a bevy of barn cats to name. Noah said naming the cats was unnecessary, but it sounded like fun to Caroline. All the animals that lived here deserved names because, despite the pretty millwork on the house's gables and the wide-planked flooring that would look incredible with a little T.L.C., it was the animals that made the property feel alive.

The animals and the wildly gorgeous flower garden, that is.

When Uncle Vestal and his long-departed wife were in their prime, they had carefully tended to this place, as their ancestors had for generations—all the way back to the founding Vestal family. It gave her hope that the house could someday feel like home to her too—and maybe even look like something Mom and Dad would have owned—not in scale, but in beauty.

That would take time.

Without Mom's decorator's eye, Dad's bottomless bank accounts, and electricity, this house would be far more rustic than the homes Caroline remembered from childhood.

Still, between her and her siblings, they could make this a charming place to live.

Her eyes lifted to the flaking paint around the upstairs windows. Thread-bare curtains that belonged on the set of a horror movie hung inside the six-over-six glass panes. Uncle Vestal probably hadn't cleaned those windows in years—inside or out. To make this house lovely, it would take every sanding block in the tool shed, every bolt of fabric in the linen cupboards, and every ounce of... where did one procure house paint in Good Springs?

And wallpaper?

And plumbing fixtures?

There was so much she didn't know about home rehabilitation, but she would absolutely find out.

She would trade, barter, and D.I.Y. until her fingers bled and Lena smiled. However she had to make it happen, she would. For them all, but especially for Lena, who had never experienced their former homes the way Caroline and Noah had. Lena didn't even know their old life in America existed—not their true past, anyhow. As the youngest member of the billionaire Engler family, Lena had been a toddler the last time the family vacationed at their cabin in Maine, so she didn't remember it or their Boston house or the beach condo—or Mom and Dad.

And that was the way Caroline and Noah had sworn to keep it.

They couldn't tell Lena they'd spent a lifetime lying to her, but they could make up for it here at their new home in Good Springs.

Two stout *woofs* echoed across the yard.

Caroline paused on the back porch with one hand on the squeaky doorknob and one hand holding the freshly cut flowers. The spunky herding dog named Nipper bound between rows of apple trees and alerted Noah to a wagon turning onto the property. Two men rode on the wagon's bench seat, and the long flatbed behind them was piled high with fertilizer.

Noah jogged to meet the wagon by the barn, and before he reached it, a second wagon turned onto the property.

Caroline waved to the men before stepping into the mudroom. The screen door clattered behind her. "Here comes Noah's helpers for the day."

Lena craned her neck around the kitchen wall, a light brown ringlet dropping in front of her hazel eyes. "Who is it today?"

Caroline wiped her shoes on the mudroom rug. "John Colburn is driving the first wagon. Connor Bradshaw is with him again. Two men are on the second wagon. One looks like the village elder who stopped by on Monday—the man who Noah said owns a big horse farm. Mike?"

"Noah called him Mark." Lena sidled up next to Caroline by the screen door, close enough their arms touched, though the younger woman was two inches shorter. She peered out. "Yes, that is Mark Cotter."

"Who's the man with him?"

Lena shrugged. "I haven't met him."

"You don't *meet* any of them, dearest. I go outside and meet them while you watch from the kitchen window."

Lena's smile curved up on the left side more than the right, just like Mom's had. "And then you kindly give me all the details when you come back inside. The details you remember, that is."

Caroline gave the unfamiliar man a second look. "He's wearing one of those silk neckties I like. What's it called? A cravat? Very classy. He isn't really dressed for farm work, but it's refreshing to see a man with style."

There was no way the man heard her from all the way across the yard, yet at that instant, he faced the house, his hair barely skimming his collar at the back.

Lena ducked away from the screen door.

Caroline gave her a silly wink. "Handsome too, isn't he?"

Her sister dashed up the two steps from the mudroom into the kitchen. "Are you going out to greet them?"

"I would love nothing more, but they are standing near two wagons full of composted manure, and they already have their shovels and wheelbarrows ready. Noah said the haze stunted the younger pear trees. The men are probably here to help spread the fertilizer he needed."

Lena crinkled her petite nose.

Caroline mirrored the gesture. "Exactly."

"If the men stay for lunch, perhaps we should serve it on the lawn by the porch."

"Good idea. Especially after you spent yesterday scrubbing this floor." Caroline whirled past her and found a tall cup for the bouquet. "What do you think of the flowers?"

"Very pretty." Lena pulled a stockpot from the shelf beside the cookstove. "I wasn't concerned about the floor."

"Just about having stinky men in the kitchen?" She arranged the bouquet and sent Lena a sidelong glance. "You would invite them inside despite their morning of spreading fertilizer if the scholarly Mr. Philip Roberts, overseer of Falls Creek and master of dreamy correspondence, were among them."

Lena's skin flushed pink from collar to crown. "Caroline! You promised to keep that a secret." Though she raised her voice, a nervous chuckle took out all the punch. "I've only received one letter from him, and it wasn't *dreamy*. Philip is wise and writes striking prose. Still, I don't want Noah to hear or he might…"

"Act like a protective big brother?"

"Precisely. Philip is older than me and—"

Caroline ignored her sister's lingering blush. "Don't worry about Noah. It's just you and me here." She pointed up. "And the bats in the attic."

"There aren't any bats in the attic."

"Fine, then the rats in the cellar."

"Too many cats on the property to have a rat problem."

Something was different about Lena since they broke their journey in Falls Creek and she connected with Philip Roberts. She sounded more sure of herself than she had back in Northcrest. Maybe it was her correspondence with a gentleman or maybe it was the relief of being out from under Mother Vestal's thumb.

Either way, Caroline thrilled at the prospect of seeing her sweet sister flourish in their new life—for all of them, really—in their new village, new house, new neighbors, and hopefully, some pleasant surprises along the way.

* * *

Lingering notes of laundry soap hung in the air inside the sunlit farmhouse until late afternoon, then the spicy zip of Lena's luscious potato soup took center stage. Caroline's sister made every recipe even better than Mother Vestal had taught them. Cooking suited Lena, just as staying inside the house did.

Not Caroline. She couldn't finish the laundry fast enough this morning so she could carry each sheet and towel from the spin tub to the clothesline, hoping all the while to glimpse the men working in the orchard.

By lunchtime Noah's helpers were gone, but the flapping linens looked as majestic in the sunlight as the sails in the bay had during the yacht regattas of Caroline's childhood.

And later, while Lena peeled potatoes and chopped veggies for dinner, Caroline found dried garlic in the cellar and pulled fresh shallots from the weed-filled vegetable patch for Lena's spicy blend. She volunteered for any chore that might give her a moment out of the house and the possibility of meeting a passerby.

Now the midsummer sun bowed behind the trees to the west, the day's work was done, and her arms were weary from an afternoon of weed-pulling.

Caroline shook out a quilt, filling the parlor with the crisp aroma of fresh laundry. She tri-folded the quilt and covered the sagging cushions of the ancient sofa with it, then repeated the process with a second quilt. As she tucked a soft sheet over the extra bedding, Noah shuffled into the room. "What's all this?"

"I found more blankets in a wardrobe upstairs and washed them. Hopefully, this will make the sofa more comfortable for you to sleep on."

He rubbed a towel over his damp hair. It looked dark brown now, but when it dried, the sun-bleached strands would make him resemble Dad after a summer of sailing. "Thanks, Care-Care."

She hated when he called her that, especially now that his voice was old enough to sound like Dad's, but she loved her brother too much to hurt his feelings by saying anything after all these years. She shifted her gaze to the moonlight that silhouetted the roadside trees beyond the parlor window. "You can take my bed. I don't mind sleeping in Lena's room until you get a mattress for the bedframe upstairs."

"Nah. This works for me." Noah sniffed the air. "What's that smell?"

"There was lilac in the laundry soap."

Even though Lena was bathing in the washroom down the hall, Noah lowered his volume to a near whisper. "It smells like the air freshener in Grandma's minivan? Remember that little candle-shaped thingy that hung from her rearview mirror?"

"Laundry soap smells better than composted manure."

"Hey, I took a bath."

She pointed at the pile of dirty clothes he'd left in the hallway. "Throw those in the mudroom for the night. I'll do the laundry after breakfast tomorrow. Lena and I worked out a chore schedule."

While Noah carried his pungent work clothes to the mudroom, Caroline fluffed two feather pillows and smoothed a blanket on top of the sofa.

He sauntered back into the parlor, finger-combing his hair. "Thanks for doing all this."

She whisked the parlor's velvet drapes closed. "I don't want you sleeping on the sofa for long. I won't be able to do the farm work here if you hurt your back again like last year."

"That was from falling off a ladder, not from sleeping on a couch."

"Regardless, you own the biggest orchard in Good Springs; you should have an actual bed to sleep on."

He shrugged a carefree shoulder. "I don't mind the couch."

Of course, he didn't. Still, she wanted this home as comfortable as possible for him—for all of them—and as soon as possible. That would require having a crop to trade with. "Any predictions for the harvest?"

"The long winter didn't bother the apple trees, so the late summer and autumn varieties are fruiting nicely. Mark Cotter fertilized them during the cold spring for Uncle Vestal. We fertilized the pear trees today, but they will need a little extra attention. The early-winter apples are blossoming now."

"Plenty of bees?"

Noah nodded once.

"How do the cherry trees look?"

A boyish smile brightened his sun-kissed face. "We can probably start picking by late autumn."

She couldn't restrain her smile either. "Lena cleaned and organized all the pans and pots today. Found stacks of pie pans. She said she'll be ready to make your favorite as soon as you bring in the first basket of cherries.

He shook his head. "First week's harvest isn't good for pie. We'll take those fresh to market. The best baking comes from the second week of cherries." He sat on his temporary bed and held up Uncle Vestal's orchard notebook, which he'd been reading since they arrived. "Maybe you and Lena can figure out how to soak some cherries in syrup to taste like the ones that came on top of ice cream sundaes. Remember those?"

He was speaking at a soft volume, but it was too loud for the topic. Caroline gave him the warning look he usually gave her and lifted her chin toward the washroom.

His brow crinkled. "The water's running. She can't hear us. Remember that ice cream place that Dad liked by the marina?"

They would never have a new life in the Land if they didn't let the old one go. She took a step back toward the doorway. "Can we barter something for a new mattress, or should I learn how to stuff one myself?"

He lifted his feet up to the makeshift bed and stretched out his long legs, satisfaction humming his voice. "I told you, this will do for now. You always want to improve everything the second you think there's a problem. What's the hurry?"

The hurry was that she was eager to start her new life, eager to make this house a home, eager to get out into the village and find friends. But if anything made Noah drag his feet, it was an eager person prodding him. She flicked a tired wrist. "Sleeping on the sofa might hurt your back again, that's all."

"Nothing can hurt me here. I'm a property owner." He flexed one bicep muscle. "I'm a superhero now."

"Shhh. I'm glad you're happy to have your own place, but let's not fill it with references from... you know." She checked the washroom door. Still closed. "We made a promise and the Vestals are depending on us to keep it, even if we are finally out of their house."

He sat up straight and pointed the old notebook at her. "No one has been more careful to keep that promise than I have."

She took a second step backward. "I know. You've been awesome about it. Seriously."

"Just remember: before the Vestals rescued us, I made a promise to Mom and Dad that I would take care of you girls." His voice was barely above a whisper. "*That* promise matters most. And if the only way I can provide for us is to stick with the Vestals' story, that is what I have to do."

Slippers scuffed along the hallway, and Noah relaxed into the sofa. He glanced behind Caroline and then directly at her.

She bolstered her voice, flushing out any trace of the emotion she didn't want to bring to their new house. "Right, well, when we have a crop to trade with, a new mattress for you is at the top of the list." She looked back at Lena and smiled. "Isn't Noah a dear for giving us the pleasant bedrooms downstairs?"

Lena beamed at her big brother and offered him their customary hug goodnight. "Yes, quite a dear. Thank you. I adore having my own room."

"That makes it all worthwhile." He kissed the top of Lena's head, then looked at Caroline. "Doesn't it?"

"Of course." One glimpse of her sister's trusting eyes and Caroline's heart thudded with the joyful anticipation of creating the home Lena deserved. "We will all finally have a happy home of our own here, and that makes everything worthwhile."

CHAPTER TWO

Jedidiah Cotter checked his reflection in the glass door of Dr. Lydia Bradshaw's medical supply cabinet. A professional appearance was a patient's first indicator of a physician's competence—whether or not the patient realized it.

He straightened his silken cravat and smoothed his hair as best he could in the scant light that came from Dr. Bradshaw's desk lamp. Sometimes it was unbearably dim in this medical office. His boss's conservation of lamp oil was admirable, but often he wished for a patient to call so he could justify turning up all the lights.

When the construction was completed on the house the village was building for him, he would make sure his medical office would always be brighter than this.

He left his lonely reflection and sat at Dr. Bradshaw's desk. When he had his own office, it would also be far more practical than this dainty space. The people of Good Springs who came to him for healthcare wouldn't find doily-covered side tables, faded cross-stitched samplers on the walls, or flower-filled vases on the windowsills. His patients would receive the same excellent medical care Dr. Lydia Bradshaw provided only without the girly frills.

Not that there was anything wrong with Dr. Bradshaw's style. It was simply that—her style. Jedidiah had his own preferences, and he wanted nothing more than to work in a medical office arranged to his liking, located in his home, under his authority.

And far, far from all ties to his corrupt family back in Stonehill.

No one could have been more ready for the responsibility. He had completed a detailed sketch of his future office's layout, planned his order for the array of medical instruments he would need, and spoken to the printer about creating blank patient charts, which would be more efficient than Dr. Bradshaw's handwritten forms.

Only one factor in his plan was outside his control: when.

When would he be titled and free to manage his own medical practice?

"Soon," Dr. Bradshaw had told him last week. "Very soon, indeed."

He leaned back in the wooden chair at her desk. Though Dr. Bradshaw was doubtlessly a respected professional, her desk shelf was lined with ceramic figurines and bud vases. The display was as unmistakably feminine as her decision-making process, which vacillated between sentimentality and sensibility.

No matter how much he esteemed her professionally, he detested waiting on someone else to decide about his circumstances, especially someone without true authority over his titling. It seemed in Good Springs it was the overseer and the elder council who controlled everything.

Those men had decided Good Springs needed a second doctor. They had selected him as the most eligible candidate. It made more sense that the council—rather than the village's other physician—should pronounce him free to work autonomously.

Then he would finally—finally!—be the master of his life, the captain of his circumstances.

But not yet.

At present, Dr. Bradshaw held the power of his livelihood in her lace-gloved hands.

So often he'd found that the person in authority was usually the least deserving of that power. And the least trustworthy.

Thus far, Dr. Bradshaw seemed faithful to her profession and to her patients. The Good Springs overseer, John Colburn, who happened to be Dr. Bradshaw's father, also seemed forthright. John was training a newcomer to the Land to inherit his place as overseer. And that newcomer happened to be John's son-in-law, Connor Bradshaw.

In Jedidiah's experience, the more family members there were in a circle of power, the less each remained uncorrupted.

But perhaps the Colburn household differed from his family. Perhaps Good Springs differed from Stonehill. Perhaps life here flowed more graciously, more righteously, just as the founders had intended life in the Land to be. He'd read all of their writings, and the life they planned when they left America in the 1860s was the life he longed for.

Which was why he'd left everything he knew in Stonehill—including his influential and idolatrous family—and agreed to settle in Good Springs in a village-supported position as their second physician.

He pushed away from Dr. Bradshaw's desk and perambulated the cozy medical office. The blankets on the patient cot and the knickknacks on her bookshelf were as ladylike as the embellished porcelain cups she used to administer gray leaf.

With his fingertip he traced the flowery vine painted on a teacup. Elegant, but gray leaf tea was a lifesaving medicine, not a beverage for afternoon sipping during a social call.

Come to think of it, since the haze had dissipated around the Land and the sunshine had returned the seasons to their natural rhythm, many of Dr. Bradshaw's office visits seemed more social than medical. Half of the villagers who came to this cottage asked for *Lydia* instead of *Dr. Bradshaw*.

But that wasn't why Jedidiah had moved to Good Springs. He'd been summoned here by the village council not because Dr. Bradshaw lacked professionalism, but because since becoming a mother—and especially during the haze—they felt she had lacked time. Time for her patients as the sole physician in this growing village, time for her family, time for her research, time to breathe.

She needed him to be titled and practicing medicine independently, as much as he did.

A polite tap on the office door broke his thoughts. As he returned the teacup to the medical supply cabinet over the worktable, the door gently opened, letting in the evening song of midsummer crickets.

John Colburn stepped inside but stayed on the mat, his hand still holding the door knob. "Good evening, Jedidiah."

"Good evening, sir."

"Have you spoken to Connor?"

"Not since breakfast."

"Well, we have good news. Since the mill completed the lumber order and Levi has readied the frames ahead of schedule, this Sunday after the church service, the elders will announce a community work day to raise your house—Wednesday, if the weather is fair. All able-bodied men in the village will convene on your property on a scheduled rotation to complete your new home."

It wasn't his property yet, nor was it his home. Not until he was titled. He could live there once it was built, but ownership depended on employment. That had been made clear in their agreement. Maybe this meant his time to be titled was coming soon, just as Dr. Bradshaw had predicted. His eager feet crossed the rug with quick strides. "This is good news, indeed. How long do you think it will take?"

John scratched his trimmed gray beard. "The men will quickly build the frame and roof. The interior will take longer, since Levi is awaiting the pipes from Southpoint. However, when our village works together, we do not waste time."

"Efficiency is commendable." Jedidiah's next question burned in his throat, but as soon as his gaze met that of the overseer's, he looked away. Dr. Bradshaw would announce when it was time for him to be titled, so asking John about it might seem presumptuous, impudent even.

The last thing he wanted to do was irritate his new overseer. If he was going to be a part of this community, he needed to gain and keep the overseer's approval. And Dr. Bradshaw's and Connor's.

Everyone's approval, really.

It was exhausting.

He forced himself to look the older man in his striking blue eyes. "I'm grateful to be welcomed to your fine village, sir."

A soft grin broke the intensity of John's gaze. "It is not my village, son, but the Lord's."

"Of course." He sank his hands into his trouser pockets. "My gratitude remains. I will work on the house with the men when my duties here allow, and if I can be of help to them on their properties, I'm at their service."

John nodded once. "Your help was most appreciated this morning at the Vestal orchard. I know it was your morning to rest." John lifted his chin at the empty patient cot across the room. "Perhaps no one will come to you this evening and you can get some sleep."

"I will be fine."

John scanned the medical office. "I have heard nothing but praise for you among the villagers, Jedidiah. Everyone seems quite impressed, Lydia especially."

"Thank you, sir."

He stepped back across the threshold. "Oh, and there was a letter for you in the messages Revel delivered today."

Jedidiah tapped his vest pocket. "Dr. Bradshaw gave it to me earlier."

"Excellent. Good night, Jedidiah."

"Good night, sir."

Once the door was closed, Jedidiah withdrew the letter from his vest pocket. He smoothed its rumpled corners. A drip of water had smeared his mother's methodical handwriting on the envelope. It must have been raining the day she had someone take it to the Stonehill overseer's house for Revel to collect on his messenger route. She wouldn't have taken it herself. She had plenty of help around the house to scurry at her every request.

Help was her word for them. *Servants* more like. Perhaps even a more severe term would be more accurate, considering they were meagerly compensated and unable to get out of his family's grasp. His father made sure of that. With the household help, with the farm help, and certainly with the workers in his mines.

Jedidiah reached under the desk and stuffed the letter into the front of his satchel, where it would remain unopened. He had escaped Stonehill and owed his family nothing. He would honor them with an annual letter, as he had promised, and nothing more.

He was making his own way now, just like the new family he had helped Mark deliver fertilizer to this morning—the Vestals. There had been a lovely woman on the house's back porch, holding a flower bouquet, wearing a simple day dress and a dazzling smile. A gray cat had pranced around her ankles while she waved to the men. Then she'd disappeared inside.

Was she one of the Vestal siblings? Was she unattached? Was she as friendly as her smile?

Regardless, just like that new-to-Good Springs family, Jedidiah also had a chance to start fresh here, a chance to be part of something bigger than himself—if they let him. Dr. Bradshaw, John Colburn, the elder council, the people of Good Springs. He needed them all to permit him to work, to trust him, to respect him.

The rattle and stomp of an approaching wagon commanded his attention. Though he'd only been working here for two weeks, his six-year apprenticeship with Dr. Ashton in Stonehill had trained his feet to rush toward that sound.

Moonlight draped a rickety wagon that halted between the medical cottage and the back of the Colburn house. A man jumped down from the bench and met Jedidiah at the side of the wagon, where a shaky woman cradled a limp child.

Jedidiah gathered the child into his arms and rushed her into the medical office. His hands sensed pulse and temperature and he listened for her breath while his eyes evaluated coloring and hydration, all before the child's parents had entered the office behind him.

All other thought erased from his mind. Neither official titles nor village approval nor pretty women nor his past or his plans meant anything when a life was at stake. Patient care was everything. This is what he was here for, what he was created for.

CHAPTER THREE

A determined wind whipped the laundry as Caroline pinned the last damp towel to the clothesline. The change in the atmosphere drew her attention to the unsettled morning sky. Stacked clouds to the east were thickening as they rolled in from the sea.

Her belly tingled with delight.

Oh, how she loved a good rainstorm!

The clatter of thunder, the thrill of running for cover, the sharp aroma of ozone in the air.

Despite her gleeful anticipation, the vague echo of her departed parents' voices played in her mind. *A lovely rain shower on land can be a nightmare at sea, and a dangerous storm a sailor's demise.*

And it had been for them.

Those ancient memories had slowly lost their sting over the years. Caroline still worked hard to sift out the pain and to keep all that Mom and Dad had taught her alive within her heart.

Across the property Noah's wooden ladder clattered as he hoisted it over his shoulder and carried it toward the barn. He wore his leather work gloves and had his long-handled pruners tucked through his toolbelt. The urgency in his steps made Caroline regret hanging the wet laundry outside. If Noah was hurrying out of the orchard, those clouds would indeed deliver on their threat.

Dad had always said: *When the sky speaks, a smart sailor listens.*

Nipper was close at Noah's heels, yapping as if his new owner needed herding rather than companionship. The pulsing breeze swished through the acres of fruit trees, filling the farm with a whirl of sounds that muffled the milk cow's bellow and horses' nickers coming from the barn.

Caroline gripped the clothesline, briefly stilling its bounce. If the encroaching clouds stayed for the day, the morning wash would never dry out here. She sighed and unpinned her laundry, sidestepping the fickle gray tomcat that wove between her feet. "We'll have to find somewhere to hang this in the house to dry. Perhaps the upstairs hallway will work. What do you think, Winston?"

The cat ignored his new name but responded to Caroline's voice with a half-purr, half-meow and followed her up the porch steps. That was new.

She opened the screen door for them both. "Want to enjoy the storm from the comfort of the house with me?"

The cat turned around, darted away through the porch railing, and dashed down to the cellar.

"I guess not. Suit yourself, Winston."

Before she closed the door, voices murmured from the side yard. She set the heavy laundry basket on the mudroom floor and stepped back out into the wind. "Hello?"

An auburn twenty-something no taller than Lena shepherded two small children around the garden's edge. The woman's green eyes shone like polished jade as she spotted Caroline. "Hello, there. It's our day to bring your family some provisions. I'm Bette Owens from next door." She held a little girl's hand in her left and a covered basket in her right. "We brought eggs from our hens. This should last your family a week."

"Thank you very much." Caroline met her at the bottom of the steps, grateful for the fresh food the villagers were bringing daily but wishing it wasn't necessary at the same time. "You're too kind, Mrs. Owens."

"Call me Bette, please. Mrs. Owens is my mother-in-law, and she'll go by nothing less."

Caroline almost laughed, but wasn't sure if Bette was joking. She offered a smile instead. "I'm Caroline—" she almost added *Engler* but stopped her mouth, accustomed to its yearning to say her real surname. "My sister, Lena, is inside. And my brother, Noah, is in the barn."

Bette beamed. "It's so nice to have new neighbors— young neighbors. Not that we didn't adore your uncle, God rest his soul, and the late Mrs. Vestal too." She lifted the little girl's hand in hers. "This is my daughter, Josie. Sweetie, say hello to Miss Vestal."

"I prefer Caroline."

The dark-haired child buried her face in her mother's skirt. The pink ribbons streaming from her thin braids flapped in the wind.

Caroline smiled at her, even though the little girl wasn't looking. "Hello, Josie. It's nice to meet you."

Bette allowed her timid daughter to stay tucked against her legs, just as Caroline had let Lena hide in her skirt when she was that little. "How old is Josie?"

"She just turned four." Bette pointed at the young boy who had wandered to the cellar steps to pet Winston. "That's my son, Simon. He's six."

The boy shot an angry look at his mother. His hair was just as red and his eyes just as green as hers, but his voice was full of fire. "No, I'm sixteen."

Bette gave Caroline an apologetic look and spoke quietly. "My husband died last year. Simon has become quite contrary since he lost his father."

A surge of remembrance tightened Caroline's throat. "I'm sorry for your loss."

The young mother kept her voice down. "It's a whole different life, raising two children alone. I can handle it with the Lord's help, but I worry about my son sometimes. He admired his father so."

"I understand." Caroline swallowed her old friend Grief before it could join the conversation, then she held up the egg basket. "My sister will be thrilled for your gift. She does all our cooking, and we don't have chickens yet. I'm not even sure how many hens we should get. There were chickens at the Vestal farm back in Northcrest, of course, but their keep wasn't my chore." More like their adoptive older brother, Eli, didn't let them near *his* chickens. Or *his* horses. Or *his* anything, especially once he was married and Father transferred the farm management to him. "I know very little about keeping chickens."

Bette's smile returned. "Oh, I do enjoy keeping a flock. We have over thirty hens. Jack," her eyes darkened briefly, "my late husband, built a beautiful hen house beyond our cottage. He said the chickens were mine, since nothing else on the property was really mine. It will all go directly from Mr. Owens to Simon one day. Never was Jack's, so it never was mine." She cleared her throat then lifted her chin toward the Owens's property, though none of the buildings were visible from here. "You should come by the cottage sometime. I'll show you my coop."

"I would like that very much. Uncle Vestal built a coop between the barn and the orchard. It's empty at present." She didn't want it to stay that way for long. If they had several laying hens, they wouldn't have to trade for eggs, let alone be given food by widowed neighbors. She returned Bette's smile, wishing she had something more to offer her new friend. "Perhaps you might give me some tips on starting my own flock when the time comes."

Bette patted her arm. "It would be my pleasure. Well, we best move along. These two are spending the day at my friend's house in the village. She and another woman and I all take a turn each week on Fridays watching the children. Thus, each mother has a quiet day once every third week. Today is my day to myself."

"Sounds wonderful. How will you spend it?"

"Making hats. That's my trade—learned from my parents. Straw summer hats are in demand since the weather has warmed. My inventory will go quickly at the market tomorrow. I can make them twice as fast when I'm alone." She took Simon's hand and pulled him away from the cat. "Hopefully, we can beat the rain to town. Good day, Caroline. It was a pleasure to meet you."

Caroline gave the sky a quick check. "Do you have far to walk?"

Bette scooped Josie onto her hip and tossed her voice over her shoulder to Caroline. "It's about a mile to their house in the center of the village."

"Take care. It was lovely to meet you." Caroline called over the wind, "And thank you for the eggs!"

The breeze caught the edge of the cheesecloth covering the basket in Caroline's hands. She peeked inside: at least three dozen eggs, some brown, some white, a few speckled, attesting to the diversity of Bette's beloved flock.

The wind susurrated through the trees as she watched Bette and her children scurry down the road toward the village. If only she had a car, she could traverse the distance in a matter of minutes.

But there were no cars in the Land.

Caroline looked to the north where Bette's in-laws' property spread out of sight. Surely the Owens family had a buggy or even a small buckboard for trips into the village. Maybe they did, but Bette couldn't handle the horse. Or maybe they didn't allow Bette to use their wagon. Recalling Bette's tone when she mentioned Mrs. Owens, the latter seemed plausible.

As Caroline climbed the porch steps, she glanced back at Noah's newly inherited barn, with its row of horse stalls, spacious storage rooms, and high hay loft. Noah had parked his long covered wagon inside the barn when they arrived six days ago, and there it remained. It was a rickety hand-me-down from Father and Mother Vestal. Its cover required constant mending, and it threatened to lose a wheel no matter how many bolts Noah tightened or how many joints he greased. At least Father had given them some sort of transportation when he sent them to Good Springs.

The two horses Noah inherited here gave him a total of four, so they could all ride horseback if they had to go somewhere for some reason, and had a horse to spare.

Once they had fresh produce to trade at the market, Noah would need to take the wagon into the village on Saturdays.

As Caroline opened the screen door, the wind pushed it wide with a bang, causing Lena to jolt. She closed it behind Caroline. "Who was that?"

"Bette Owens and her two children, Josie and Simon. Bette lives in a cottage on her in-laws' property next door. Little Simon is to inherit it all one day. Josie seems sweet but shy, like you."

Lena reached for the basket. "What's in this?"

"See for yourself." She handed off the basket and hurried to the kitchen window to check if her new friend was still visible on the road. "Bette's husband, Jack, passed away. It traumatized Simon."

Lena lifted the cheesecloth from the basket. "Gracious! That's the most eggs I've seen since Eli used to bring them in from his coop."

"And he would set his egg basket on the kitchen counter and say only Rilla could touch them."

"Well, she was his wife."

"I still can't believe Mother made that woman *the lady of the house* as soon as Eli got married."

Lena raised her eyebrows and tilted her head. "You said once we left Northcrest you wouldn't grumble about it anymore."

"You're right. I'm sorry." No sooner had the words come out of her mouth and a low rumble vibrated the floorboards. Her stomach fluttered with excitement. "Thunder!"

She left Lena with the bounty of eggs and dashed into the parlor window for a better view of the road. Bette and her kids were out of sight. The fun of the approaching storm was smothered by worry for the young mother alone on the road with little children, trying desperately to walk a mile to a friend's house and a mile home before the rain started. Then, after a few hours of work, she would have to make the walk again to pick them up.

If only Caroline had a way to help them. Noah's wagon was too difficult to ready by herself and too rickety to trust, especially with children. Images of her childhood bicycles and scooters played in her mind. She'd seen strollers—baby prams mostly—here in the Land, but Josie and Simon were too big for that. Bette needed some sort of transportation on days like this, but Caroline had no way of helping her.

Nothing rankled more than seeing a need and not being able to fill it.

A delicious clap of thunder rattled the house. Noah was safely in the barn, and the animals too. Lena was in the kitchen, happily adjusting her meal plans to include the fresh eggs. All was well with their family, but not everyone was safe at the moment.

Caroline lowered herself to the sofa and leaned over its back to stare outside. The land across the road had been cleared before they moved here, and now stacks of lumber frames waited to be raised. The same man who she'd seen hammering those frames all week had been here early this morning, covering the remaining lumber with a black tarp. The locals must have been better at timing a coming storm than she was.

No one was visible on the road in either direction at the moment, but the storm's first raindrops were stirring the dirt. Bette and her children were probably racing to the village, soon to be sopping wet and miserable.

* * *

Jedidiah angled the brim of his hat to keep the rain off his face so he could unload wooden boxes from the Colburns' wagon. He stacked the last crate beside the covered lumber pile on the land that John and Connor were calling *Jedidiah's property*. He still dared not claim it as his own until his title was confirmed by the elder council.

That was the deal. He knew from watching his father conduct business never to take an arrangement for granted until a deal was done. This arrangement with the Good Springs elder council differed greatly from the deals his father made with unsuspecting workers back home.

So long as the elder council here was swift in granting Jedidiah his medical title, he wouldn't have to worry about ever going back to his father's house— whitewashed tomb that it was.

Connor carried a folded oilcloth to the supply crates. "Here, take this end."

Jedidiah pinched the coated fabric's edges and helped Connor cover the boxes of brackets and nails and fittings. "Sorry, I couldn't get out of the office to handle this before the rain started."

Connor tilted his head as he adjusted the cloth and water streamed from his hat brim. "If I can land an aircraft on a pitching platform in the middle of a typhoon, I can unload building supplies in a little rain."

Jedidiah didn't need Connor to define those words for him to understand his overall meaning. Since coming to work in the medical cottage with Dr. Bradshaw, Jedidiah had eaten many meals at the Colburn family table where

Connor spoke about his life before arriving in the Land. Still, he didn't understand what exactly Connor's former occupation as an *aviator* was, nor how the flying machines he spoke of could stay aloft in the sky, nor what a *platform* was, nor the purpose of the electronic gadgets he mentioned.

Nor did he care.

If the topic wasn't medicine, it didn't pique his interest.

But if he wanted the community to accept him as one of their own—especially the council, which included this jovial man from outside the Land—he had to try. He tucked the edges of the oilcloth under the crates and secured it with a few loose bricks, then looked to the east. "That should hold it for now. I'll come back to check on everything after my shift in the medical cottage. The clouds don't look too fierce."

Instead of checking the sky or hurrying back to the wagon, Connor anchored his thumbs in his belt loops and surveyed the building site. "The men cleared out a full acre for you, so you'll have room for a stable and a horse. And there's space to build an addition onto the house when you have a family." He turned back to Jedidiah and raised a thick, black brow. "If you have a family, that is. Do you have a lady friend back home, waiting to move out here once you're titled?"

It was not the question he was expecting from Connor. Maybe from the village's aged matchmakers, but not from Connor. "No. No lady friend back home. Why? Have there been… inquiries?"

Connor's stout laugh rose above the distant thunder. "Nope. But there will be once you have a house." He waved a hand for Jedidiah to follow him back to the wagon. "Just have a polite response ready for when the well-meaning villagers try to set you up with an underaged niece or a neighbor's babysitter or some undateable cousin."

He might not understand Connor's past, but he appreciated anyone with an honest sense of humor. He chuckled as he closed the wagon gate, only looking away from Connor's half-grin long enough to secure the latches. "Did that happen to you after you arrived in the Land?"

Connor nodded once. "All the time, before I was engaged to Lydia."

Jedidiah hadn't been drawn to the women in Stonehill. Or perhaps they hadn't been drawn to him. Being the second son of the village's chief employer, he'd watched his elder brother, Henry, enjoy the fairer sex's attention. But no one involved was sincere.

If Henry could have gotten away with it, he would have built a harem to rival Solomon's. But even with their father's powerful hold on Stonehill, the village overseer had his limits. Besides, the women who admired Henry only wanted the power his inheritance would bring.

Maybe that was why Jedidiah held little hope of finding genuine love and having his own family. People weren't genuine.

As Connor drove the wagon toward the road, the tri-colored stray cat Jedidiah had spotted here yesterday slinked from under the lumber pile's cover. So she did live here. A twinge of joyful anticipation briefly made him feel like a young boy again.

With her pregnant belly hanging low, the curious cat stalked over to the newly deposited building supplies and sniffed around the oilcloth as if hoping a snack had been left along with the boxes. Jedidiah would bring something for her next time. He certainly knew the feeling of being a stray. And once the house was complete, it would be nice to have a cat around the place.

The wagon swayed as they rolled from the cleared property to the dirt road. Across the road the Vestal siblings' prim two-story farm house looked as old and proud as the tales of the Land's founders. Its gables were straight and sturdy, but in need of fresh paint. The threadbare curtains that had hung limply inside the upstairs windows yesterday morning were gone now. The window sashes were halfway up, and a figure moved about inside one room. Perhaps it was that of the lovely woman he'd seen on the porch when he'd gone with Mark to help the orchard's new owner spread fertilizer. That woman had worn an apron over her day dress and carried a handful of garden flowers, making her look like a schoolbook drawing of a Renaissance-era maiden. But her smile and wave had proclaimed confidence beyond any maiden.

Was that her he just saw pass the clouded window?

Raindrops pelted his hat as he watched the window until the house was out of view.

CHAPTER FOUR

By afternoon, the flush of rain ebbed to a steady drizzle. The morning's damp laundry hung from a makeshift clothesline strung through the upstairs hallway. The towels were still damp but stiffened from the breeze that circulated through the half-open upstairs windows.

With her morning chores completed and the lunch dishes washed, Caroline had the afternoon to tackle the upstairs rooms—or to make a plan for how to tackle them, at least. Noah needed a bedroom and a proper bed first, and he deserved the biggest room in the house. After all, this was technically *his* house.

She paced to the end of the upstairs hallway to the largest bedroom, determined to conquer it for her brother. The door creaked on its heavy hinge when she swung it open. Dusty sheets covered the heirloom furniture. The sleeping floorboards awoke beneath her feet as she crossed to the west-facing window and stepped over the pile of tattered curtains she'd removed last night. A film of neglect clouded the windowpanes. She inched the window up higher to let more of the breeze in.

Drizzle still misted the flower garden below, the road in front of the property, and the empty lot beyond. Being in a room no one had lived in for decades gave her the creeps, but from the window she had a clear view of the puddle-dotted road. Noah would appreciate this view, not for the road but for the sunsets on fair days.

Just as his orchard surely appreciated today's rain.

She gripped the corners of a sheet that covered a narrow chest of drawers and folded it to prevent the dust from puffing into an unbreathable plume. Her fingers traced a carved leaf pattern on the dresser's edge. The nature design would suit Noah. Swiping a damp cloth over the wood unveiled its beautiful grain, and rubbing a soap bar along the drawer grooves silenced their squeak.

The rag bundle tied to the tip of her broom handle helped clear the cobwebs from the cornice molding and baseboards. The exquisite carvings of the trim throughout the house proved the orchard could and would provide a comfortable living for them as it had for previous generations. No doubt once Noah filled the harvest crates and Lena amassed her inventory of jams and preserves, Caroline could trade every last bushel and jar at the village market. The three of them would make an unbeatable business team.

But first, she had to get this house livable before Noah aggravated his back injury by sleeping on the sofa or Lena realized she wanted to cook for a family of her own and not her two older siblings for the rest of her life. Thank goodness the overseer of Falls Creek lived too far away to be a temptation because even a modest parsonage might be more appealing to Lena than this house in its present condition.

But its days of neglect were over.

A rolled-up rug towered in the corner behind the bedroom door. She wiped the dust from its thick edges, wishing she had a vacuum cleaner like the ones the maids used at their Boston house. After shifting the empty bedframe to the edge of the room, she unrolled the wide rug. Its chunky weave was nothing like the carpets back home, yet its intricately detailed leaf pattern and muted colors gave the room equal bursts of masculinity and hominess.

It would be perfect for Noah.

Between every chore, Caroline checked the road for Bette. At half past four the laundry was still damp, the drizzle was still falling, and she still hadn't seen her new friend make the trip back to the village to collect her children. Maybe Bette had passed by while she was scrubbing or dusting or hefting the bedframe atop the centered rug in the now spotless room.

Even if Bette and the kids made it safely home—which they likely already had—the whole situation left a queasy guilt in the bottom of Caroline's stomach. Surely there was something she could do for the sweet widow next door.

She swiped the escapee strands of hair off her sweaty forehead and piled the dirty rags outside the bedroom door to add to tomorrow's laundry, then stood back to survey the result of her hard work. The room was ready, save for the bed. She'd done all she could do until they had a mattress for Noah. After dinner, she would bring him up here to show him his new room.

Pride at the shining dresser, the washed walls, and the homey rug delighted her heart. Maybe she should show him now. He was probably just doing odd chores in the barn while it rained anyway. Ten minutes in the house to see what she'd done for him wouldn't interrupt his day too much. How pleased he would be at the pleasant surprise!

She dashed downstairs and passed Lena on her way through the kitchen. "Go look at the room."

"What room?"

"Upstairs. The big one on the end. It's going to be Noah's. The door is open. Just go look at what I did."

Lena matched Caroline's excited grin, then brushed her flour-covered palms together over the sink and hurried up the stairs. Without waiting to hear her sister's reaction, Caroline tugged on her work boots, tied on her rain bonnet, and marched to the barn.

The mist dampened her hands as she held them out before her. Sweet summer drizzle!

Winston sprang from the cellar steps and followed her, not minding the mist on his fur but weaving around the puddles. When they reached the open barn door, the cat launched ahead of her toward the back storage rooms, disappearing into the shadows.

She lost sight of him but found Noah under the low light of an oil lantern. He was leaning over a workbench, his fingertips blackened with grease. His wind-tossed hair and his stiff posture while he worked reminded her of Dad.

"Got the sails mended yet, skipper?"

"Nope. No sails for me these days." A faint grin gave a glimpse of his orthodontically straightened teeth. Thank goodness, Mom had the foresight to have his braces removed before they left to sail around the world. "Only pruners and shears and harvesting nets."

"What have you been doing in here all afternoon?"

He lifted his chin at a rack of shining farm implements. "Oiling some of Uncle Vestal's old tools."

She glanced at his work. "Nice job. Now, come see what I did."

He held up two dirty hands. "Can it wait till I'm done here, Care-Care?"

She tossed him a shop rag. "It won't take ten minutes."

"Lena doesn't want me traipsing through her kitchen like this," he pointed at his dirt-caked shoes, "and I want her to have control over her own space for once in her life."

"Just leave your boots in the mudroom and don't touch anything."

"You're going to get me into trouble. Straight to bed with no dessert like Nanny used to threaten."

She tugged on his elbow and laughed. "Lena isn't cruel like that, but I will be if you say no. So come on. You're going to love your surprise."

He dropped the rag on his workbench. "*My* surprise?"

"That's right. Your—"

"Hello?" A baritone voice called from out front of the barn. "Hello in there? Mr. Vestal?"

"Coming," Noah replied as he strode to the barn's open doors. "Mr. Colburn. It's good to see you again."

A broad-shouldered silhouette moved in the filtered light outside the doorway. The overseer stood beside his horse, reins in hand and brimmed hat tipped forward. He met Noah under the barn's eave. "I was passing by and thought I might check on Good Springs' newest residents. Did the rain wash away the fertilizer we spread yesterday?"

While Noah answered him, dried hay crinkled under Caroline's boots as she crossed the barn to greet their visitor.

She hadn't spoken to John Colburn since they first arrived in the village last week, and she'd been too excited about their new home to pay much attention when he gave Noah the deed and directions to the property.

When the middle-aged man spotted Caroline approaching the doorway, he removed his dew-speckled hat. "Good afternoon, Miss Vestal."

"Good afternoon, sir. Do call me Caroline. Wonderful rain shower this morning, was it not?"

John's gaze had already returned to Noah, but instantly snapped back to her. "Yes, I supposed it was." Amusement warmed his striking eyes. The black-rimmed irises were the sort of blue she remembered seeing in the clear sky above the harbor on crisp New England autumn days.

Though she wanted to talk more, to ask all about John's family and life and the village and the people of Good Springs, she kept her mouth closed and her feet in their expected place—a pace behind her brother—while the men talked business, as Mother had taught her after their adoption.

Just because Caroline had learned how to behave and speak to blend into society in the Land didn't mean she had to like it.

But she would do whatever she must for Noah and Lena, to keep their new home and to live their lives peacefully and abundantly in the Land while the rest of the world suffered from war, famine, disease, and nuclear fallout.

At least that was what she and Noah surmised had happened from the vague third-hand details they heard from the accounts that had circulated the villages since Connor Bradshaw's arrival several years ago.

If only they could have an honest conversation with the former naval aviator. What had happened to the outside world during the past twenty years? Why was the United States now called the *Unified States*?

No! Move forward in life, not backward. She had a purpose in this place—not just to sustain a living in Good Springs, but to be a part of the community. Her skin tingled with anticipation as she imagined the friends, the fun, the being included. Maybe she could do something significant for the village, maybe make the difference in people's lives she'd always dreamed of making.

She couldn't look away from the overseer's eyes while he and Noah talked about harvest schedules and how the workers would rotate among the villages' farms. Their plans only mattered to Caroline because it meant an orchard full of people would be here several times this autumn. While Noah got the help he needed to harvest— help he would return to the other village farms—Caroline and Lena could serve an outdoor buffet lunch and make cider and she could get to know more people and hear their stories.

John turned his attention to her. "Do you agree, Caroline?"

She shook the fantasies of social plans and cheery buffets from her mind. "Agree with what, sir?"

He chuckled a short laugh that blended fatherly kindness with deep understanding. "You are much like my Bethany." He looked at Noah. "My youngest daughter has always been easily distracted and is even more so now that she is expecting twins."

Having someone other than her siblings say she was similar to anyone thrilled Caroline to the core. She sidestepped Noah. "Mr. Colburn, would you like to join us for dinner this evening?"

He flicked a glance at Noah, whose brow was furrowed at Caroline.

She ignored their surprise but corrected her only misstep. "You and Mrs. Colburn, of course. Our sister, Lena, is a wonderful cook. She considers it her duty, or rather, her mission in life, to create heavenly dishes out of the simplest ingredients."

Noah tried to stop her. "Caroline—"

"Not that the food we've been so generously blessed with over the past week by our new neighbors here isn't heavenly, of course. We're most appreciative of all we've been given."

"Caroline—"

Despite Noah's embarrassment, she touched John's forearm to keep his attention. "Our gratitude is precisely why we would be most honored to welcome you and Mrs. Colburn to our humble table."

"Thank you, Caroline, but not tonight. Mrs. Colburn went to Heaven many years ago, and I already have plans for this evening." John patted her hand once, then removed it with the rare skill of setting boundaries while not insulting her eagerness. He'd met her type before.

Noah finally exhaled, but Caroline didn't take her eyes off the overseer. "Another day, perhaps?"

A faint smile moved his short gray beard. "Another day." He looked at Noah. "Will your household be attending church this Sunday?"

Noah nodded. "We would have been there last Sunday, but my sisters were tired from our journey to Good Springs."

"I understand. We look forward to seeing you there. The bell rings two hours after sunrise."

A stirring she'd never felt rushed through Caroline's system. It made her want to save her seat in the chapel right now and also to remove herself from John's intense gaze and hide, lest he see right through her. The reasonable thing to do was somewhere in between. She took a small step backward. "Good day, Mr. Colburn."

He nodded politely, but his soul-bearing eyes held no pretense. "Good day, Miss Caroline."

She left her embarrassed brother in the overseer's powerful presence and marched through the barn, past the workbench and horse stalls, and into the dimly lit storage area at the back. "Winston? Are you back here, kitty?"

The cat didn't respond to her calls nor to her kissy noises, so she flung the barn's back door open, letting muted afternoon light and the sweet orchard breeze into the barn. "Winston? Kitty-kitty?"

A meow, then a clatter, then a sharp thud roused the horses in their nearby stalls.

Caroline inched toward the noise in a dark storage area that was stacked high with barrels and empty fruit stacking crates and rusted farm implements. "Winston?"

While her eyes searched the rafters above a tall clump of equipment covered with a frayed tarpaulin, something moved against her stockinged legs. She jumped back a half-step before realizing it was the cat.

Blowing out the extra air she'd sucked in, she bent to stroke him. "Oh, Winston. What are you doing back here? Hm? Did you find a mouse?"

The cat meowed once and dashed away, keeping the conversation brief, just like everyone else she'd met in Good Springs thus far. That would not deter her from making friends of the cat, nor of the neighbors, nor of the overseer, nor anyone else she met.

As she followed the cat out of the storage area, something about the bulbous stack under the hay-speckled tarp intrigued her. She leaned around the corner to check the barn entrance. Noah was walking back inside and John Colburn was riding away. She was already covered in filth from a day of cleaning Noah's new room. Might as well have a peek under the cover.

A wheel smiled at her from the ground, so she peeled the tarp up higher. The sturdy metal wheel hugged an axle, which was attached to a solid wooden frame. No signs of rot, so probably gray leaf wood. She lifted the cover higher and there waited the thick, multi-layered leather cover of a delightfully stylish buggy.

"Uncle Vestal drove a buggy?"

Overflowing storage boxes filled the floorboard and also the back seat and the cushioned driver's bench. Fencing material and feed sacks covered the tarp, but the buggy's top didn't sag under the weight.

Whoever built this vehicle had built it to last.

Maybe it had been waiting for her all this time. She didn't have a crafting skill such as hat-making like Bette, and no one would barter for her kitchen creations like they would for Lena's, but with a smart little buggy, she could start a taxi and delivery service and trade for the materials she needed to transform the old house into the home her siblings deserved.

And she would certainly get to know people as she drove them throughout her new village. Imagine the conversations! The friendships!

She ran her fingertips along the dusty wheel. It would take effort to clean and ready the buggy, and it belonged to Noah, but she may have just uncovered an answer to her prayer.

* * *

Both of Caroline's siblings stared at her with mouths agape and eyes wide, both with a forkful of food hovering outside their surprised lips. With those expressions, they looked at her more like their adoptive family in Northcrest used to than like Englers. Mother and Father Vestal had always told Caroline to stay home, to stay quiet. To mind her own business. They would have choked on the idea of her starting a business.

Mom and Dad, however, had always encouraged her in all her young entrepreneurial ideas. They supported her when she tried to sell lemonade and to sell her made-in-kindergarten crafts online and to start a neighborhood dog-walking service.

Of course, her grandma had made the one and only purchase from her online store. And since several acres of landscaped grounds hid their palatial home behind an ornate security gate, the public never saw her lemonade stand. Nanny had kindly bought a cup with her pocket change and then helped her take down the sign, fold up the card table, and stash the jugs of untouched lemonade in the pool house refrigerator.

And with the nearest neighbor living in their own gated mansion, her naive seven-year-old self could only slip her handmade pet sitting business cards to the landscaping crew, but none of them had a dog she could walk.

She would honor that enthusiastic little girl by pressing on where past dreams had fallen flat.

Undeterred by her siblings' reactions, she elaborated on her plans. "I was thinking after we go to the market tomorrow morning, I'll unbury the buggy and clean it up to have it ready for church on Sunday." She smiled at Lena. "Wouldn't that be lovely to ride to church in a covered buggy?"

Lena looked at Noah and chewed her food instead of answering Caroline.

He lowered his fork to his plate and gave Caroline a you-know-better look. "A taxi service? Really, Caroline? Here?"

"Sure. Just like in the old storybook Mother Vestal had." She pinched off a corner of the egg bread Lena baked this afternoon. "Besides, the river boats go up and down the rivers and barter for their service, which we appreciated on our journey south. It cut two days off our trip. I'm sure people would be very happy to swap something for a ride to an appointment in the village on a blustery day. Take Bette, for instance. She told me that two Fridays out of three she walks her small children to a friend's house so she can have a day alone to work. Today, she had to walk in the rain."

Noah slowly sipped from his water cup and glared at her over its top rim. "Walking to town in the rain might be inconvenient, but people are accustomed to it. If they didn't like it, they would drive their own buggies."

"Most people don't have one. I only ever saw two in Northcrest."

"Their wagon, then. I imagine every family here has something to drive when the need arises."

She shook her head, mouth too full to speak.

"Then they prefer to walk or ride horseback. Either way, no one will barter for buggy rides."

She ignored his naysaying. "Bette has a thriving chicken flock and knows all about keeping them. She is willing to teach me, but we don't have any chickens. I could offer her a trade. I would drive her children to town on those Fridays and she would give us a starter flock of laying hens."

The corners of Lena's surprised eyes turned up with delight. "Fresh eggs whenever we want them? I could preserve dozens for the winter months when the hens don't lay."

Noah upturned a hand. "Caroline, we don't know how people do things here."

She raised an eyebrow at him. "Here in the Land?"

Lena was none the wiser, but Noah knew exactly what she meant. He flattened his tone. "Here in Good Springs. There was a reason Mother was terrified of gossip in Northcrest. She always said if the wrong church lady took offense with a particular family, the rumors would ruin their livelihood."

Caroline let her weary eyes roll. "How?"

"Accusations get people removed from the church. No church, no community. No community," he pointed a thick finger at the window, "no help to harvest an orchard that size."

"So driving a sweet widow's children to their friend's house might offend some busybody that may or may not exist here?"

"That's the point: we don't know who exists here or what the local culture will tolerate. All I know is John Colburn is including me in the harvest schedule for the village, which means I will have help when it's picking time. We can't afford to offend the wrong people, especially our first year here."

She shrugged. "We won't. I won't. That's what you're worried about, isn't it? You're acting just like

Mother Vestal. Haven't I proven I know how to behave to keep from—"

"How about the way you behaved with John today?"

"That? I was just being friendly."

"When you get excited to meet people, you forget—"

"Please, both of you." Lena's soft voice broke their elevated tones. "Please don't argue."

Noah shot Caroline a silencing glare. "We aren't arguing."

There was no point in trying to make the house beautiful for her family if her plan to achieve that upset them. The dining chair's old wooden slats creaked when she slumped her shoulders against it. "I just want to do something—to produce something—of value. Something that will freshen this old house while you," she pointed at Noah, "are working hard to make the orchard profitable. And while you," she pointed at Lena, "are keeping us alive with your incredible cooking." She took another bite of the bread. "This is scrumptious, by the way."

Now it was her turn to give Noah a look. "It's important to me. Yes, I want to meet people, but mostly I want to do this for us… to barter until the harvest comes in so we can have a mattress for your bed and new faucet handles for the bath. Little things like that will make this place more comfortable for all of us. But, it's your buggy in your barn on your property, so, according to tradition, Lena and I need your approval to do, well, anything—"

"Don't be like that. The Land's traditions place as much responsibility on me as they do restrictions on you girls. I'm simply doing what I'm supposed to do, Care-Care."

He rarely used her childhood nickname in front of Lena. Maybe she was getting through to him. She leaned forward, planting her elbows on the table in a way neither her mom nor her adoptive mother would have permitted. "Noah, I'm capable of more than laundry and dusting and mopping. I'll keep doing those chores, of course, but I can do more. Let me take the buggy and see if I can use it to earn a few supplies that will make the house better for us."

A flash of empathy softened his eyes. He stared at his plate and shoveled another forkful of mashed potatoes into his mouth. He didn't speak while he ate, nor did he look up.

Lena's gaze bounced between them.

Caroline met her sister's anxious eyes and gave her a half-grin and a brow wiggle—their secret smile that meant everything would be all right.

Lena returned the faint brow wiggle and waited with her while Noah thought and ate.

What man could make a decision until he'd thought, and what man could think until he'd eaten?

Finally, after Noah's bread sopped up the last of the pan gravy from his plate, he leaned back in his chair and crossed his work-toned arms over his chest. "You can't leave your chores for Lena to do while you go taxiing people around the village."

"I won't."

"Because you girls agreed on your chore division already, and Lena has enough to do as it is."

"I won't ask her to do anything extra."

"And if this buggy loses a wheel or the top leaks or whatever, I can't stop my work to fix it."

"If I can't fix it myself, I'll barter with someone who can."

"And if it breaks down while you are who-knows-where—when it breaks down—you must keep the horse safe. The horse matters more than the buggy."

"I know—" She almost teasingly added *Dad*, but stopped herself in front of Lena.

"And if Bette doesn't like the barter you offer, you must drop the subject. I don't want our neighbors annoyed with us over your idea."

She chuckled and mocked offense. "When have I ever annoyed someone with my ideas?"

He didn't return her humorous tone, but his knowing eyes lit up. "Lemonade?"

Lena started clearing their dishes. "What lemonade?"

"Nothing." They both answered in unison, drawing a double take from Lena.

Caroline quickly stacked plates. "I loved lemonade when Noah and I were children."

"Oh." Lena pushed the foot pedal below the deep-basined sink to fill it. "I have only tasted lemonade once. Rilla made it when she and Eli were courting. I didn't care for it much. Whenever I have a lemon, I can think of a dozen dishes to add the juice to rather than squeeze it into sugar water and gulp it down."

Noah waited for Lena to finish her innocent comments before he continued his unnecessary instructions to Caroline. "You matter more than the buggy and the horse combined. Keep yourself safe foremost. Tell your customers you won't drive in storms or after dark. And we don't know the men here, but every town has its scoundrels. You must stay vigilant."

"I will."

"Some horses won't give a smooth ride, and some won't pull a wagon for more than a few yards. We don't know which of the two horses Uncle Vestal left us was trained for the buggy, if either."

Caroline's insides jittered at the possibility her idea would work. She sat back down across from him. "Probably the big brown one. The draft horse."

"They're both draft horses."

"The one with three white stockings."

He drank the last of his water. "Get the laundry done early tomorrow. I'll help you unbury the buggy after we go to the market. If it's fit to drive, we'll see if either horse is good at pulling it. You won't be in business long if your horse is stubborn."

"My horse?"

A sly smile lifted the corner of his mouth. "I already have two horses from Father. I figured the two we inherited from Uncle Vestal should be yours and Lena's."

A dish clanked sharply in the sink as Lena flinched. "Oh, I don't want a horse. Not of my own. I prefer to stay home, except for church. I found several novels in my room to keep me entertained. I'll help with the market when we have fresh produce to sell, of course. But I don't want to go anywhere, so I don't need my own horse."

Noah took his cup to the sink and gave Lena's shoulder a reassuring squeeze. "If you must ride somewhere, you'll need a horse that knows you. But don't worry, I'll take care of him."

She leaned her head against him, compressing the loose strands of her wavy hair. "I'll just barter with Caroline for a ride in the buggy. A slice of pie for a ride to the village. Does that sound fair?"

Caroline joined her siblings at the sink. "How about this: you can have any ride anywhere anytime you want, and I'll make sure you have everything you need for your happy kitchen life?"

Lena chuckled. "That suits me perfectly fine."

Noah pulled two dishtowels from the drawer and tossed one to Caroline. "All right, but if we take the buggy to church, I'm driving."

Caroline snapped the towel open and shot him a grin. "It's a deal!"

CHAPTER FIVE

Dappled mid-morning light sparkled between the overhead trees along the road into the village while Jedidiah ambled leisurely from the Cotter horse farm to the Saturday market with young James and Tabitha. Mark's children had begged their parents to let them walk to the market with Jedidiah instead of riding on the wagon with them at the break of dawn, claiming their parents' business would be boring, but walking with Jedidiah would be fun.

Jedidiah had tried not to smile until Mark and Doris did.

He appreciated the children's enthusiasm for his company, but not as much as he respected his gracious hosts. Though a distant cousin on Jedidiah's father's side, Mark behaved nothing like the Cotters of Stonehill—nor did he seem to know what they were truly like. Mark and Doris's generosity in offering room and board to Jedidiah without meeting him proved Mark's commitment to his place as a village elder and as a trusted member of Connor's emergency response team.

Jedidiah's boarding hadn't been an emergency, but getting a second physician to move to Good Springs had been urgent. During the haze, the people here had suffered in spirit in a way that affected their health, and

Dr. Bradshaw's time had been stretched too thin. Since she had lacked a qualified candidate to apprentice under her and Jedidiah was nearing the end of his apprenticeship in a much smaller village that had already had two physicians, the elders of both villages thought it best to offer him the position here.

And Mark and Doris immediately opened their home to Good Springs' new physician, giving him a private room and even a horse for when he needed to ride out to patients' homes.

Jedidiah never dreamed anyone bearing the Cotter name could live as openhandedly as Mark and Doris did. Even little James and Tabitha reflected their family's joyful grace. The children skipped beside him now, galloping circles on the road to stay near him while burning up the endless energy of childhood.

Tabitha paused her skipping and took Jedidiah's hand. "Can I have some cim-a-nun bread from a baker?"

Her sweet voice warmed his heart more than the soft summer wind. "You certainly may have cinnamon bread, but let's get you saying it correctly so the bakers will know what you want. Can you say *cinnamon*?"

She squinted from the sunlight as she looked up at him. "Cim-a-nun."

"No, try saying it slowly like this—*Cin*."

"Cin."

He kept himself from chuckling. "*Na*."

"Na."

"*Mon*."

"Mon."

"Now put it all together. *Cinnamon*."

"Cim-a-nun!"

James laughed his bubbly five-year-old chuckle. "Say *cinnamon*, Tabby."

Tabitha ignored her big brother and walked closer to Jedidiah, her tiny fingers clutching his hand. When her pace slowed a bit with momentary exhaustion, he scooped her up and set her on his shoulders to carry her the rest of the way.

Someday he might have his own happy son skipping circles around him and his own tender daughter riding on his shoulders.

Someday. Maybe.

There were a great many issues a man must settle in his life before he sought such responsibility. He needed a livelihood, which he was securing even now; a home, which the village was providing in exchange for his commitment to be one of their physicians; and a godly wife, by which those precious children might come. Even the writer of Proverbs warned how hard she would be to find.

The road's sandy gravel turned to cobblestones when they approached the center of the village. This was the sort of place where he could imagine himself raising a family—a notion he'd never entertained in Stonehill. The morning sun brightened the steeple and the front of the white chapel as they walked through the shadow of the stone library. Even the buildings in Good Springs evidenced the long-lasting benefits of intentional living.

Many of the village's farmers, craftsmen, and artists were already at their booths in the vacant lot beside the stone library. Growers were arranging their wooden crates of vegetables, bushels of fresh flowers, and packets of heirloom seeds. A tanner was laying out piles of leather, its tangy aroma giving the ocean breeze a masculine edge. Woodworkers were dusting handcrafted furniture, and a spinner was organizing skeins of wool yarn and woven tapestries. Traveling merchants were setting up displays of items acquired by trade with other villages in the Land.

Jedidiah was here to locate one particular item. He scanned the market for Bethany Foster's booth as he lowered Tabitha from his shoulders. "Let's find the pottery yard's display and see if they might have a food dish for the cat I told you about."

Tabitha's energy surged back, and she danced an excited stomp. "Feed Patches! Feed Patches!"

"Yes." He smoothed her baby-fine hair. "I need a bowl to feed... Patches."

When it came to small children, all a person had to do was mention a stray cat and it would be adopted, named, and have a place in a home that wasn't even built yet.

That was the sort of optimism he wanted in his life.

"There's Mama!" Tabitha squealed, spying her mother at the baker's booth. "Cim-a-nuns!"

The little girl dashed to her mother with her brother close behind her.

Jedidiah meandered toward them. The children yanked on their mother's arms and pointed to the treats they wanted. Before he reached them, Tabitha already had a full mouth and sticky fingers.

Doris smiled at Jedidiah. "It seems your little friends forsook you for sweet breads."

"That's all right."

"I'll have to clean her up before she can go near the sellers' booths. You should go about your business in case you get called to an emergency."

He gave Doris's shoulder a squeeze. "Very well. Goodbye, children."

Tabitha and James barely let their eyes move from the treats in their hands to him before he walked away.

Beyond the vegetable booths and wool spinners, Jedidiah spotted the pottery yard's display. There was only one table of bowls and pots and plates for sale this week. With Bethany carrying twins she must not be working as much these days. Her young assistant was behind the table in her stead, bartering with a woman Jedidiah had very much hoped to meet.

The lovely lady reached for the only stoneware bowl small enough to suit a cat. Perhaps his intriguing, soon-to-be neighbor also wanted the bowl to feed a pet. Perhaps she needed the bowl for spices or for orange peels or to use as a soap dish. Perhaps he could challenge her to a game of Pick-a-Number with the little dish as the prize.

Every clever remark that popped into Jedidiah's mind seemed childish, conflicting with every cell in his body that wanted this woman to know he was a mature man, master of his life, full of wisdom and practical skill, a competent man to be—

She returned the bowl to its place on the table and walked on with a simple smile for the girl behind the booth.

Jedidiah forgot about the dish and followed her to the next booth, staying back a few paces while watching her posture as she spoke to a trader about a mattress that was stacked on the junk that remained on his wagon. She kept her hands folded daintily in front of her bodice as any demure woman would, but her straight spine and uplifted chin hinted at an innate strength, almost a defiance.

Her full voice was edged with honey as she spoke to the trader. "I have nothing to trade you at the moment, but my family now owns the Vestal orchard, so we expect to have plenty in a few weeks."

Jedidiah gave the mattress a quick check. From his angle of approach, he could see a stain of mildew along the mattress's edges. Perhaps she hadn't noticed it. He slipped closer to her and the trader, listening but not interfering.

The trader tapped greedy fingertips together. "Well, I can't save a mattress for that long. It's too bulky to cart from village to village while I wait for your harvest to come in. But since you look like an honest girl, I reckon I could part with it on promise."

"On promise?"

"Yeah, you take that there mattress now and promise me a dozen bushels of your best fruit come harvest."

Jedidiah forgot about his desire to impress the woman and stepped forward, glaring at the trader and pointing at the mattress. "That mildewed heap isn't worth half a bushel of anything, and you know it. How dare you try to swindle a lady, sir!"

The trader cocked his greasy chin and leaned across the table that separated them. "Do you own that orchard she's talking about?"

"No."

"Then this doesn't concern you."

Jedidiah's collar grew warm. "It's starting to."

"Gentlemen, please." She spread her feminine hands across the air between them and lowered her noble chin at the trader. "I have no intention of sending my family into debt, even if the deal were a great bargain, which it isn't." Then she set her gaze on Jedidiah. "And I appreciate your gallantry, sir, but I can make my own trades. Good day, gentlemen."

When she turned on her boot heel and sauntered away, Jedidiah followed in the wake of her soft scent. "Your name, please, miss?"

"It's Caroline." She stopped walking and retied her bonnet straps. "I suppose you have a better bargain on a ratty old mattress to sell me?"

When she finished tying and straightening the bow, he took her hand without it being offered and shook it. "Nice to meet you, Miss Caroline. I'm Jedidiah Cotter."

Amusement curved her generous lips. "Oh, I know who you are—the manure delivery man."

"Pardon?"

"You came to our property this week with Mark Cotter to spread fertilizer." Her smile grew, but she turned her attention to her gloves. "And as much as I appreciate your kindness in helping my brother with his orchard and," she glanced back at the trader, "your attempt to save me from a bad deal, I'm not buying anything today. We need a mattress so I was curious about the price, that's all."

He let her take a step away before he spoke up. "I have a spare mattress. A new one."

Her feet paused.

"Two were donated for me when I came to Good Springs to complete my medical apprenticeship—one for my bed and one for the patient cot in my new office, but a patient cot must be a stiff canvas, not a cloth-covered feather bed. The person who donated it said for me to do as I wish with it—use it for trade or find a family who needs it."

She turned an ear to him. Whether it was the new mattress that got her attention or the fact that he was a physician, he wasn't yet sure. Women responded to abundance.

He continued his offer. "It is yours, if you want it."

"In exchange for what?"

So she was a savvy business woman, after all. How intriguing! Now it was his turn to flash a smile. "How can I sell what cost me nothing to receive?"

She turned to him fully. "That's very generous. I can only offer my gratitude, as I said: I have nothing to trade with—at least not yet."

"It would be my pleasure to deliver it to your house this afternoon. It's a gift to your family."

"What a lovely surprise!" Her suspicious smile softened with pure delight. "I've never met so many gracious people in my life as I have since coming to Good Springs."

"Nor I." When she continued walking, he stayed in step beside her. "I've found it unsettling to be the recipient of such generosity. John Colburn told me I will get used to it, but I doubt that is possible. Nor would I want to."

"Exactly!" Her voice raised with excitement, the same way little Tabitha's did when she spoke of cinnamon bread. "It makes me think that if everyone gave whatever extra they had to someone who needed it—not to get anything in return or to win someone's favor or praise—the entire world would be a much pleasanter place."

The passion in her idealism scattered his usually logical thoughts and stilled his tongue.

Her chipper words continued as she walked across the market. "Not that I could imagine any place more pleasant than Good Springs, at least from what I've seen in the short time I've been here—one week. It seems like longer than that. Mostly because we've been working to get the house and orchard in working order." She pointed a thumb back at the market. "See, we have beds—the three of us, my brother and sister and I—but my brother's bed has no mattress. He's been sleeping on an old couch, and I fear he will hurt his back again. He will be so grateful to you for the new mattress."

Here she'd been talking about how unselfish generosity would make the world more pleasant and he had offered the mattress to her because he wanted to win her approval. To think he wanted to be a trusted member of the community and he was the one with insincere motives. His insides sank.

She immediately stopped talking and angled her regal chin. "What's wrong?"

"Nothing." Though everything in him wanted to stay and learn every detail about her and absorb her positivity, he was probably not seeing her hidden motives either. "I must leave. The mattress will be at your farm today. I'll see to it." He walked away, each step making his feet feel twice their weight. "Good day, Miss Caroline."

* * *

Caroline smoothed the pleats that flowed from the waist of her best dress and then tied on the matching bonnet. Mother Vestal never would have allowed her such a lovely garment, but Father had bartered with the seamstress in Northcrest for both of *his daughters* to have a new dress for their new life. It was almost sweet until he added: *How else are they going to attract husbands?*

Lena's dress was a pale blue while Caroline's was a soft green. Neither was allowed a printed pattern, since the dresses were to be worn only on Sundays, and Mother had nothing nice to say about women who wore printed fabrics to church. Caroline had requested a slightly more fitted bodice and the addition of lace cuffs while the seamstress was taking her measurements, but the prune-faced woman almost spat straight pins in disgust.

As if having a smidge of style made a woman a wanton fiend.

Mom was the classiest and most moral woman Caroline had ever known, and she wore smart sweater sets and tailored trousers to church—a sight that would have made the self-righteous gossips in Northcrest light-headed from such sharp disapproval.

Caroline might never own a modern sweater set, but she didn't have to worry about the Northcrest gossip here either.

"Come on, Caroline!" Noah called from the twin-rutted driveway outside.

After a glance at the wardrobe's mirror, she grabbed her Bible from the nightstand and hurried out of the house, the screen door clattering behind her.

"It's about time!" Noah scoffed, giving her a double take when she finally emerged. "John Colburn said they ring the church bell two hours after sunrise."

Lena was perched on the buggy's backseat. She leaned forward to shine her beaming grin at Caroline. "I have my own bench. I don't have to balance on a crate in the wagon bed anymore. And it's cushioned!"

Caroline lifted her dress skirt, gripped the side handle, and climbed the convenient iron step to the front seat, where she sat beside Noah who couldn't have looked more handsome in his black Sunday suit, complete with matching waistcoat and starched white shirt. "Very dapper."

He straightened his cuffs like a yacht club preppy. "Me or the buggy?"

"Both." She chuckled at him. "The muscles in my forearms are burning this morning, but this is worth all the work." She ran a gloved finger along the freshly washed brake handle. "Do you want to release it, or can I?"

"Go for it."

She shifted the pole rod that stuck out of the floorboard between them, and the rudimentary braking system clanked below the buggy. The horse fidgeted, aware the noise meant he was about to go to work. "That's right, Captain! Take us to church!"

Noah raised an eyebrow at her. "You named him *Captain*?"

With Lena in the backseat inches behind her, Caroline couldn't tell Noah that the oddly shaped white patch on the horse's face reminded her of a communication device from her favorite old science fiction television show. Instead, she pointed forward and said, "Engage!"

Noah pressed his lips together and nodded. "Nice."

Morning dew sparkled on the tips of the tall grasses in the ditches along either side of the narrow road. Every few hundred feet, the road widened enough for a second wagon. She would need to learn the driving customs. Which driver pulled over if two met?

Outside of the village, wooden fence posts held sagging boards to mark property lines or to contain horses and cattle, but as they neared town, the pastures gave way to mowed yards and ancestral family homes.

In the village's center, the gravel road changed to cobblestone and the buggy's rhythm changed with it. The chapel's white steeple towered above a row of gingerbread cottages.

Lena tapped Caroline's shoulder. "Aren't they lovely?"

"Yes. So lovely. I wonder who lives in them." She couldn't wonder long as she was trying to watch how Noah directed the horse off the road to the sandy lot beside the church where two other buggies were parked.

No sooner had he set the brake and the bell rang out in a series of two-beat clangs that must have carried for miles. People were already walking to the chapel from all directions—along the road they'd just driven from the north and from the opposite direction. From the side roads and from the darling Christmas-card-worthy cottages. All in their best dresses and suits, shoes shined and collars starched.

Whether they were dressed up to please each other or out of respect for the overseer or because they thought a good effort might hide their sin from God, she could not guess. Nor did it matter to her. She only wanted to meet them all and learn their stories and tell them hers.

That is, the parts of her story she was allowed to tell.

Her gaze followed the gleaming steeple up to the clear summer sky. Maybe someday soon she would find a soulmate, one absolutely trustworthy person. Then finally, she could share her secret. Finally, she could be truly known.

Noah walked a pace ahead while Lena stayed so close to Caroline's side that their dress skirts ruffled together.

Every face outside the chapel was new to her, and Caroline met each one with a smile. Some returned her pleasant greeting while some glanced from her, then to Lena, whose gaze was fixed on the ground.

John Colburn stood at the top of the chapel steps, wearing a plain black suit. He briefly greeted each family before they entered, causing a line of waiting congregants.

Each stone step she ascended brought a thrilling quiver to Caroline's stomach. When it was their family's turn, John shook Noah's hand, then folded his own and said a simple *good morning* to her and Lena.

Perhaps men didn't shake women's hands here.

A slender woman with a baby bump and a mop of perfect auburn curls stood at the front of the sanctuary, playing a hymn on the violin. The soft notes of praise filled the atmosphere like an heirloom fragrance.

Everyone who entered seemed to know where to sit, heading directly to the same place they probably sat every week for years, just as their parents had before them and their parents before them. Half of the seats were already filled, and half of those people watched Caroline and her siblings dither in the aisle. All were silent.

The long chapel had two sections of wooden pews, split by a center aisle. Noah slid into the back pew on the right and Lena followed him, leaving space for Caroline beside her. The two pews in front of them were empty.

Caroline leaned around her sister to look her introverted brother in the eye. "I'd rather sit closer to the front so we can meet people."

He held a finger to his lips and whispered, "They don't talk in the sanctuary before church here."

She matched his quiet volume. "You will dash out as soon as it's over, and we won't meet anyone."

He shook his head tightly at her, then looked forward at the violinist in the same way the other contemplative attendees did.

When in Rome, she supposed.

Try as she might to gaze blankly at the front of the chapel and listen to the music and still her thoughts, every person in the room was a closed book to her, a fresh story ready to be told. The back of every head hid a face she hoped to see, eyes she wanted to look into.

Then she scanned the room for the man she had met yesterday at the market. He'd called himself Jedidiah and said he was a physician. He'd left her looking forward to his promised afternoon delivery of a mattress for Noah. The mattress had arrived on a farmhand's wagon, but Jedidiah hadn't come. The farmhand said he had been called into work at the medical office.

Caroline craned her neck to see if Jedidiah was sitting up front, but he wasn't. Maybe he was still at work. She stretched around Lena to whisper to Noah, "I wanted to thank Jedidiah for the mattress, but I don't see him."

He only pointed forward, directing her attention to the service.

The chapel doors closed and John walked down the center aisle to the lectern at the front of the room. The violinist ended her sweet song, and John prayed. When he taught from the Bible, words of wisdom flowed from his lips like summer rain to the parched ground of Caroline's soul. What deep truths had she been denied all those years in Northcrest!

Her heart softened with each scripture verse the overseer quoted, and new insights popped from the sacred text. In one hour of John Colburn's teaching, she learned more about the grace of God than she had in her entire lifetime.

John taught they were to live lives that exemplified the grace God had given to them. No wonder the community had poured out one blessing upon another on their family since they'd arrived. She wanted to be a part of the bestowing too.

After John led the congregation in the *Doxology*, he left the lectern and sat on the front pew while an older gentleman stepped to the front and read community announcements from a palm-sized notebook. A young couple would be wed next Sunday after the service; this week the elder council would meet at the Colburn house instead of the chapel because the sanctuary floors were being waxed; if anyone had unreturned library books, they should return them before school started this week; at sunrise on Wednesday, the men of the village were to meet at the site of the new physician's home to help with construction.

That was the cleared lot across the road from the orchard. That would be Jedidiah's home. She would have a friend next door in Bette and a friendly man across the road in Jedidiah. The out-of-town orchard wouldn't seem so remote with friends living nearby. Her fingers tingled with the verve flowing through her system.

Caroline's attention drifted away from the man speaking and she scanned the backs of those sitting in the same row as John Colburn. Connor Bradshaw sat next to the overseer and had a squirming little boy on his lap, then a young woman she presumed to be Lydia, Connor's wife and John's daughter, who was also the village physician.

Beyond them, she didn't know who anyone else was, but she wanted to meet them all—and to speak to John again, to tell him how much she appreciated his teaching. Hopefully, she would sound more intelligent than she had during their last conversation. Now that she'd heard him teach, it made sense that he wasn't interested in chatting with her that day. He was probably too wise for small talk.

Or their house was his last stop on a rainy afternoon and he'd been ready to go home.

The man at the front of the chapel broke her thoughts with his final announcement. He pointed in her direction as he told the crowd to be sure to greet Good Springs' newest residents: *Noah Vestal and his family.*

She smiled as every head turned to check them out.

Lena's quivering fingers gripped Caroline's hand. Poor girl was probably about to faint from the attention.

Caroline squeezed back to reassure her.

Noah gave a nod to the onlookers, and slowly all the heads turned back around.

What if one of those faces had been that of her future soulmate and he'd heard *"Noah Vestal and his family"* and assumed she was Noah's wife?

Since Lena was the person sitting beside Noah, maybe they would assume she was the wife. Or maybe since Lena was several years younger than them, people would assume Lena was their daughter.

Either way, thanks to the old guy squinting at his notepad, Caroline would never get a date.

Not that it mattered. She had work to do. A mission to accomplish. *Bigger fish to fry*, as Dad used to say.

Her goal was to make her siblings happy, not to get married and leave them forever. And she could be content with that life if she could leave the house for a little while each day in her buggy.

When the congregation was dismissed, Caroline held her ground at the end of the pew, not letting Lena flee or Noah slip out like they were probably aching to do.

A tall man with light brown hair and a young face that favored John Colburn opened the chapel doors, allowing in a flood of late-morning light. Probably John's son. Noah had said John had five grown children, four of them daughters.

Most of the villagers turned in their seats and chatted with each other. A few children dashed outside to play, then several more followed, exploding with the energy they'd held back while sitting still for an hour's sermon.

A family of four passed her pew. Caroline smiled and said hello to them all, hoping for a reciprocal greeting. The children didn't notice her, but were focused on the other kids playing outside. The man nodded once at Noah, and the wife met Caroline's eyes, then instantly looked away.

Okay, so not everybody would have an outgoing personality. That was normal in a crowd this size.

Lena nudged her to leave, but she ignored the push.

An elderly couple hobbled past. "Welcome to Good Springs," the man said, and kept walking. The lady never looked at them, too focused on her cane-assisted walking.

Caroline thanked him, then almost gave in to Lena's nudge, but caught sight of a familiar face. "It's Bette!" She pointed across the room. "Come, Lena. You must meet her. You too, Noah."

Her jovial neighbor gave a little wave as they hurried through the crowd toward each other. "I'm so glad to see you!"

"Me too." Caroline would have pulled her into a big hug, but little Josie slid between them and raised her arms for her mother to pick her up. "I want you to meet my sister and brother." She glanced behind her. Lena had been stopped in the aisle by the man who rode the mail route across the Land. She was blushing as he handed her a letter, which she immediately tucked into her Bible. A middle-aged couple were talking to Noah.

Caroline pointed at them. "That is Lena there, and Noah is behind her."

"Yes, I saw them earlier," Bette's green eyes shone, "when you arrived in a buggy."

While she spoke to Bette, several women passed and interjected a warm greeting. It seemed having one friend made it easier for others to see she was friendly.

The happy greetings were broken when an older lady with a stern brow grabbed a handful of little Simon's shirt. She ushered him over to his mother. "Bette, this boy is begging for a spanking. Poked a hole in the seam of his best pants during the service. I made those pants so he would have something decent to wear to church. How could you allow him to behave thus?"

"I'm sorry, Mother Owens. I didn't see him doing it." Bette's countenance fell while she gently drew her resistant son toward her and out of the woman's grip. "Simon, apologize to your grandmother."

The boy refused, slipped from her hand, and plopped down on an empty pew, his mop of coppery hair covering his forehead.

Bette shifted Josie to the other hip and sighed to her mother-in-law. "I'm truly sorry."

The woman's jowls wobbled as she shook her disappointed head, then she turned her glare on Caroline. "Did I see you arrive in a buggy this morning?"

"Yes, ma'am. We—"

"You drove a buggy to church?"

"Well, it was in the barn and—"

"Oh, I know who it belonged to. Your dear uncle had that built when his beloved wife couldn't walk to church anymore. That is who deserves a buggy ride on a Sunday morning: those who've given decades of life to their community. Not you young people who can walk plainly on the two feet the Lord gave you. It's not what's done, young lady!"

Caroline glanced at Bette, whose dismayed expression intensified. When Bette looked at her, they locked eyes for only a second, but it was long enough for a schoolgirl recognition to flash between them.

She didn't know what the proper response to Mrs. Owens should be and didn't have long to consider. The older woman spotted her next victim and turned her prickly voice to them.

Caroline leaned close to Bette. "Bless you for what you must endure."

"I'm sorry about her."

"Don't be. I'm not." She lifted her chin at the sulking boy on the pew. "Is he going to be all right?"

Bette pressed her lips together. "I haven't given up hope yet."

"And you must never give up hope." She patted her new friend's arm. "I have an idea that might help you, at least on Fridays anyhow. It would help me too, actually."

Bette angled her head. "What is it?"

While Caroline proposed her barter, Josie wiggled to get down and dashed over to an older man who stood near Mrs. Owens. The man swooped her up like any stout grandpa would and planted a smacking kiss on her cheek that made her wipe her face and giggle. At least one of Bette's in-laws was kind to the children.

Bette's smile grew with Caroline's explanation, but she kept her volume down to reply. "If you drove the children to the village on those days, I could get in an extra two hours of work. And I would very much enjoy helping you start a chicken flock. Only you won't want four hens and a rooster—not right away. Start with five hens at first."

Caroline felt a cartwheel coming on but restrained herself. "Wonderful! Five hens. Wow! I'll be over with the buggy on Friday morning. Should I pull through the yard to park beside your cottage?"

"No, no. I will walk the children over to your house." She glanced across the chapel at her mother-in-law. "It's best that we keep our arrangement out of sight from some people. For as long as we can, anyhow."

Caroline nodded her agreement. They were grown women and didn't need anyone's opinions ruining their smart solution. Or their budding friendship.

Her heart swelled with excitement. Her first barter had been accepted. She was helping her community already and would earn a profit for her family too. Mom would have been so proud!

Lena and Noah stood at the back of the church, their eyes begging her to leave. She hooked her arm through Lena's and smiled up at Noah. "I got my first customer."

He responded with a quick wink and led them out of the chapel to the buggy where Captain was waiting to take them home—and anywhere else Caroline would need to go with her new business venture.

CHAPTER SIX

The trees' summer foliage thickened and fruit swelled on the orchard stems, promising a bountiful harvest for Noah. The vegetable patch beyond the kitchen window yielded more beans than Lena could cook and more tomatoes and cucumbers than she could slice, and so the canning and pickling began mid-season.

Caroline's heart sang for her siblings' delight in their new life, and for hers too. They all had plenty to eat, thanks to God's provision through the earth and through the gracious villagers. They each had a private bedroom in their old-but-solid house. In the past month, she'd already bartered rides and deliveries for new curtains and window screens, yet there was still much to be done to make this place a lovely home.

She slid a basket of her hens' eggs onto the kitchen counter, then gave her family a quick wave goodbye. "I'm leaving to drive Josie and Simon to the village. And it's my first day to pick up the weekly food collection at the chapel and make those deliveries." She looked at her brother. "How was your new pillow?"

Noah set his empty coffee cup by the sink and ran his fingers through his hair. "Best sleep I've had in… years."

She knew when he'd last slept in a bed that suited him—long before their family's ill-fated sailing trip twenty years ago. "See, I told you I could barter my buggy service to get your room comfortable before harvest time."

"You were right again, Care-Care. Usually are."

"Plus, I'll get more materials each week with this new delivery route. I told Connor we all agreed on needing new bathroom fixtures before the exterior paint."

"I won't have time to paint anything until long after harvest." Noah shuffled toward the mudroom and pointed at her arm as he passed. "What did you do this time?"

She checked the fresh bruise that now spanned her forearm. "I slipped down the porch steps this morning. It looks worse than it feels. Doesn't hurt too much."

"You wouldn't admit it if it did. Will you be back by lunch?"

Lena turned from the soapy dishes in the sink. "We have plenty of fresh veggies from the garden, so I can make your favorite."

"A big salad?"

"Yep, a big salad."

"Sounds delicious," Caroline pulled on her driving gloves, "but since it's my first time making these deliveries, I don't know how long it will take." She counted off the stops on her fingers. "I have to go to the Colburn house and to all three of the schoolteachers' homes and to the pressman's and to Jedidiah's house. Connor said he will have directions ready for me when I get to the chapel. I might be gone most of the day."

Noah tugged on his work boots. "Leave Jedidiah's delivery for last since his house is the closest to us. That way you can have lunch here and do your afternoon chores before you have to go back to pick up Bette's kids."

"I'll figure out my routing myself, thank you very much." She pointed out the screen door at the clothesline. "And don't worry about my chores. I'll mop the kitchen floor after dinner, and I had the laundry rung and hung at sunrise."

Lena chuckled at the silly rhyme, then looked out the window over the kitchen sink, even though Jedidiah's new house couldn't be seen from that view. "How convenient to have a doctor living nearby!"

Noah scowled beneath the rim of his sweat-ringed field hat. "I hope you don't plan on needing him."

"No, I didn't mean that… I just meant..."

Caroline shewed a hand at her brother. "Don't tease her." She gave Lena their brow-wiggle-grin. "I must dash. If I'm not back by lunch, save me that big salad for dinner."

Noah was already halfway to the barn, which still cast its morning shadow over the yard, when Bette walked her children to Caroline's buggy. Eager to get to her hat making work, Bette said a quick thank you to Caroline and a goodbye to Josie and Simon as they climbed aboard the buggy.

Caroline waved to Lena, who stood inside the kitchen window, and then gripped the reins. "Ready, Captain?"

Josie giggled in the backseat while the buggy rocked along the driveway to the road. Simon sat beside her, his frown set at the horizon in preparation for another silent Friday morning ride to town.

Caroline offered him her usual opening to friendly conversation, hoping to improve his mood. "Simon, what sort of games do you and your friends play each week?"

He didn't answer. He never did.

She turned to flash Josie a smile. "You look beautiful today, sweetie. I like your braids."

"Thank you. Mama gave me blue ribbons. Do you like them?"

"I do! Very pretty."

The morning sun made Simon's hair seem redder and his frown seem deeper.

Caroline wished she could reach the boy somehow. Perhaps if he knew how she and Noah and Lena had been orphaned, he would find her to be a kindred spirit. Maybe she would have a talk with him sometime when they were alone. Not now. Josie was too happy and free with the warm breeze and her new ribbons to be reminded of life's pain.

Caroline glanced back at Simon again. Every child processed devastating loss differently. Apparently, Simon's reaction to the horror of losing his father was angry withdrawal.

When their parents died, Noah had grown quiet but was resolute to keep his promise to Dad. Lena had been too young to remember—consciously, at least—what happened. Caroline had cried. She had shivered for what seemed like weeks and refused to leave Noah's side. At night when Lena had curled up beside her in bed, Caroline clung to her tiny sister for her own security.

But when the initial shock wore off, Caroline and Noah started telling each other what Mom and Dad would have wanted them to do. Mom would have wanted Caroline to take care of Lena, to raise her to have hope, to look for the light in every shadow. Dad would have wanted Noah to be strong for his sisters, to protect them, to provide for them.

Captain snorted as Caroline parked the buggy along the cobblestone street outside the gingerbread house where Josie and Simon's friends were waiting on the porch for them.

Simon jumped down from the wagon with a thud and traipsed straight to the house, only speaking to one boy who was about his age.

Caroline lifted little Josie from the backseat and planted a smacking kiss on her cheek as she set her feet on the ground. "Have fun today, sweet girl!"

From the gingerbread house, Caroline only had to pass five more cottages to arrive at the chapel. Its steeple gleamed in the morning light, urging her eyes upward, reminding her—as Mom always said—where she really came from and where she was ultimately going.

One of the chapel's tall narrow doors was already propped open with a brick. Connor must have arrived early. Or it was John inside. Or both.

A ping of delight straightened Caroline's posture at the thought of getting to speak to John Colburn without her embarrassed brother beside her, huffing so slightly only she could catch his meaning.

She tapped her knuckles on the open chapel door as she walked inside. "Hello?"

Her eyes slowly adjusted to the scant light inside the hallowed building as she shuffled through the entryway to the sanctuary. She wished it were Sunday so she could sit in the pew and listen to John Colburn expound the Word of God. The chapel's wax-scented air was cooler than outside, its shadows more sacred. She peered beyond the rows of pews toward the office at the other end of the building.

"Hey, Caroline." Connor's chipper American accent flowed from the office doorway.

She'd missed the relaxed way her countrymen said her name, though she hadn't thought about it in years. It was best not to think of it at all. "Hello. I'm here to pick up the deliveries."

Connor raised a half-sheet of paper as he sauntered along the outer aisle and met her near the back pew. "I just finished writing out directions to each house for you. Good Springs has seven village-sponsored positions right now—each one gets a basket the elders filled with the village's donations. One of the physicians and the overseer live at the same address," he winked, referring to his wife and his father-in-law, "and the pressman is married to one of the primary school teachers. So you only have five houses to deliver to."

She accepted the paper he handed her. "Okay." As soon as the casual but foreign word slipped from her mouth, she clamped her lips shut.

He didn't react. Maybe since so many people knew about Connor and the fresh terms he'd brought to the Land, he didn't suspect her of being an outsider.

He opened a hand to several baskets on the entryway floor along the wall. They were filled with pints of strawberries and cucumbers and varying-sized parcels wrapped in brown paper. "You have eight bushels to distribute today."

"Eight?"

"The overseer receives a double portion. It's honor for all that he does and also necessary because an overseer's home is always open to travelers." He lifted one of the laundry-basket sized containers. "I doubt all of these will fit in your buggy at once, though."

She scanned the directions he'd written. "Not a problem. I'll make the deliveries to the south side of the village first, and then come back here and pick up the others to go north."

"This must not be your first rodeo."

She chuckled at the old American expression. "Nope."

He raised a dark eyebrow at her.

She ignored it and hefted a basket to the door too, wanting to earn the materials she needed fair and square. "You don't have to help me load the buggy. I can do it all myself."

He kept walking. "That isn't how it's done in the Land, and you know it."

She said no more while they hauled the heavy loads to the buggy, but everything in her wanted to ask him about his experience since coming here. Did he miss things like pizza delivery and going to the movies and driving a car? Did he wish he could show his son the beauty of his native country? In summertime, did he yearn for an air conditioner?

What had really happened to the country her family sailed away from twenty years ago that turned it into what he called the *Unified States*?

He slid the first basket onto the floorboard of the backseat, then turned and took the next from her arms. "You know, Caroline, I enjoy living here, and you will too."

For a moment, her jaw froze. Did he mean here in the Land? Had she said her thoughts out loud? Could he tell somehow where she was really from? Mother Vestal had worked with her and Noah's speech for years.

He lowered his chin, a knowing smile exposing his perfectly straight teeth. "Good Springs is a wonderful village."

"Oh, yes." She released a whoosh of breath. "Good Springs. Of course. I already enjoy it very much. As do my brother and sister. We're quite fortunate to live here now."

He slid the second basket onto the buggy floorboard and faintly echoed her. "*Fortunate.*"

Captain turned the buggy smoothly from the dirt and shell road onto the Colburn property. Caroline didn't have to double check the directions to know this was the correct house. The two-story home with its stately brickwork and proud chimneys reminded her of the old houses frequently found in small downtown boroughs in America—the type of houses that had bronze history placards out front, were photographed for lifestyle magazines, and were occupied by hipster website developers.

She pulled the reins and parked on the narrow driveway at the back of the house by the little white cottage where Dr. Bradshaw worked. The main house's back door was open, but no one was in sight. Between the big house and the medical cottage, a sweep of all shades of daisies and lilies and marigolds lined a flagstone path.

Caroline set the break and gave Captain a scratch on the neck as she passed the front of the buggy to lift one of John's two baskets from the floorboard. The scent of lavender rose from the package nearest her face—soap, perhaps. Beneath it seeds shifted restlessly in another package. Apparently, everyone took turns giving part of whatever they produced to support the people who spent their lives taking care of the village.

"Miss Caroline, allow me." John Colburn hurried from the house and reached to take the overflowing basket from her.

"Oh, thank you." She allowed him his chivalrous gesture, then smiled and retrieved the second basket from the floorboard. "I'll carry this one."

A half-grin puffed the edge of his gray beard. "I could tell you to leave it and I would carry that one too."

She matched his cheeky grin. "And I could tell you it is my job to deliver both baskets."

His bright blue eyes widened under uplifted brows. "Yes, you are much like my Bethany. I suspect you are about her age."

His interest in her energized her work-weary muscles. She forgot about the heavy load she was carrying. "I just turned twenty-nine on the fourth."

"Twenty and nine? Then I am mistaken. Bethany's twenty-first birthday will be next month. The older I get, the more everyone looks young to me." He lifted his chin at the doorway for her to enter first. "Set it there on the table, please."

Lingering notes of freshly baked muffins warmed her soul. It almost smelled as good as what Lena had made yesterday. She set the basket on a long table that commanded half the kitchen's dining area. An empty stone fireplace stood opposite it. Light shone on the grate from a room on the other side. A double-sided stone fireplace. Beautiful!

She glanced around the wide kitchen as she lowered the heavy basket to the table. Delicate curtains framed the open windows, dining lanterns hung from the ceiling's wooden crossbeams, and stacks of heirloom cookware waited on shelves beside the iron stove.

The Colburn house wasn't decorated to look old, nor was it filled with mass-produced artificial character. No, this ancestral home was a living testament to unbreakable family traditions, time-tested craftmanship, and faithful hospitality that spanned the generations.

She slipped off her leather driving gloves. "My mother would have loved this house."

John cocked his chin. "Your birth mother?"

She almost swallowed her tongue, then realized he meant the fictional woman who had supposedly died in their supposed home village of Stonehill. Unable to meet his piercing eyes, she forced her most congenial smile and pointed at the oven. "Smells delightful in here. Do you bake?"

His gaze didn't falter. "I do. Mostly bread and rolls, but my grandson enjoys blueberry muffins. He would live on them if allowed."

The sparkle of pride in his eyes as he spoke of his grandson drew Caroline in. She faced him fully. "Your family means everything to you and yet your sermon last Sunday on the gift of singleness was so poignant. I never heard such a message and thought it must be a comfort for your congregation to know singleness can be a gift from the Lord. Are there many other widowers here?"

He straightened his shoulders. "A few. There are also several unmarried men your age in the village."

"Oh, I wasn't concerned with age... or with men. That is good to know, of course." She chuckled at her own nervous chatter and waved the subject away with a dismissing hand. "It seemed to me there are about three times as many people in the church here as there were in

Northcrest. The singing is much more joyful too. The heartfelt prayer and worship and your sermons have revived my own devotion."

"I am glad to hear it." His gaze softened. "If your work keeps you in the village until lunchtime, you are welcome to eat here."

Her mom would have referred to John Colburn as a *silver fox*, but all Caroline could think was how flattering it was to be found interesting by this wise and discerning scholar—interesting enough to be invited to lunch, that is. Nothing could stop her smile. "Lunch here? With you? I would be delighted."

"Excellent." He began unpacking the basket. "Lydia took Andrew with her to a neighbor's house, but they will be home by noon. And Connor will be here by then as well. They have been wanting to get to know you."

Her facial muscles relaxed as her smile lost its motivation. He was only inviting her to lunch for his daughter and son-in-law's benefit. She slipped her hands back into her driving gloves. "I would be delighted; however, I only have two more deliveries on this side of the village and then I must pick up the rest of the baskets at the chapel and head north."

His eyes turned to her, but his hands kept drawing packages out of the basket. "Another time, perhaps."

"Certainly," she replied, just as he had on that rainy day by the barn. "I must be going now."

Before she reached the door, he said her name in the crisp lilt of the Land. "Miss Caroline?"

"Yes?"

"Do be careful while you drive. Some might consider such an occupation to be hazardous for a woman."

She squared her shoulders. "I don't."

"Even still, please take care." He followed her outside. "The main roads are well maintained, but you will find some narrow ways rocky and the ditches deep. Do not be deceived by tall grass."

"Thank you, sir."

Every motion of climbing aboard the buggy, unlocking the brake, and guiding Captain back to the road was done without thought. John Colburn found her worthy of protecting, thought she was the same age as his twenty-year-old daughter, and wanted Lydia and Connor to get to know to her. He didn't see her as interesting, and he certainly didn't see her as beguiling; he saw her as a child, a new friend for his kids.

A new villager under his care as an overseer.

And somehow that only made her respect him more.

She blew out a weary breath. Why had she wanted his admiration? Not because she found him attractive, but because something about his fatherly demeanor reminded her of what it was like to have a father—an actual father who was genuinely fond of his daughter.

Once on the road and no one was in sight, she wiped the single tear that slipped down her cheek. Oh, how she missed Dad.

* * *

Jedidiah pushed and turned the screwdriver for one final twist, then stood back to examine the fruit of his morning's labor. The new supply cabinet in his medical office would soon be filled with the instruments and bandages and prepared gray leaf tea medicines that would heal wounds, cure diseases, and save lives for decades to come.

Mid-day sunlight flooded into his office through a wall of north-facing windows, precisely how he had imagined it would. Everything was meeting his expectations, save one important issue. An empty certificate frame glared at him from the opposite wall. Connor had called it odd to hang an empty frame, but for Jedidiah, that emptiness demanded to be filled.

Connor had only shrugged and remarked, "Whatever works for you, man."

It did work for him. Any reminder of unfulfilled desire pricked his hide like a burr under a saddle. Dr. Lydia Bradshaw had given the elders her report of his apprenticeship being sufficiently complete and his professional abilities being superbly proven, yet they still hadn't awarded him the official title of Doctor.

Thus the empty frame.

The roll of wheels hummed onto his property. The tracks remaining in the construction site's leveled dirt led to the east side of the house. His office's north-facing windows gave him the ample sunlight he wanted, but he didn't have a view of who was arriving. It was probably the delivery of village support the elders had told him would be distributed each Friday.

Just in case the visitor wasn't a delivery boy with a sack of flour but was a person in need of medical care, he buttoned his waistcoat and smoothed his hair. Before he reached the front door, the bell rang, sending brass clangs through the house. It must be someone needing urgent attention to ring the bell with such vigor.

The thrill of action erased his mind of all but emergency medicine. He yanked open the stiff new door. "Yes?"

The pretty lady he'd thought about since the market last month smiled from the stoop. She had a bushel basket full of parcels in her arms. "I'm sorry if I startled you. Your sign says to ring the bell. I'm delivering your weekly support from the village."

His professional verve settled, but his heart rate didn't. Every ounce of interest he'd felt for her at the market stirred afresh inside him. He took the heavy basket from her arms. "Yes, of course. Thank you, Miss Caroline."

She rubbed her empty hands together. "I'll be making these deliveries every Friday. Connor said it's usually one basket of goods, but sometimes more during harvest season. Where should I put your deliveries if you aren't home when I arrive?"

"Good question." He stepped back from the doorway into the empty front room, which had a squat corner stove and a single basin sink but no dining table or cabinets yet. He wouldn't want her go into the medical office if he was tending to a patient, nor would it be appropriate for her to enter his private bedroom.

He carried the basket to the area where he planned to build a countertop and set it on the floor between the stove and sink. "This spot is best, unless the stove is warm, then put it there. I hope to have cabinets built in here soon. Until then, the floor will suffice. Keep the area around the door clear for patients."

When he turned back around, she had stepped inside and removed her gloves. Her summer dress had three-quarter sleeves with unruffled cuffs. A long bruise blackened her forearm from wrist to elbow, yet her smile was as happy as a lily on a lazy afternoon. "Very well.

And do you prefer I ring the bell or knock when I make deliveries? I wouldn't want to disturb your work."

"Knock once and let yourself in if I don't answer."

Her gaze traced the bare walls. "This house is so charming. It was fun to watch the men build it. I love the smell of new construction, especially the gray leaf lumber." Her delicate fingers pointed to the window where the top of her house was visible over the tree line near the road. "The day Noah was here helping to raise the walls, my sister and I watched from our upstairs window. The frames all went up so quickly. When can you treat patients here?"

He wished he had a comfortable chair to offer her. "As soon as they come. I don't have the instruments and furnishings yet, but I always have my medical bag with me."

"Ah." Her response came as if she understood, but her porcelain brow crinkled. "How will people know when to come here?"

"The elders haven't advised me of their plans yet, but I'm expecting an announcement soon." Her interest in his situation made his feet cross the floorboards to stand closer to her. "Dr. Bradshaw said she treated patients in her cottage for a year before the elders officially titled her as the village doctor."

Sympathy filled her hazel eyes. "A year? That seems like a long time to wait to start your own practice after all your training. I suppose the elder council here moves slowly and intentionally with their decisions."

"I suppose."

"Doesn't make it any easier to wait, does it?"

"No, it does not."

A soft grin widened her full lips. "When they soon announce you're accepting patients, the people on this side of the village will start coming to you immediately. Then the elders will see everyone has accepted you as their doctor, and they will have no choice but to issue your title promptly."

"I like your optimism." Despite what he said, his insides burned. His father always spoke to people with that type of flattering reassurance to gain their trust, then immediately offered a small favor. Once the favor was accepted, they owed him. And his father knew how to compound a debt until he owned a man.

But Caroline seemed different—genuine, if that was even possible.

She opened her hand to the unfurnished room. "Uncle Vestal left the storage room in our barn piled high with old furniture and things. There are several good chairs and such that you might find useful. Noah wouldn't mind if you came over to pick through it."

Ah, there was the favor. Soon he would be in her debt.

Her sweet grin never faltered. "After your kindness of giving him a mattress, it's the least we can do for you."

She was right—he had given the first favor. Maybe he was the one being insincere. If so, he had misjudged her. Again.

If he wanted the village to accept him, he had to accept them, no matter how vulnerable that made him. Why couldn't he be relaxed about things like Connor was or be able to see people's motivations clearly the way John could?

All he could do was try to ignore the examples his parents had set for him and build his own life. When he'd said goodbye to them, he'd meant it. He folded his hands behind his back and gave a slight bow. "A couple of chairs would be useful, that is, if your brother says it's all right."

She shooed away his uncertainty. "Oh, I'm sure he won't mind."

"Ask him, just the same."

"I will as soon as I get home. I have to warn you though: that storage room is full of rusted junk too. Bring your gloves. There are a few treasures, though. That's where I found my buggy, and now look—I have my own business."

"So you enjoy driving?"

"I adore it!" She pushed a strand of stray hair off her elated cheek. "Every morning, I do my chores as quickly as possible so I can take the buggy for a drive."

Her childlike air got a chuckle out of him. How could anyone live a decade into adulthood and still be that happy?

"Plus, it gives me a reason to get out of the house. I almost dread being done with my driving each day."

Ah, there it was—the clue to her effusive joy being a facade. Something wasn't right at home. But what would make a grown woman live with her grown siblings and yet have to find excuses to leave the house all day?

He caught her fingertips and lifted her hand. When her eyes bulged with surprise, he examined the bruise on her arm. "What happened to you?"

"Oh, I'm so clumsy." She rolled her ever-expressive eyes. "I slipped on the dewy porch steps this morning. Winston likes to weave between my ankles when I take the laundry basket to the clothesline. I didn't see him, and down I went. I saved the clean laundry from hitting the ground, though."

"Winston?"

"One of the cats."

"Is it painful?"

"Yes, but not as bad as it looks."

He kept her fingertips in his hand. "Come with me."

"Winston has claimed the back porch and our cellar. Noah says he's a good mouser, so we tolerate his attitude." She kept talking in a chipper tone while she followed Jedidiah through the short hallway into his office. "I probably startled him by being outside so early, but I had to hang the laundry before I left to drive. What are you doing?"

He knelt by his medical bag and withdrew a jar and a cotton ball. "Roll your sleeve above your elbow."

She obeyed, but kept talking. "I've seen at least a dozen cats on our property. We don't know if they were Uncle Vestal's pets or if they are strays. Winston is my favorite, probably because he's a bit of a grouch. What's that?"

He smoothed the ointment over her bruised skin. "Gray leaf salve. It's only half strength, so it won't make you drowsy."

"How clever! Did you make it?"

"No, Dr. Bradshaw did. Have you ever used gray leaf medicine before?"

"Nope. Never needed it."

She didn't speak like any of the women he knew in Stonehill. He looked away from her forearm to check her eyes and saw nothing but sincerity. "How is that possible?"

She shrugged. "Just fortunate, I suppose."

The lid clinked when he capped the medicine jar. Caroline looked at it and then at her fading bruise. "It's already healing. That is incredible! Thank you."

He couldn't take his gaze off her. Such sweetness usually aroused his suspicion, but with her, it only allured him more. Still, he had to ask. "Were you alone when you slipped?"

"Just me and Winston."

"Did you get any other wounds?"

"No." She glanced away from the disappearing bruise long enough to lower her brow at him. "Why?"

"Just curious."

Her gaze returned to the area that was bruised. It was completely gone. "That is amazing! Absolutely amazing. You'll certainly have a waiting room full of patients in no time." She straightened her sleeve. "Thanks, Doctor."

He shook his head. "Don't call me that yet."

"Oh. Sorry." She squeezed his arm gently, warmly, then sauntered to the door. "But see how easily it comes. We will call you Doctor Cotter very soon."

"For now, it's just Jedidiah."

"Can I call you Jed?"

"Not if you want me to answer."

She paused at the open front door and laughed warmly. "I'm on my way home for lunch now. Would you like to join us? My sister, Lena, makes the best food."

For the first time in six years, he wished he could shirk his medical duties. He followed her onto the stoop. "I can't. Dr. Bradshaw is expecting me at the medical cottage for my shift."

"Well, do come by when you have the time. We will hunt for chairs in the barn, all right?"

For that smile he would do anything. "All right."

She pointed at her forearm. "And thanks again for the salve."

"It was my pleasure." He followed her to her buggy and the waiting horse. "Please, be careful."

CHAPTER SEVEN

Caroline gave the purring Winston a quick pet down his silky back, then sidestepped him and climbed to her buggy's front bench seat. With reins in hand she peered over Captain's vigilant ears, hoping to see Jedidiah's house through the tree line across the road.

It was no use, and she knew it.

The only clear view of the charming physician's new residence was from Noah's window, but her brother had shooed her from his upstairs bedroom when she'd tried to look out early this morning. At least Noah hadn't realized her fascination with Jedidiah; he was still worried that she found John Colburn intriguing.

Well, she did, but not in the way Noah feared.

Not anymore, that is.

They were simply all so interesting—every person she'd met in Good Springs—with their complex pasts, subtle signals, and controlled passions.

Especially Jedidiah Cotter, soon to be *Doctor* Jedidiah Cotter.

Perhaps she would throw a party to congratulate him when he was titled. A small party, of course. Invite only the nearby neighbors. Surely that wouldn't overwhelm Lena. And maybe the downstairs redecorating would be done by then—just the essentials. Paint, wallpaper, maybe reupholster the sofa.

She strained her neck, trying to see the house across the road.

Nope, nothing but shrubs. Shrubs and the feral mama cat who often dashed over from Jedidiah's property to hunt in Caroline's flower garden. The cat's midsection was slimmer. Perhaps she'd hidden her litter of kittens somewhere around Jedidiah's house.

Maybe that would be a good excuse for Caroline to cross the road. *I just came to check on the kittens.* She glanced down at Winston. *I think my cat might be the father.*

She snapped herself out of the imaginary conversation with Jedidiah. Why should she care whether he was home today? He hadn't crossed the road to her house one time in the week since she'd invited him to come for lunch and to look through their barn's storage room for furniture for his new office.

Besides finding him intriguing, she desperately wanted to repay his kindness after he'd tenderly healed her bruised arm with his miraculous potion.

Okay, so the gray leaf tree's medicine probably wasn't miraculous.

She stood up in the buggy for a better view.

All right, so her interest in Jedidiah was more than simply wanting to repay his kindness.

Ever since those sweet moments in his office, she'd wondered about him every day and dreamed about him every night. It was silly. She wasn't a boy-crazy teenager. Never had been. She was a successful twenty-nine-year-old businesswoman.

Granted, she lived in a hidden land settled by pioneer folk whose descendants were still blissfully living like it was the 1800s, and her business involved a horse-and-buggy taxi and delivery service. It wasn't like she was so committed to a demanding career in a twenty-first century urban center she couldn't spare the time to daydream, especially about a brilliant and handsome physician who now lived across the road.

Still, she had a job to do. She should be watching for Bette's kids to cut through the path behind the hen house for their Friday ride to town. She shouldn't be pining for a sign that Jedidiah was home. Besides, she would find out whether he was there when she made his weekly food delivery later today.

Noah lumbered from the barn to the house with Nipper prancing behind him, tail wagging. With nothing around the orchard to herd, the peppy herding dog assumed his job was to nip the heels of any person trying to leave his territory. Noah was carrying a full bucket of milk for Lena to churn into delicious butter, and the dog let him get as far as the clothesline before giving his boot a peck.

"Hey!" Noah corrected Nipper, then glanced at Caroline. "The hybrid varieties Uncle Vestal planted at the back of the orchard are ready to harvest. I'm going pick for samples this afternoon if you want to join us. Lena's excited to test the hybrids' flavors."

"Sure. I should have an hour or two between drives."

"Cool." He pointed a thumb toward the Owens's property. "Where are Simon and Josie?"

Caroline pretended she was standing up in the buggy to scan the property for the kids. She shielded her eyes with her hand, even though the morning sun was behind her. "I don't see them. They should be here by now."

"Maybe you ought to go to Bette's cottage and check on them." He pursed his lips. "Or I can go, if you need me to."

That pulled her gaze from the road. Noah was too busy with harvest preparations to hike next door and check on the neighbor kids simply because they were a few minutes late. She caught a peculiar glint in his eyes. "Ah, I get it."

He switched the bucket to his other hand and nudged Nipper away from it with his foot. "You get what?"

"Do you want to check on the kids or do you want to check on their pretty mama?"

"Cut it out." He furrowed his brow beneath his new straw hat—a hat he'd traded way too much for so he could impress Bette at the market last Saturday. "I was only offering to go over there as a favor to you."

Just like she was only peering toward the road to look for the kids.

Well, apparently she and Lena weren't the only Engler siblings with secret crushes.

She wrapped the reins around the brake pole and hopped to the ground. "Thanks, but I can take care of my business myself."

When she breezed past him, he mumbled. "You sound like Mom."

She didn't look back. "And I can run my business as well as she did too."

As she cut across the yard in front of the flower garden, Ed Owens's buckboard wagon rattled down the road. Josie and Simon were sitting in the back, scowling, their little feet dangling from the tailgate. Mr. Owens didn't tap his hat when his eyes met Caroline's like he usually did. He turned his face to the road ahead and cracked the whip above his anxious horse.

Caroline waved to Josie.

The little girl only stared shyly in the manner she had when they first met.

Something must have happened to Bette for her not to come over and explain why Mr. Owens was taking the kids to the village this morning. But if something was wrong with Bette, she wouldn't be having her usual Friday work day and so the children wouldn't be going to their friend's house.

Caroline's gait picked up speed as she rounded the hedgerow that marked the border between their front yards. Fresh wagon tracks creased the short grass on the dewy drive. Mr. Owens never drove his grandchildren anywhere. Bette must be in trouble.

Just as Caroline launched into a jog, the screen door at the side of Mr. and Mrs. Owens's two-story house clattered. "Where do you think you're going?"

Caroline halted. "Mrs. Owens? Is everything all right?"

Sue Owens waddled her full frame down her porch steps. "Nothing has been right since you hitched up that buggy and started flaunting your inheritance around the village. I don't know what your uncle was thinking, leaving all that he earned to your brother, but I do know this: our dear Mr. Vestal would rise from his grave in shock if he saw the buggy he bought to care for sweet Mrs. Vestal in her feeble years being driven for profit— and by a woman, no less. A brash unmarried woman."

Caroline's stomach flip-flopped. "I don't know what—"

"Oh, you know what exactly you're doing!" The older woman's jowls reddened. "You are just like the woman the Proverbs warn men about, with your alluring looks and playful smiles."

Her mouth went dry while her thoughts scrambled to keep up with the insults being hurled at her from her neighbor's porch. Mrs. Owens seemed disapproving of, well, everything, but Caroline hadn't been accused of anything so outrageous, even in Northcrest. Her knees locked for support. "Mrs. Owens, I don't appreciate being—"

"Well, I don't appreciate your brazen behavior in our village, driving from one man's house to the next, using your charm for profit. A buggy service is an immoral occupation for a woman—especially a single woman. As long as Bette is a part of this family, she will not be a part of something so base."

No one had shown any sign of not approving of Caroline's business—or of her. She was slowly but surely growing her business and also making friends, and she intended to keep it that way. The louder Mrs. Owens's voice grew, the harder Caroline's pulse pounded in her ears. She forced a smile but matched her slanderer's volume. "I have done nothing wrong."

Mrs. Owens stomped down her painted porch stairs, but stayed on the last step. "My grandson told me about you driving him and his sister to the village as a trade with Bette for chickens. Why, everything that woman has was my son's and will be my grandson's one day. Bette has no right to make such trades for such luxuries, especially with the likes of you."

Caroline took her eyes off the hollering tyrant on the big house's porch steps long enough to peer down across the yard beyond a vegetable patch to the tidy yellow cottage the late Jack Owens had built for his lovely young bride. Bette was standing in the doorway, her hand over her mouth, her fiery red hair disheveled.

While Mrs. Owens continued her ranting, Caroline gave a discrete wave to Bette.

The young woman didn't return the wave, but only curled her hand over her heart. From this distance it looked like her hand was clutching a handkerchief.

Knowing her new friend needed her support, Caroline tried to squeeze in a polite *excuse me* to the venomous Mrs. Owens and hurried to the yellow cottage.

The indignant ramblings increased in pace until Caroline was halfway past a second barn. Finally, the distant screen door clattered, and silence returned to the Owens's sprawling property.

Caroline let out a full breath when her feet reached the stone pavers outside Bette's cottage. "Are you all right?"

"I should ask you that. I can't believe she said those things to you." Bette wiped her eyes, the crying making her green irises seem even fiercer. She stepped back into the house for Caroline to enter. "What am I saying? Yes, I can believe she said that to you because she's spoken to me the same way many times since Jack died."

Caroline closed the door behind her and leaned against it. "She yells at you?"

"Often." Bette opened a hand to one of the four mismatched chairs around her cozy kitchen table. "I've never heard her speak to anyone else in such a manner, though. She seemed to like me just fine when I came here to marry Jack. But as soon as Simon was born, she started ignoring me and only speaking to the baby in my arms.

You know the way people talk to your child, but say things meant for you. 'Your mother shouldn't have dressed you so warmly on such a fine day, should she?' And 'Your mother had best learn to tidy up this place, hadn't she?' Things like that."

Caroline lowered herself to the kitchen chair but couldn't relax. "I don't have a child of my own, but my adoptive mother used to talk like that to my cat."

"Adoptive mother?" Bette paused with her hand on the kettle handle. "I'm sorry. I didn't know."

"Didn't you? I thought everyone knew. They did in Northcrest, and I assumed people talk as much here as they did there."

Bette pointed out her little kitchen window toward Caroline's new home. "So Mr. Vestal was your..."

"Our adoptive father's brother. Uncle Vestal had no children of his own, and Eli, our adoptive brother, is inheriting the family farm in Northcrest."

Bette sat opposite her at the table while the kettle boiled. "The inheritance traditions can be so harsh. Noah wouldn't have had anything if your Uncle Vestal hadn't left him the orchard here. You and your sister would have been desperate."

Caroline patted her hand. "God would never leave us desperate. And neither would Noah."

"And after having been orphaned as children too. I can't imagine."

"No need to try imaging it. From the sounds of your mother-in-law, you have plenty to deal with already."

Bette stuffed her handkerchief into her apron pocket and returned to the whistling kettle. "Jack was their only surviving child. He was everything to Ed and Sue. When Jack couldn't find a suitable wife here, Ed wrote to the overseers in the other villages. My overseer in Woodland thought we might be a good match." She poured steaming water over waiting coffee leaves and let it brew. "I only saw Jack twice before we were married. Ed and Sue were there both times. It didn't matter to us, because we were instantly taken with each other."

Caroline spotted a framed sketch of Bette and a man on the wall by the door. She stood to look closely. "Is this him?"

"That's my Jack."

"You made a beautiful couple."

"And two beautiful children." A wistful smile lightened Bette's expression while she poured two cups of the dark drink the people in the Land called *coffee*. "Jack was so happy to have a son, he cried when Simon was born. And so happy to have a daughter, he laughed when Josie came." Her smile weakened. "But everything changed when we lost him."

Caroline met Bette at the table and accepted the cup she offered. "I don't know what it's like to lose a spouse—"

"Nor I both parents."

"But I do know the ache of grief. When did Jack die?"

"It's been over a year now. Someone told me the first year is the worst, so I thought the pain would ease up, but it hasn't. It has changed, but it hasn't left."

Caroline shook her head, unable to respond until her memories released their grip on her throat. "It's been twenty years since we lost our parents. I can assure you, sorrow respects neither clock nor calendar."

Bette pressed her lips together. "Josie is fine because she was so little when her father died. But Simon is a different boy now. Sue blames me for Jack's death since I didn't find him for hours after he fell from the barn loft and broke his neck. Ed ignores her horrid behavior. He doesn't blame me, but he doesn't stop her either. I'm not welcome in their house anymore, even though it will one day be my son's home."

"Have you ever thought of leaving? Taking the kids and moving back to Woodland?"

Bette's eyes widened. "That's not what's done. I don't know what they did in Northcrest, but in my family and here in Good Springs, the founders' traditions are of highest importance." She lowered her voice as if someone would hear her otherwise. "But yes, I often fantasize about running off, finding a new home and a new life. Being loved again. Not that I could ever replace my Jack, but... well, I am a young woman. Even if I never marry again, I don't want to be alone forever."

Every word echoed in Caroline's heart. "If it weren't for my brother and sister, I would be all alone. If I even think of life without them, it sets off a sort of panic in my heart." Everything in her wished she could tell Bette the whole story. It would relieve years of yearning for a loyal confidant. But she wanted to protect her family—especially Lena—even more. She traced the wood grain in the table as she continued. "I don't want fewer people in my life; I want more. I would have a hundred friends if I could find them. I guess I think the more people I have in my life, the less likely I will be left all alone." Her cheeks warmed. "It sounds childish when I say it aloud."

Now it was Bette who reached across the table to touch her hand. "Well, I know we've only been neighbors for a few weeks, but as long as it's up to me, you will never be all alone. You might have to cut through the back of the property to avoid Sue's hollering, but you're welcome in my home any time."

The joy of making her first real friend since a long-ago childhood in a far-away world seeped into her striving heart, filling the cracks and softening the scars. "I'm grateful Mrs. Owens threw a fit this morning."

"Grateful?"

"Sure. Otherwise, I wouldn't be here having coffee with my new friend." She raised her cup and affected her voice with pomp. "I propose a toast to new friendships that help to heal old wounds."

Bette smiled. "Here, here!"

* * *

The sandy road crunched beneath Jedidiah's polished shoes as he ambled home from a two-day shift at the medical cottage. Dr. Bradshaw had expressed her appreciation for his diligent work after an accident at the mill sent them multiple patients—two needing broken bones set and another requiring surgery. He'd stayed with the patients last night so Dr. Bradshaw could sleep, and he was willing to again tonight, but she insisted he go home to rest—after a hearty meal at the Colburn table, of course.

He yawned as the sun slipped behind the trees to the west. No matter how tired he was, his eyes wouldn't close until all the light was drained from the sky. He'd always been that way. And since late summer evenings with a clear sky lasted longer, he needed to find something relaxing to do.

After working endless hours all week, he yearned for the comfort of good company. A happy face, casual chatter.

A friend.

His dinner at the Colburn house with his boss and the overseer and the overseer's apprentice was pleasant enough, but still felt like work. All they spoke of was the mill accident and the patients' progress and other villagers who needed house calls.

As he set his medical bag on the shiny new gray leaf flooring inside his front door, a basket of the packages and produce the elder council called *village support* greeted him from the floor between the stove and sink.

Caroline had put it exactly where he'd said to.

Yes, it was her smile he longed to see, her joyful chatter he wanted to hear. Her company he needed.

His father had always demanded silence upon arriving home from work, but as Jedidiah lit an oil lamp waiting in his empty house, he realized it was the rhythmic purr of a feminine voice prattling about the day's tedium that he yearned to hear. One week in his own home proved he was opposite the nature of his father.

And he suspected Caroline was the opposite of his mother.

Perhaps the people of Good Springs were nothing like the people of Stonehill. If so, he was only hurting himself by not building a new life in every way—socially, as well as his career.

He crouched by the brimming basket and plucked a folded note from its top. Caroline's handwriting was a neat but simple script, lacking the fervor of a physician and the reserve of most women he'd known. Her cheerful, rounded lettering captured his eye as much as her words. She wrote that since he hadn't gone to her house to look through their storage room for furniture for his new house, she had *taken the liberty of rescuing four chairs from the heap,* all of which she had *cleaned and tightened, but dared not guarantee their appeal.*

Her humor gave him a much-needed smile and she wasn't even present.

Yes, he would accept her invitation to *come over when convenient and select or reject the waiting chairs—* as she had put it.

He changed his clothes, washed his face, and gave his shoes a quick shine, then remembered the letters Revel had given him when their paths crossed in John Colburn's driveway.

The letter from his mother remained ignored in his jacket pocket, but the other he would deliver to the youngest Vestal sibling per Revel's request. He glanced at the envelope. Apparently, the reclusive Lena Vestal had a correspondence with Philip Roberts of Falls Creek. Intriguing.

Delivering the letter would make the perfect excuse to visit the Vestal home. He put out the oil lamp on his way to the door, leaving his empty house with its unfurnished office and unproductive silence for the recently revived farmhouse across the road.

The setting sun still illumined the western sky, but to the east it reflected off the Vestals' house, giving the white exterior a rosy glow. A curved line of stone pavers led through ankle deep grass to the front porch. The bed of perennial flowers that flanked the porch had enjoyed the warm summer and reseeded themselves bountifully, crowding against the fading daylilies.

This must be where Caroline had cut the bouquet she was holding the first time he saw her. She looked effervescent that day, standing on the back porch with flowers in her hand while talking to a tomcat. Jedidiah had been there with Mark to spread a wagon full of manure in the orchard. How he'd wanted to drop that shovel and run to meet the girl with the flowers! But duty had called.

Not tonight, though.

No work tonight. No patient charts or medical exams. No trying to impress someone who could influence the elder council to speedily grant his title before his family found a way to ruin it.

The only business tonight was simply a man delivering a letter and a woman offering second-hand furniture for the village's new medical office. And those issues were only excuses to see each other. For him, at least.

Hopefully, for her too.

He climbed the front steps and gave the door a polite knock. No one answered. As he raised his knuckle to try again, the muffled sounds of laughter hummed from a distant room inside the house. He backed down the steps and looked up at the second floor windows, but saw nothing.

As he shuffled through the grass to the side of the house, the gentle clink of pots and pans being washed flowed from an open window. The lingering aroma of some baked wonder caught him by the nose and pulled him to the back porch. Before he ascended the steps, Caroline's gray tomcat rubbed against his ankles to mark him as part of its territory. He slid his leg away from the bold feline, but it only tried again.

Caroline opened the screen door. "Evening, Jedidiah. I thought that was you walking across the yard."

"My apologies. I tried the front door but—"

"No apology necessary. We never use the front door, so I forget it exists. Its hinges are rusted in place. Besides, you're our neighbor. Back doors were made for neighbors. Come in, come in."

Her smile was brighter than the setting sun, and just as with the sun, something told him staring too long would only hurt him.

Though he tried to avert his gaze, his eyes refused to obey. He withdrew the letter from his jacket pocket and offered it as he stepped into the mudroom. "When I left work, Revel was riding into the village with a full messenger bag. He asked me to deliver this to your sister."

A half-grin played on Caroline's lips, almost as if she doubted his motive, but was going along with his scheme anyway. She cast her voice over her shoulder and into the kitchen. "Lena, you have mail."

Noah appeared in the doorway between the mudroom and kitchen. He gave Caroline a quizzical look. She shooed him away to pass the letter to her younger sister. "This came for you today."

Noah's eyes landed on Jedidiah and he swooped a hand toward the kitchen. "Welcome. Come in."

"Thank you."

"Have you eaten dinner?"

Jedidiah slipped off his hat. "Yes. At the Colburns' after my shift."

"You got here just in time for dessert, then." Noah ignored his giggling sisters—Lena trying to open her letter while evading Caroline's curious fingers. He pointed at a spread of freshly picked fruit lined up on a tea towel on the kitchen table. "We were about to sample the first fruits of harvest."

Jedidiah examined the plump and unusually colored produce. "I've never seen apples with peels of both green and red, nor cherries that bright, nor peaches that large. Are these typical for Good Springs?"

"No, they're all selectively bred varieties. From what I read in Uncle Vestal's farm journals, he experimented with cross-pollination for years."

Jedidiah's ears tingled in delight. "What traits was he hoping to achieve?"

"Early ripening fruit. Sweeter flesh." He picked up a particularly golden peach. "Thinner skin that was difficult to bruise when harvesting, but easier to bite through when eating."

Caroline left Lena alone with her letter and brought Noah a paring knife. "Uncle Vestal wanted to have fruit ready for market earlier in the season that would look great and trade well."

"And we are grateful. For the past few years, he wrote nothing about the dozens of hybrid trees that he'd planted at the far end of the orchard. It makes me believe this is their first fruiting." Noah took the knife from Caroline and held up a peach. "And it is our pleasure to be the first to sample them. If they are indeed ready and we start picking at first light in the morning, we'll have several bushels to take to the market."

Caroline waved Lena over. "Come on! He's going to slice the peach first."

The younger woman gently folded her letter and tucked it into her dress pocket, keeping her hand over it as if the paper itself held the key to her heart. "I'm coming."

Noah offered the knife to Lena. "You will be the queen of canning and preserves once the full harvest is in. Would you like the honor?"

She shook her head rapidly. "You do all the orchard work, Noah. You deserve the first taste."

He shrugged jauntily. "Very well, then." He pressed the knife through the peach's fuzzy skin with a mouth-watering slice. It swished through the fleshy center until it hit the pit with a click. Noah made short work of rounding the blade, then dropped the fruit to the table and sucked in a shocked breath. "What the devil!"

Jedidiah assumed Noah had cut himself and reached to take the knife, but instead he caught the look of disgust on Noah's puckered face. He followed the man's gaze down to the open fruit on the table.

Caroline leaned in for a closer look. "Oh, no!"

Lena squirmed back, clasping the kitchen sink with both hands. "What are those things?"

Noah set the knife on the table, his devastated hands moving in such minute increments he could have caught a fly. He didn't have to; they had caught him. "Those are buckle worms."

Lena kept her distance. "Buckle what?"

Caroline stayed by her brother. "Maybe just that one peach got infested somehow. Check the apple."

Noah took a slow inhale through flared nostrils. He trapped the apple on the table and sliced off a quick section. Whitish, half-inch long worms wiggled in surprise as they poured onto the tea towel. Without a word, Noah chopped a bulbous cherry in half, revealing more tiny worms. "They're in everything! These fruits came from trees that were an acre apart."

Lena arched over the sink, grasping her stomach.

Caroline glared at the invested fruit. "What exactly are buckle worms?"

Shattered words slipped through Noah's gritted teeth. "They're a type of fly larva."

"Like maggots?" Caroline stayed near Noah, but put a comforting hand on Lena's back. "In fruit?"

Noah didn't answer her, so Jedidiah did. "These are the larva of what the founders named the *Atlantic shake fly*. Fishermen sometimes find shake flies on dead sea life that has washed ashore. They lay their eggs in the decomposing flesh and..." He stopped his explanation for Lena's stomach's sake and lowered his volume. "I've never heard of them infesting vegetation, and certainly not three different species of fruit. Must be something about the hybrids that attracted them."

Noah raked his fingers through his hair. "I'm responsible for the largest orchard in Good Springs. This village is depending on our harvest, especially after the haze reduced so many other crops this year."

At that Caroline and Lena both snapped their gaze to their brother, shocked by the thought of losing the entire harvest.

Caroline pinched the edges of the tea towel that the wormy fruit was on and rushed the whole mess out the back door. The screen door closed softly behind her.

While her older brother was overcome with disappointment and her younger sister with disgust, it was Caroline who remained calm and took care of what needed to be done. She was the anchor that steadied this family. And she did it with grace—such grace as Jedidiah had never witnessed in a woman.

She had the perfect disposition to be a physician's wife.

Lena shuffled away from the sink, whispered *excuse me*, and disappeared down the hallway.

Noah paced from the kitchen into the parlor, hands planted firmly on his hips.

Outside, a flash of fire beyond the clothesline gave an orange glow to the darkening back yard. A moment later, Caroline returned empty handed.

Noah stepped back into the kitchen. "Where'd you put it?"

"The burn barrel."

"Smart. Thanks."

"You're welcome."

Deep shadows lined his eyes, making him appear a decade older than he had moments ago. "I'll have to burn all the branches—or at least the branches of all the infested trees. The whole orchard might be infested."

Caroline washed up at the sink. "And it might only be those particular trees. We won't know until morning. It's getting too dark to go climbing around out there now. Can't risk you falling and hurting your back again."

He whooshed air between his puckered lips. "I know, I know."

Jedidiah wasn't sure if he would be more of a comfort to them by staying or leaving. He threaded the brim of his hat through his fingertips as he dithered near the doorway. "Let me know if I can help with... whatever you discover tomorrow. It is my day off—unless there is a medical emergency and Dr. Bradshaw needs me, of course."

Caroline snapped open a fresh kitchen towel and dried her hands. "So kind of you, Jedidiah."

He slipped on his hat with the resignation of a man who hadn't received what he'd come for and wasn't even sure what that was. He mindlessly watched Caroline wash the table, then after offering Noah a nod, he left the homey kitchen for his empty house. "Goodnight, all."

"Wait!" Caroline hurried to the door behind him. "I have those chairs for you in the barn. They're just inside, near the door. Let me show you." She removed a lantern from a wall hook in the mudroom and ignited the flame. "Won't take but a few minutes."

At the chance to spend more time with her, energy surged inside him and invigorated his being, save for the part of him that possessed the manners he'd learned from reading the founders' writings. At such a time, he should help them with their situation instead of accepting her attention for his. Before he could respond courteously, she slipped past him and led him across the yard to their barn.

Her guiding arm held the lantern before them, even though the fading dusk kept the path to the barn visible. "I set out the best four chairs I could find. They need sanding and painting, but I cleaned them as best I could." She offered a relaxed smile. "As I said in my note, if you like them, take them. If you don't, leave them. I won't be offended."

"That I believe."

She paused with her free hand reaching for the barn door latch. "That I won't be offended?"

Now it was he who grinned. "You don't seem like you'd be easily offended, which is a rare quality."

"Is it?"

He reached past her to unlatch the barn door while her hand still hovered near it. "It is." He pushed the latch open while keeping his eyes on her, watching for some reaction, some signal that she thought more of him than just a name on her delivery route, that she had asked him here for a more important matter than chairs.

Her smile faded as a thousand questions flickered behind her eyes. His closeness had certainly elicited the reaction he intended. Though he missed the smile that was becoming like oxygen to him, pulling her mind out from behind her cheerful veil was necessary if he was ever to discover the real Caroline.

And it had worked.

Her gaze left his and wandered his face to his lips.

He could have counted off the seconds to eternity as he lost focus on her eyes too. She wasn't simply the only person in his thoughts; she was the only person in his world, and forever would be.

He leaned closer, slowly, as if she were a butterfly that had momentarily lighted on his sleeve. Any swift movement would scare her away. He halted, his breath only inches from hers, giving her the final say in closing the space between them.

Never had he wanted to entwine every future moment of his life with another person, nor considered any woman honest enough, pure enough, but this woman before him was piercing his heart without even knowing it.

Or maybe she knew.

With a blink her lashes fluttered and her gaze shot to his. Her casual smile returned and brought normal time back with it, leaving a chink in his heart that let the yearning spill out.

Her voice hadn't yet regained its full authority. "I can be offended, though."

He didn't speak, waiting for his pulse to regain its regular rhythm while he relished the victory of capturing her full attention, if only for a moment.

"Why just today, Mrs. Owens—you know Sue Owens next door? Well, she lambasted me for no reason at all." Her volume increased with each phrase until it was solid again. "She said absolutely horrible things about me. Yelled them. I was most certainly offended." She brushed past him and stepped into the barn, then held the lantern over four ladder-back chairs. "No cushions. They probably got thrown out decades ago."

A horse whinnied to her from the back of the hay-strewn barn, a whiff of manure in the air.

He ignored it all and glanced at the chairs, still stunned by the whip of emotions that had suppressed his logic. "The chairs will do fine. Thank you. Why did Mrs. Owens yell at you?"

"Because she doesn't approve of my buggy business. Seems to absolutely hate me." Her nimble fingers trailed the top rail of one chair. "You could have cushions made. I would offer to make them, but I'm a lousy seamstress."

"I don't care about cushions. Was Mrs. Owens the person who complained about your business to the elder council?"

Caroline's fingers froze on the chair. "She complained to them?"

"Someone did."

The whites of her eyes shone in the faint lantern light. Her words came out on a desperate whisper. "To the elders?"

A jolt of remorse ripped through his being. He was only trying to make conversation as effortlessly as she usually did. But with this? How could he have been so thoughtless? He propped an anchoring hand on the chair's high back. "I'm so sorry, Caroline. I thought you knew, seeing as how the debate is about you."

"What debate?"

"About whether you should be allowed to barter your delivery services and buggy rides, about it being a risky occupation for a woman. Dangerous roads and such. And," he hesitated, knowing he shouldn't say it, but she deserved to know the whole truth, "how it might look bad to some—an unmarried woman alone with any man who paid her."

She lifted her fingertips, though they'd lost their alacrity, and pointed them weakly toward the Owens's property. "That is the sort of rubbish she was yelling at me this morning."

The lightness that usually carried her from one conversation topic to the next wasn't a skill he possessed. He did, however, know the feeling of being in trouble, especially with an insulted female. He held up a halting hand as if this woman whom he adored had suddenly been replaced with his angry schoolteacher or aunt or, worst of all, his mother. "I know nothing about the elders' council debates, except what I overhear from others in the village—people who aren't on the council, so I should have ignored it as gossip."

She laid her hand over her heart. "People are gossiping about me?"

The skittish back-scrabbling in his voice made him feel like a ten-year-old. Instead of making it worse, he took a long breath. "Caroline, I'm so sorry. I assumed you were aware. Please forgive me for mentioning it."

Her volume sliced in half again, leaving no trace of insult but only sorrow. She stared into the blackness of the barn beyond them. "The elder council approved my delivering the weekly baskets. They are paying me in materials to fix up our house. How could they suddenly see my business as something bad?"

"I shouldn't have said anything."

"No, no. I'm grateful you did. How else would I know that my nasty neighbor had complained about me and that the village's supposedly wise elder council is taking her complaints seriously?"

He gathered her shaking fingertips in his hand. "They shouldn't. All it takes is one elder to raise an issue and they must debate it. Mrs. Owens probably complained to her husband—Mr. Owens is on the council—and made him raise the issue."

None of this was changing her demeanor. He gently tugged on her fingertips. "Believe me, I'm on your side."

"You are?"

"Yes. And I always will be." He waited for her distant stare to free her to look at him. "From what I've seen these past few months, this village's council is difficult to predict and slow to move. There has been no word on my titling, even though Dr. Bradshaw recommended it weeks ago."

Sarcasm edged her voice. "They're probably too busy debating letting women drive buggies."

He rubbed his thumb over her fingertips. "Bitterness doesn't suit you. The reason no one mentioned it to you is probably because it's nothing. Mrs. Owens might be one of those types who complains about everything."

He was a physician; he should be better able to handle people, especially in moments of distress. He had let his own emotion cloud his thinking, but it was time to regain control with logic. "Has the overseer told you to stop your work?"

"No."

"He hasn't questioned you about it at all?"

"Not once."

"Then he is probably on your side too."

The hardness in her face softened. "You're right. John has always seemed very pleased with our arrangement. He has even suggested other villagers who might need my services too."

He mirrored her optimism outwardly, even though he didn't quite feel it inwardly. "And has anyone other than Mrs. Owens seemed displeased with you?"

"No. Everyone else has been so grateful— encouraging even—that I'm available to take them wherever they need to go."

"There you have it."

A slight curve parted her lips. "Oh, Jedidiah, you had me scared there for a moment." She withdrew her fingertips from his hand and motioned as she spoke. "I want to get to know the people here. It's been so long since I've had a—"

She clapped her mouth shut as if plugging a dam before a great secret flowed out.

"A what, Caroline?"

She grinned faint-heartedly and flicked a dismissing wrist. "Oh, it's nothing. I was hoping to make friends here, that's all. I certainly don't want enemies. I needed to earn extra things for the house, and I also thought a buggy business would be a good way to meet people."

"And so it is."

"I just wanted the people here to like me, to enjoy my company."

This was his chance, if ever he would have it. There was much he did not know about Caroline Vestal that kept his suspicion roused, but there was also too much beauty and joy in her he could not ignore. He discreetly wiped his sweaty palm on his trousers. "I can't speak for all the people in Good Springs, but I enjoy your company... very much."

Her long-lashed eyes were unblinking as she gazed at him, her thoughts unknowable. Finally, with the lantern in one hand, she lifted a chair with the other. "Thanks, Jedidiah. You're so kind. Grab those chairs and we'll carry them outside."

CHAPTER EIGHT

After hanging the laundry and sweeping the horse stalls, the muscles in Caroline's arms were warm while she gave the cow its morning milking. Winston dodged her determined boots when she trudged out of the barn with a full milk pail. The cat launched ahead of her, scaring the songbirds from the sun-dried flower garden.

She'd only been covering Noah's barn chores for him for a week while he was clearing the infected trees from the orchard, yet Winston already knew the new routine. "You aren't going with me into the chicken coop. If you try, I'll call Nipper over to herd you back to the cellar."

Winston meowed his doubt at her, then rubbed his face against the porch railing, marking his territory.

She switched the heavy pail to the other hand and opened the screen door. The leftover aromas from Lena's breakfast cooking smelled a thousand times better than the barn on a late-summer morning. "Lena?"

"Coming." Lena dusted her hands on her apron, leaving flour marks across the calico cloth. "Wow! The cow gave all that?"

"I forgot to milk her last night. Don't tell Noah."

Lena took the pail and set it on the kitchen floor. "I'll make butter."

"Mm. Your butter makes all these extra chores worth the effort."

Lena smiled, basking in the pleasure of pleasing her big sister, then returned to her bread bowl and kneaded the dough therein. "Who is helping Noah today?"

"Mark Cotter. I heard him talking to Noah while they were getting saws and ladders out of the barn, but I was too busy milking to go look."

"Oh," Lena looked out the kitchen window, "I thought I saw two men arrive."

Caroline's heart gave an excited thump inside her chest. Maybe Jedidiah was here too!

She craned her neck to see around her sister at the window. Mark's wagon was parked by the barn, but the men had already gone to the far side of the orchard to finish cutting and burning the infested trees. "What did the men look like?"

Lena shrugged. "I couldn't see either man's face from here. One man was rather portly."

Mark Cotter wasn't portly, and neither was Jedidiah. If the dapper physician wasn't here, it didn't matter to Caroline who came to help in the orchard.

Her tired feet shuffled away from the window and to the cabinet. In the second drawer down, she found a rag to line her egg basket. As she stepped into the mudroom, Lena popped her head out of the kitchen. "Who were you hoping to see?"

Her dishonest shoulders shrugged. After six nights of replaying Jedidiah's sweet words in her mind, followed by her pitiful lack of response, she could only conclude the opportunity was gone.

A man she admired—*the* man she admired—had told her he enjoyed her company.

She'd told him to carry some rickety chairs out of the barn.

Oh, he had carried them all right—straight across the road, into the darkness, and out of her life.

She couldn't blame him.

He'd been vulnerable by daring to make the hardest connection of all, and she had ignored it.

Outwardly, at least.

Inwardly, she'd lost her breath, and her mind. She'd done the only thing she knew how to do—keep going as if nothing had happened.

Lena cocked her head, a knowing grin curving one edge of her smile, just like Mom. "Who, Caroline? Tell me."

She busied her hands by straightening the rag in the egg basket so she didn't have to look her sister in the eye. "It doesn't matter."

"Are you intrigued with someone?"

Lena sounded like a woman raised in the Land despite being born thousands of miles away. For some reason Caroline could listen to all Lena's secrets and care about all her concerns, but she couldn't bring herself to speak of her own. The woman standing before her was in her twenties, yet to Caroline she would always be a little girl who needed protection. She forced a smile. "You know me: I'm intrigued with everyone... and by everything." She raised the egg basket. "Off I go now to visit my intriguing hens."

Lena didn't hide her disappointment. "Fine. But I told you about Philip's letters."

"You had to. You're the only person in this house who receives mail. Besides, I saw the way he looked at you when we were in Falls Creek." She blew her sister a kiss over her shoulder as she closed the screen door. "I'll be back with eggs for you."

"And I will make butter for you."

Caroline chuckled. "And that will make my day, sweet sister!"

She dodged Winston and started for the coop, glancing up at the puffy clouds that floated lazily across the morning sky. Noah always said she had a gift for finding the silver lining of life's clouds.

So where was the silver lining to brushing off Jedidiah's delicate advance?

The only positive aspect she could think of was probably the best thing for her: He said he was on her side and always would be.

She had most wanted a friend in Good Springs and so far she'd made two. Bette understood her grief, and Jedidiah, well, he seemed to understand her. Or at least he seemed to be trying to.

As Mom used to say about Dad, there was something wonderful about a man putting forth the effort to understand a woman.

Whenever Mom said that, Dad would swoop her into a kiss that made Caroline and Noah cringe and make puke faces then laugh and hide their eyes. But Caroline always peeked. She wanted to see how her dad loved her mom then, and she wanted a man to love her like that now.

She hadn't truly admitted to herself how she wished Jedidiah would be that man until the moment after she'd dismissed his effort. Now that possibility was gone, yet it was all she could think of.

As she reached for the latch on the coop, Mark Cotter walked a wincing Noah out of the orchard.

Caroline rushed over to her brother. "Noah? What's wrong?"

With one arm over Mark's shoulder, Noah spoke through clenched teeth, his puckered face cherry red. "It's my back. Something's wrong. It locked up."

"Oh, no!" She looked to Mark, who was balancing half of her brother's bodyweight while they inched toward the house. "What should I do?"

Mark lifted his chin toward the road. "Go get Jedidiah."

She dropped the egg basket, gripped her skirt to raise the hem, and set off sprinting through the sun-dried grass, praying the man she needed was where she needed him to be.

* * *

Jedidiah checked his patient's pulse. All signs indicated he'd administered the perfect dosage of gray leaf tea to remove the pain, relax the hyper-contracted muscles, and restore the herniated spinal disk while his patient slept comfortably for the next twelve hours. The patient had dealt with a similar injury before and probably would throughout his life, especially since he reported it was a condition his father had frequently endured.

Jedidiah made one more note before slipping the thick paper chart onto the side table next to the Vestal's parlor sofa. As he did, someone knocked on the back door. This wasn't Jedidiah's home, so he waited politely in the parlor.

The soft tap of feminine boots crossed the kitchen floor. It had to be Caroline since Lena had already retired to her bedroom for the night. The footsteps continued down the two mudroom steps, then the screen door rattled open. Caroline's pleasant voice murmured to the visitor. The low hum of a man's voice conversed with her.

Only one person in the village would have come all this way this late in the evening to check on Noah Vestal. Jedidiah wished he had brought his coat with him when he dashed out of his house this morning at Caroline's breathless plea. The only time he didn't think of his appearance was when his medical training was activated by someone needing emergency care. While she had related the details of Noah's back injury, he simply grabbed his medical bag and rushed out, wearing the shirt and waistcoat he'd come home in after an overnight shift at the medical cottage.

There wasn't much he could do now to improve his appearance before speaking to the village overseer. John Colburn didn't seem to mind when work depleted a man of his formality. Still, Jedidiah needed to display all the professionalism he could muster so that maybe—just maybe—the overseer would urge the elders to move ahead with his titling.

As he walked from the parlor to the kitchen, he could barely make out the words in their quiet conversation.

The male voice held a questioning tone. "But you didn't say *hereditary*; you said *genetic*."

"Did I?"

"Yes, ma'am. Where'd you learn that term?"

"I don't know. Probably from a doctor or a book. Why?"

"You know why."

Caroline's respectful tone grew syrupy. "Do excuse me if I misused the word. I simply meant—"

Jedidiah smoothed his hair, squared his tired shoulders, and stepped into the kitchen. "Good evening—

" He stopped short of saying the overseer's name when his eyes landed on the visitor.

"Hey, Jedidiah," Connor responded from the other side of the kitchen. He gave Caroline a side glance, but kept his voice aimed at Jedidiah. "How's Noah doing?"

"He is resting comfortably under the gray leaf medicine's influence."

Connor nodded knowingly. "He'll feel much better this time tomorrow." He looked at Caroline then. "John said for you not to make the deliveries tomorrow. He's having me handle it for a while."

The lantern light gleamed off Caroline's widening eyes. "Why? Did he say why?"

Connor spread his palms. "Because you don't need to worry about taking care of village deliveries while you're tending to your brother and doing twice your normal work around here." His gaze returned to Jedidiah. "What's the prognosis?"

"It's good. I expect him to be able to walk tomorrow without pain. He should not return to work for a few days—"

"Tell John I thank him for his concern, but we had a deal." Caroline stepped forward, blocking Jedidiah's view of Connor. "I need the business to earn trade to fix up this house. I've already been doing the barn chores since Noah has been clearing out the infested trees, so I really don't see why John would take my deliveries away from me."

Connor patted the air as if calming a spooked mare. "When any family in Good Springs encounters difficulty, John makes sure they have as little extra burden and as much support as possible. It's the way things are handled here. It's for the best. You can trust John's judgement on these things. Okay?"

Her countenance dropped, along with any fight she had left in her for the day. "Okay," she repeated with a tired voice.

Connor squeezed her shoulder. "The orchard's harvest is your family's livelihood. That is where you need to focus your attention. Don't worry about trading buggy rides for house paint and doorknobs right now. Okay?"

"Yeah, okay."

The man from the outside world gave Caroline a peculiar look. His eyes narrowed briefly, but whatever thought played upon his expression didn't affect his voice. "After the harvest season is over, the buggy will be waiting for you to play taxi driver."

At this, she looked up with a glint of hope in her eyes. "So the elders are not forbidding my business?"

Connor's dark brow furrowed. "I'm simply relaying John's message. Don't worry about the village deliveries right now. Stay home and take care of your brother and your chores. Since the harvest is as important to the village as it is to you, we will have men out here every day helping to pick and store the fruit." He released her shoulder with a nod of satisfaction that his message was getting through Caroline's emotions to her logic. "Okay?"

She echoed his affirmation one last time, in the same inflection he used, almost as if it were her native accent. And with the next breath, she smiled sweetly. "We've been overwhelmed by the kindness of everyone—almost everyone—since we arrived. Tell John we appreciate the help."

Connor tipped his hat to Jedidiah. "I'll relay Noah's condition to Lydia."

"Very well. Unless something changes, I will be at the medical cottage in the morning as scheduled and give her a full report then."

Caroline followed Connor to the door, and Jedidiah followed Caroline without knowing why. He needed to leave too, but he wanted to stay with her and speak to her alone while he had the chance.

He waited until Connor was riding away before stepping out of the mudroom and onto the little wooden porch behind Caroline's moonlit figure.

While the screen door closed, he deeply inhaled the floral-scented night air. "Is that jasmine?"

"Primrose."

"You inherited quite a flower garden. It blends in the air beautifully with the orchard's aroma."

She entwined her arms in front of her like a child and stared blankly toward the moon-draped orchard, her only response a weak hum of agreement.

He'd given her an opening to talk about her beloved flowers, yet she hadn't taken it. He stepped down next to her on the bottom porch rung. "Caroline, your brother will be fine."

"I know."

Sadness edged her voice, tugging at his heart. Despite wanting to pull her into his arms where they could cry together, he maintained his professional demeanor. "And your family and the orchard will be fine."

"Yes, I know."

"And you will get to drive your buggy again soon."

"It's not just the driving I enjoy." She scooped her skirt under her as she sat on the porch step. "It's the people. Getting out of the house and seeing lots of people, even if for only a little while. I wasn't allowed a social life in all my years in Northcrest. When I learned Noah inherited this property and we were moving here, I determined to get to know as many people as possible."

Jedidiah knew the thrill of saving a life and the satisfaction of repairing a body, but once a patient was well, he preferred his interaction with them to end. How could he be so drawn to a woman he barely understood? Dr. Ashton always said that understanding came from learning and learning from intentional study. He sat beside her, ready to learn. "Why do you enjoy talking with strangers so much?"

"You sound like Noah."

"Pardon my question. I meant it with genuine interest."

She shrugged. "To me, they aren't strangers. I guess it's because everyone has a story. If a person can't tell their own story, the next best thing is to hear someone else's. I love to hear everyone's story. Even if they don't think they are telling me theirs, I hear it in their simple comments and what concerns them. Even in their opinion of the weather."

"The weather?" He leaned his elbows back on the porch's scuffed wood planks and gazed up at the stars and the oval moon. "Well, it is my opinion that tonight's fine weather is a generous gift from the Creator, so that we might take this moment to pick out which of Abraham's stars we think is named for us."

She snapped her head toward him. "That's the most beautiful thing I've ever heard."

"Good." He didn't take his eyes off the sky, but could feel her surprised smile. "So, did you hear my story in it?"

She went silent for a moment, and in that moment he felt more was being said between them than in a thousand audible words.

But the longer the normally loquacious woman remained silent, the more he feared she hadn't heard him. And for the first time in his life, he wanted to be heard, to be known, but only by her.

He glanced her way.

She was gazing up at the stars too, and so he returned his attention to the sky, but kept his voice quiet enough to prove he wanted privacy. "I come from a most difficult family. I mean my parents no dishonor, but the older I got, the more I realized how ungodly their characters were. I cannot express the degree of my disappointment in them, especially in my father. I took very few pleasant memories when I left home to apprentice with our Dr. Ashton in Stonehill."

At the edge of his vision, he saw her turn her face to him. If he was going to tell her anything about himself, which she deserved to know before he courted her, he couldn't look directly at her until he'd said what he needed to say. "With Dr. Ashton's blessing, I left the past behind in Stonehill and came here. My greatest desire is to forge my own life in Good Springs with intentionality in God's ways. To do so, I had to sever the binds with my family."

"You aren't speaking to them?"

"I told them I would only write to them once per year, and I prefer the same from them, until they are repentant for their sins against God and their workers." He touched his vest pocket, which still had last week's folded letter from his mother, unopened. "My mother disregards my wishes and writes to me incessantly. I only opened the first few letters, then stopped."

"Why?"

That question was harder for him to answer, not because he didn't know the words to say, but because uttering his most private thoughts felt like standing in a crowd unclothed.

But if he wanted Caroline to enjoy his company, he had to give her the story she longed for—at least some of it. "For two reasons. First, because she is not repentant. She boasts of her devious behavior and finds it amusing to mock those they oppress. Second, because until I am officially titled here, if my father and my older brother were to both perish, I would inherit the mining operations and be expected to return to Stonehill and spend my life running a business I detest."

He didn't receive a gasp of horror as expected, nor did she assault him with questions. As interested as she was in humanity, she didn't probe. His respect for her grew more than he knew was possible.

When he finally turned his face to meet her gaze, she simply nodded once and said, "Smart man."

This was indeed a woman he could love for the rest of his life.

She toed off her shoes, crossed her feet out in front of her, and tilted her face to the sky. "The moonlight is perfect tonight, and the air. It felt like this a lot back home—well, not exactly like this—but bright and beautiful on cool summer evenings when my family would sit on the fishing pier and talk. We'd let our feet dangle over the edge. Noah was the quietest. Lena was so little she would fall asleep on our parents' lap. They would sit so close together even a moonbeam couldn't squeeze between them. We'd talk about our day and… whatever." Her lovely grin spread with the memory. "I would sit between Noah and our parents. While Lena slept, she usually had a leg hanging over mine."

"It sounds as though our families were opposite in every possible way."

"Every family has good and bad moments. I like to focus on the good. And the more I focus on the good memories, the less I remember anything bad."

Now she made him smile. "To be as joyful as you are, I find it hard to believe anything truly bad has ever happened to you in your life."

Her smile remained, but the light left her eyes. "Those parents were our real parents. We lost them when we were young, so yes, I know heart-wrenching pain."

"I'm sorry." Apparently, there was as much he didn't know about her as she didn't know about him. "So the family you lived with in Northcrest before coming here was your—"

"Our adoptive family." She lifted a hand to the orchard. "They only had one child, Eli. He inherited their property in Northcrest. We inherited this place from our adoptive father's brother. We never met him. But since he had no heir, he left it to Noah."

He scanned the silvery orchard that disappeared into the distance and the massive barn across the yard. "Such a blessing hardly makes up for enduring such a tragedy."

"We endured great tragedy, yes. But that's no reason to bemoan every moment of every day."

Even in her sadness, the light of hope shined out of her soul. He shifted on the porch step to face her. "You seem to believe the old poets' line about every cloud having a silver lining. Do you always look for them?"

"Look for them? Ha! I live under them." She chuckled at herself, then shifted to face him too, their knees touching. "I truly believe there is good to be found in any bad circumstance. Don't you?"

Now it was he who shrugged. "I don't think of circumstances as good nor bad, simply challenges to work through."

"That sounds very wise." One corner of her mouth curved up. "Not particularly fun, but wise."

She studied her fingers as she laced them in her lap. "You wondered if anything truly bad has ever happened to me. Now I have to wonder if anything truly enjoyable has ever happened to you."

Sitting here with her was the most enjoyable experience of his life and the only one he could ever imagine. When he didn't respond quickly enough for her, she playfully nudged him with her shoulder. "Come on, have you ever had a moment of fun in your life? Enjoyment, bliss, some circumstance that was truly good?"

"Yes… this."

"This?"

He slipped a hand between hers and unlaced her fingers to entwine them with his own. "This."

CHAPTER NINE

The autumn equinox announced the beginning of harvest time in the Land, with its balance of daylight and darkness, and the promise of cooler temperatures and fullness of cellars. It also brought the aching, watery pain that only an anniversary can dredge from the emotional sediment of the heart.

As soon as Caroline drove home after her last delivery for the day, she scanned the property for any sign of harvest helpers being there. No wagons, no horses. The barn doors were all still open, so Noah was still working.

She parked the buggy in front of the barn's double door, then untacked Captain and walked him to the trough by the side paddock. "Have a long drink of water and eat some hay." She latched the paddock gate to close him in. "I'll come get you for a good brush down in a little while."

She left the buggy in front of the barn and hurried inside, hoping to speak to Noah while he was alone. It took a moment for her eyes to adjust to the dim barn. Late afternoon light sent a dust-speckled stream through the back doorway. She glanced at the milk cow's stall, the horse stalls, and Noah's workroom as she dashed through the cavernous building. No sign of her brother, or his energetic herding dog.

Stacking trays full of apples filled the storage room. The harvesters had been busy today.

So had she.

The barn cast its last shadow toward the orchard, touching the first trees in the long, soldier-like rows. The clank of a wooden ladder and swish of netting drew her into the orchard. "Noah?"

"Over here." His call was followed by one stout bark from Nipper.

The dog was close beside Noah while he traipsed through the orchard, with his ladder over one shoulder and a hunk of netting over the other. The net trailed the ground behind him like a bridal train. His straw hat was tilted to one side, and his whisker shadow made him look like Dad after a full day of sailing.

Caroline reached for the netting to take a load off Noah. "Here, I'll carry this for you."

He didn't let go. "No, it's helping me to balance the ladder."

"Okay, okay." She walked beside him toward the barn. "How's your back?"

"All better. Like I told you this morning. I wish you'd quit asking me."

"I just want to help."

"Then let me be a man and take care of myself."

She raised both palms in mock surrender. "Fine, just don't overdo it."

"You sound like—" He stopped himself before he said the name.

Caroline gave him a side glance. "Ah, so you do know what day it is."

"Of course I do. I can't believe it has been twenty-one years." His voice lost its toughness. "You okay?"

"Yeah. Better than I was last year." The sun dipped low in the western horizon on the other side of the barn. She stopped outside the doorway and waited while he carried his equipment inside. "Having this place and all the work and worry that came with it has helped us both to move on."

Noah didn't respond. He simply hung the ladder in the workroom and stretched out the net to pick the stray twigs and leaves from it. When he was done, he pointed at the end of the net that was nearest her feet and she lifted it up to help him fold it.

When he stepped close to take her corners of the net, he briefly met her gaze. "How were the deliveries today?"

"Okay, I guess. It felt good to be back to work... to have something to do away from the house. Even if I only have the one route. At least I can still earn a few things for the house."

He shrugged. "The apple crop is abundant. Peaches too. I expect lots of cherries next month. We'll have plenty to trade for all the materials we need to fix up the house, and I can help you with the house projects during the winter. So, don't worry about your earnings with the buggy. You have plenty to do around here."

Now it was she who shrugged. "I suppose."

He flopped the folded harvesting net onto a pile of others and then turned to her, dirt-caked hands propped on his hips. "What's up, Care-Care?"

At some point she had to say something about that. It might as well be now. Still, her voice barely rose above a whisper. "I wish you'd stop calling me that."

He drew his chin back. "I've always called you that."

"No, Dad always called me that. You only started after he died."

"Oh. Sorry. It was unconsciously done."

She tried to smile to soften the blow, but didn't have one more left in her today. "I guess it's probably like how you don't want me to sound like Mom."

"Yeah. I get it."

"It's hard not to sound like them to each other."

He pointed out the barn's back doorway at the rows of trees. "Well, you know where the apple falls?"

She chuckled once. "Neither of us fell far from the tree. We might always remind each other of them."

He scratched his whiskered jaw with a thumb. "Maybe that's not such a bad thing."

"Maybe."

"This day is always hard." He waved a hand for her to follow him while he closed the back door and walked through the barn, straightening up for the evening. "Did you get to see Jedidiah when you made the delivery to his house today?"

She hadn't said a word to anyone about their sweet conversation on the porch last month. "No. He's never home."

After a month of not seeing him, she'd decided the sensible physician either wasn't really that interested in her or he was the slowest moving man in the Land when it came to romance. She walked out the side door to the paddock where Captain was waiting for her, then hollered back over her shoulder at Noah. "Why do you ask?"

She didn't hear a response, and as she walked Captain to his stall, she glanced around for Noah. He was pushing her buggy into its place inside the barn's big front opening. He closed the double doors and brushed his hands together. "Because I think you like him."

Captain snorted happily while she brushed the dirt off him with his favorite curry comb.

"I like everyone."

Noah carried a bucket past her on his way to milk the cow. He paused long enough to give her an I-know-better stare.

"Okay, fine. I like him."

"And?"

"And what?"

"Does he like you too?"

"I don't know. I thought so. He said he enjoys my company—whatever that means."

Noah stepped into the milk cow's stall and out of sight, but she could still hear him clearly. "For a man in the Land, that means a lot. Especially for a guy like Jed."

"Don't let him hear you call him that."

"See, that's what I'm talking about. He's somewhat stiff."

"I want more than stiff. And he is more than that... at least, when we actually have time alone. His job keeps him too busy for that, though."

"It's just part of it."

"Yeah, I know." She smoothed a hand over Captain's flank, then filled his oat bucket and hung it on the stall gate for him to eat. Somehow, her feelings for Jedidiah would be easier to explain to her horse than to her brother.

Maybe she never would find a soulmate. Not that she didn't adore the friendships she was making. But there was something else, something more, she wanted. The deep connection of one loyal companion to whom she could tell her true story—her full story. Someone who needed to know her as much as she needed to be known. But she was probably wishing for something that didn't happen for most people, and probably wouldn't happen for her. "I guess I'm destined to be alone my whole life."

Noah carried the full milk pail out of the stall. "You won't be alone. You have your flower garden."

"Very funny. The neighbor children will call me *the spinster Vestal* and throw rocks at me while I'm pulling weeds."

He grinned but didn't laugh. "Maybe Lena's boyfriend in Falls Creek has a brother you can write to."

"Goodness, don't let her know you know about Philip's letters. She'd melt into a puddle of embarrassment."

She followed him out of the barn and closed the side door behind them. "And what about you? I see how the single ladies at church look at you. One of them will snatch you up one day soon. You will marry a nice girl, and Lena will get swept away to Falls Creek, and then I'll certainly be all alone."

Nipper danced hotly at their heels, impatient with their slow pace to the house.

Caroline was enjoying the conversation too much to let the dog hurry them. "Are there any ladies in Good Springs that have caught your eye?"

"I'm too focused on the orchard to think about that."

"Don't you want a family of your own?"

He switched the pail to the other hand. "Sure. Someday. Don't you?"

"A trusted, lifelong companion who loves me as much as I love him, yes. A family? I know as a woman in the Land, I'm supposed to say I'm yearning to have children. But... honestly, I'm not. I don't mind kids. I practically raised Lena. I suppose if she gets married and I don't have anyone to take care of, my clock might start ticking."

Noah chortled. "It isn't already?"

"Nope."

"Well, don't worry, Care-Care, I mean, Caroline, you can always cook and clean for me."

She would have sharp elbowed him if he wasn't carrying something. Instead, she just laughed. "Oh, you say that now while you're single, but one of these Good Springs ladies will snap you up. And then where will I go?"

He paused at the bottom of the porch steps, his gaze darkening, his voice quiet. "You won't have to go anywhere. We have plenty of space in the house. I promised Dad I would take care of you girls, and I will keep that promise."

"I know you will." Something about talking to Noah always made her feel better. She followed him into the mudroom and breathed in the full aroma of Lena's scrumptious dinner preparations. Pots were simmering on the stovetop, but Lena wasn't in the kitchen. Down the hall, the washroom door was closed and the water was running.

Caroline took the opportunity to whisper to Noah. "So, Lena's correspondence with the preacher in Falls Creek..."

"Yeah?"

"She's doesn't think you know he's more than a pen pal. Let's keep it that way."

He set the milk pail on the floor. "Why?"

"Let her have her secrets. Goodness knows, we have ours."

* * *

Silver clinked against silver as Jedidiah arranged freshly washed medical instruments in the cabinet over Dr. Bradshaw's worktable. The air in the medical cottage was still thick with gray leaf aroma, and the bowl of refuse from a successful tooth extraction still needed to be taken to the burn pit, but the patient was better and likely home by now.

Jedidiah wished he were at home too. Not for the control of working in his own office with his own instruments and preferences. Not for the comfort of rest or the satisfaction of privacy. And certainly not for his house's empty silence. But because it was Friday and Caroline was back to making the weekly village support deliveries.

She would have gone to his house today, and he hadn't been there to see her. Again.

When he came to Good Springs, he wanted nothing more than to have the security of being a titled doctor.

Something was changing, though.

Caroline was changing him.

He still desired his official title. Without it there was no point in pursuing Caroline because if he were forced to return to Stonehill, he wouldn't dare ruin her life by taking her with him into that wasp nest. But now, he wanted something in addition to the career security and the command of his own circumstances; he wanted to share that life with her.

Not simply to share it, but to enjoy it—the way she seemed to enjoy almost everything in life.

In the little time they had spent together, she'd stirred in him desires for a life he'd never considered. Thinking of her sweet smile and blissful laugh only made him admire her more. Though they rarely spent time together, the more he thought of her, the more he felt he knew her.

Even his vague wariness when she said something odd was being smothered by his desire to be closer to her. Surely his suspicion was simply residue from being raised by people who'd deeply disappointed him. He'd felt it with everyone now, and that was to be expected. Caroline didn't deserve such unwarranted judgement. How could she ever disappoint him when she overflowed with such optimism?

Whenever he was around her, he felt her joy lifting his spirit along with hers. And while he was in the middle of this afternoon's tooth extraction, her buggy arrived at the Colburn house. He'd heard her happy voice talking to John while she delivered his baskets and wished he could leave his patient and go to her.

But he couldn't leave his work, nor resent it. For without his profession, he would have no life to offer her. And yet with his profession, he had no time to woo her into his life.

It was the one challenge he wasn't trained to overcome.

Once the medical office was cleaned and Dr. Bradshaw came to relive him of duty, Jedidiah walked the flagstone path to the main house to say goodbye to John before walking home. He needed to keep himself and his work in the overseer's attention.

The back door was open, as always. The homey aroma of roasted chicken wafted through the air. Jedidiah tapped a knuckle on the doorframe and leaned through. "Mr. Colburn?"

"John went to the Fosters' for dinner." Connor stepped out of the pantry with his sleeves cuffed and a potato in each hand. "What's up?"

The house was unusually quiet for late afternoon. He crossed the threshold, scanning the wide kitchen for Connor and Dr. Bradshaw's little boy. "Did he take Andrew with him?"

"Yep." Connor carried the potatoes to the sink and started peeling with vigor. "I get a date night with my wife."

Jedidiah, too, wished for an evening with the woman he admired. But duty came first. "Dr. Bradshaw said I was free to go home. Should I stay at the medical office in case a patient arrives while you're having dinner?"

Connor shook his head. "You've worked a ton lately, and Lydia wants you to have some rest and relaxation too. Besides, she and I have handled this for years. We can make it through an evening on our own."

"Very well." Jedidiah turned to leave, but stopped and pointed at the empty baskets by the door. "I saw Caroline Vestal is back to delivering the village support."

"Yeah. Yours will be at your house when you get home."

"Excellent. I'm glad she was able to resume her deliveries. The work means a lot to her. I'd heard there was a complaint to the council."

Connor chopped the peeled potatoes so quickly Jedidiah wondered if he might have one more patient tonight after all. "Caroline has nothing to worry about.

Some of the ladies did the same thing to Lydia while she was apprenticing to become a doctor—the Land's first female doctor. They were worried about her riding to patients' houses at night, about her being alone with male patients, stuff like that. John assured them Lydia was the right person for the job, and everything was fine."

Jedidiah slipped his hands into his pockets and felt an unopened letter from home. "Yes, well, Dr. Bradshaw was fortunate to have a father whose word can be trusted by the village. Not everyone has a family of such a good character, let alone a father who is the overseer. Caroline doesn't have such an advantage."

Connor slid the potato chunks into a boiling pot, then brushed his hands together and turned to Jedidiah. "Have you been able to get to know the Vestals much living out there by them?"

The rise of Connor's brow hinted at suspicion, but whether it was directed at the Vestals or at Jedidiah, he couldn't tell. He withdrew his hands from his pockets and straightened his posture. "A little. I don't see them as often as a neighbor should, since I am here more than there. I have been to their property thrice—most recently, when Noah needed medical attention."

"Your family probably knew their family in Stonehill. You're from the same village, right?"

Jedidiah stepped farther into the kitchen. "No, I believe they came here from Northcrest."

"They came here from Northcrest. That's where they lived after they were adopted by the Vestal family there."

She hadn't mentioned Stonehill at all. He would have remembered that fact. "Are you certain?"

Connor gave the pot a stir. "Yep. I met their adoptive father when I traveled to Northcrest a while back. He's on the village council there. He told me then how his youngest three were adopted as children from Stonehill when his distant relatives there drowned and left the kids with no one else to take them. He said he was passing his farm to his eldest son, as is tradition. That's why Noah inherited the orchard here when their uncle died without an heir."

She had told him part of the story. But why not all of it? "I'm pleased for Noah's sake, though I've never heard of an adopted second son inheriting such a living."

"It was the right thing for all of them. And apparently for us too. Good Springs needs a man like Noah running that orchard."

Though Jedidiah agreed Noah was a hard worker and certainly knew how to make the most of the orchard, there was much he did not know about the man or the family, apparently. Why had Caroline not mentioned that she was actually from Stonehill? Jedidiah leaned back against the counter. "Is their situation public knowledge?"

Connor narrowed his eyes briefly. "I wouldn't be telling you if it wasn't."

"Of course." He pushed away from the counter and paced to the doorway for cooler air. "I wasn't aware they were from Stonehill, that's all. Not that they were obligated to tell me—not as their neighbor, nor as Noah's physician. If the elder councils in Northcrest and Good Springs settled the inheritance matter openly, then there is no reason for Noah—or Caroline—to speak of their history to everyone they meet."

"Exactly. It was probably difficult enough for them to be orphaned and have to move to a new village and integrate into a new family at such a young age."

"I'm sure it was." Though the more he talked about it, the less sure he was of anything to do with the Vestal siblings. He had to ask again. "Are you certain they are originally from Stonehill?"

"Yes. I'm certain." Connor cracked the oven door to check the bird. "Noah and Caroline are about your age. That's why I asked if you knew them there. I figured you probably went to grammar school together."

"I don't remember them." With only one small grammar school in the village, he certainly would have known if they had attended it. He could remember the face and name of every child at school and could picture where they sat in class. Maybe the family had stayed clear of the village—probably because of his parents. Maybe they had been schooled at home.

Or maybe the Vestal siblings were lying about who they were and where they were from.

He didn't know Noah well enough to judge him, and Lena seemed scared of her own shadow. It was unthinkable, especially for some as lighthearted as Caroline, to be involved in deep deception.

But it would justify his suspicion.

And break his heart.

He didn't want to learn that Caroline's life was a lie, but he had to discover the truth before his feelings for her clouded his discernment.

His parents knew—and controlled—almost every inch of the village of Stonehill. They knew everyone and forgot nothing.

But he would not ask them.

He would write to the one man who'd always remained autonomous. Dr. Ashton also knew everyone in the area, and if a couple died twenty years ago and left three children who were adopted by distant relatives, Dr. Ashton would know.

He would have signed the parents' death records and may have witnessed the children's adoption.

No woman had intrigued Jedidiah like Caroline Vestal because no woman had deserved his attention the way she did. If there had been a dishonest scheme concocted to win an inheritance, it was likely the brother's doing. He couldn't imagine the joyful Caroline or the timid Lena being behind it. But if it were so, they were in danger of being accused of fraud every moment they went along with it.

He had to find out the truth—for Caroline and her sister, for the village of Good Springs, for his future happiness. But he also had to protect her from the consequences of such a scheme.

He gave Connor a nod and turned to leave. "Enjoy your evening with your wife."

CHAPTER TEN

Jedidiah paced to the expansive window in his office. The tall glass panes provided all the sunlight he could wish for, but no view of the road in front of his property. Just another proof that the fulfillment of any desire always brought an unforeseen difficulty.

And he firmly believed every difficulty brought a unique opportunity.

Such as the fact the windows' private view meant he would not have to close the curtains and thus lose his much desired light whenever he was treating a patient.

Perhaps that fact was less of an opportunity and more of a silver lining. Caroline's talent for finding those must be influencing his thinking. And surely he too would find the good in the seemingly bad news he'd received today.

The box from Stonehill that Revel delivered this morning sat empty on the floor, its contents now neatly arranged in Jedidiah's medical supply cabinet. Dr. Ashton had sent him a full set of shiny new instruments, as well as bowls and patient drapes.

And one very important letter.

It had taken two weeks for Jedidiah's letter to get to Dr. Ashton in Stonehill and the much-anticipated reply to come. Two weeks of plunging himself into his work at the medical cottage, covering every extra shift he could to keep his thoughts from drifting out of fact and into speculation. But finally today, Dr. Ashton's response had arrived.

Jedidiah unfolded the letter again to re-read it, as if this time the information would be different, the prognosis better.

But it was not.

No, Dr. Ashton did not know a family of five that was separated by the parents' tragic death and the children adopted by relatives from Northcrest. No such incident had occurred in his lifetime, and he was nearing his sixtieth year. He knew all the families in Stonehill and certainly could account for all those of the Vestal surname. No children had been orphaned in Stonehill twenty years ago. Perhaps in another village, but not in his.

Jedidiah dropped the open letter onto his unadorned desk. Reading it again only strengthened his questions and deepened the ache in his heart. He'd known better than to trust anyone. How had he allowed such a disappointment to rattle him... again?

Wagon wheels rumbled down the road. He hurried to the front room and peered out the window beside the door.

The horse and buggy pulled onto his property just like clockwork. It was Friday afternoon, and she was as punctual as a schoolteacher and as reliable as gray leaf medicine. Still, Dr. Ashton's letter proved Caroline was hiding some great deception, and that was one flaw Jedidiah couldn't tolerate.

Not if they had a future together.

And how he prayed they did!

With one hand on the doorknob, he commanded himself to wait for her to knock. It took all of his resolve not to run out to meet her, especially since he hadn't seen her for two weeks. That time apart was by his own arranging, thinking it wise while he awaited Dr. Ashton's reply.

It had only made him miss her company, her optimism. Had she even noticed he wasn't around?

He blew out a slow breath and closed his eyes, like a child waiting to be found during a game of hide-and-seek. The instant a delicate boot heel tapped the stoop, he yanked the door open. "Hello, Caroline."

She flinched, wobbling the full basket in her arms. "Oh, my!" Her delightful giggle filled his house like the music of his dreams. "I didn't expect you to be home. What a lovely surprise!"

He took the basket from her arms and locked eyes with her. "Thank you."

When he didn't move or say more, the brilliance in her smile faded. "What's wrong, Jedidiah?"

It required more determination than he'd anticipated just to break his gaze. Somehow, he managed to set the basket on the kitchen floor and return to the door.

She hadn't left the mat, concern replacing her surprise. "Did you have a bad day at work?"

"Come in." He motioned to the nearby table, which was flanked by two of the chairs she had given him. "Have a seat."

While she perched obediently on the edge of a ladder-back chair, he closed the door, the click of its latch the only sound in the room.

His dry tongue refused to cooperate. Perhaps he should simply forget the matter and consider this an opportunity to forget and forgive without demanding an explanation.

She slipped off her driving gloves, revealing one elegant hand at a time. "I know you aren't allowed to talk about your patients, but if you can't tell me what happened, can you at least tell me if you're all right? Honestly, you look like you saw a ghost."

At that, he found his tongue. "*Honestly*, you say?"

"Pardon?"

"You claim honest concern for me, yet you haven't been honest with me since we met. Have you?"

She shook her head at him, not in answer to his rhetorical question, but in disapproval of his demeanor. "I've had a difficult day too, Jedidiah, but I can still be kind."

"Answer my question."

She shot to her feet. "I don't need to be treated this way." Her words were fierce, but her hands trembled with the knowledge of being exposed. "You once told me you enjoyed my company. And today you invited me in. Then, bam! You accuse me of dishonesty." She yanked on her gloves. "Good day, *Mister* Cotter. Enjoy your delivery. Next week, I'll leave it at your doorstep and not bother you."

He let her fume but didn't move away from the door. She finally looked him in the eye and crossed her arms tightly over her green dress. It wasn't her work dress, it was her church dress. She had wanted to look her best to impress those she hoped would approve of her.

He knew the feeling.

She blew out a breath and tilted her head. "Move out of my way if you want me to leave."

"I don't want you to leave."

"Then what do you want?"

"Come with me." He peeled her angry fingers from her crossed arm and led her into his office. "You told me your family was from Northcrest. Is that true?"

The lift of her eyebrows wasn't a nod. Since it was all the response he was going to get, he continued. "So imagine my surprise when Connor mentioned that you and I supposedly grew up in the same village— Stonehill."

She pulled her fingertips from his hand and re-crossed her arms.

He would not let her defiance prevent him. "I don't remember you or your siblings ever living in Stonehill. So, I wrote to the doctor under whom I apprenticed. Dr. Ashton has lived in Stonehill his whole life and knows every family and every tragedy." He pointed to the letter atop his desk, hoping she would look at it. "Dr. Ashton replied that he never heard of a couple drowning in Stonehill and their three children being sent to live with relatives in Northcrest, who immediately adopted them. He said whomever told me such a tale was surely mistaken."

Her gaze dropped to the floor. "You checked my family's story behind my back?"

"Is Dr. Ashton correct?"

"How could you be so cruel?"

Because he wanted the truth for his reputation's sake as much as for his own future happiness. Because he was selfish and harsh and if she was lying, she needed to know he would not tolerate such behavior, not in a wife or in a friend.

Because he'd been raised by cruel people who treated him thus while they were the ones living a lie.

At that thought, his aching shoulders slumped. He would not carry on as if the judge of her when she was not his to chastise. And in the future, he would not behave cruelly. Even if she ever was his, she would be his to love.

He lowered himself to the edge of the canvas patient cot, leaving her standing in the superior position. "Please, tell me how your parents died."

Her voice was as cold as his new metal instruments. "They drowned in a boating accident."

"In Stonehill?"

"Off the coast of the Land."

"And you and Noah and Lena were adopted by distant relatives living in Northcrest?"

"Yes."

"How distant?"

She gazed up at the ceiling, whether remembering her deceased parents or beseeching her Maker or thinking of a lie, he did not know. Her voice was lighter when she spoke. "Well, we are all descendants of Adam and Eve, so we are all related, if you think about it."

He wouldn't scold her, but he wouldn't grant her a humorous way out of the conversation, either. He stood and didn't speak until she met his gaze. "I have thought about this a great deal, Caroline, but came to a different conclusion." He proffered the letter. "No one seems to know about your family's tragedy, except you three and your adoptive parents."

"You once told me you were on my side and always would be."

"And I am on your side. That's why I need the truth."

Instead of taking the letter, she turned away from him and faced the window. Her voice was smaller, tighter, as if reserving itself for private weeping later. "Just because every person in the Land doesn't know my story doesn't mean it didn't happen. My parents died. I was there. I saw them slip under the water, sink out of sight, out of reach. I know what happened. Noah was there. He knows."

"Caroline—"

She pressed her thin fingertips to her forehead. "We didn't let Lena watch. She was too young. She doesn't remember anything about it. And Noah and I agreed long ago to keep it that way."

He took a step toward her, his heart aching with every grief-stricken phrase she uttered. "Caroline—"

She closed her hands over her face. "Why can't you let this go?"

He reached for her reluctant shoulders and turned her to face him. "Because I don't want to let you go."

She didn't speak but only remained locked with her hands over her face, her head against his chest.

"Caroline, I want to love you, the real you, with everything in me. But how can I if you won't tell me the truth?"

As he bent his head to kiss the top of hers, she slipped from his arms and wiped the single tear from her cheek. "I won't talk about this anymore. I lived through it once. Since it happened when I was only eight, I've had to live through it over and over all my life. So has Noah."

His desperate hands reached for her once more, but she took another step back. "I know there is something you aren't telling me. Something important, and it eats at you. I can see it, Caroline. Please, tell me who you really are."

She smiled, but it didn't reach her eyes. "I'm your neighbor. I deliver your village support every Friday. I enjoy gardening, meeting people, and buggy driving."

"What really happened to your family?"

"Haven't I been through enough?"

With each step he took toward her, she took one toward the door. He stopped where he was. "I don't want to hurt you, Caroline."

She paused her retreat mid-step and narrowed her eyes. "And yet you do."

Before he could think of a response, she marched to the front door and let herself out.

The bright sun streaming into his office wasn't enough to shed light on what he should do. Running after her and apologizing would leave him without his integrity and the truth. Going to Connor or John with his suspicions and Dr. Ashton's letter would only create enemies out of the very person he wanted to be his friend—more than his friend.

He wanted her to be his wife.

But how could he pursue her if she wouldn't tell him the truth?

* * *

Caroline cursed her trembling fingers while she clumsily freed Captain from the buggy, each buckle and strap refusing to give her a moment's grace. "Why should I expect grace from an inanimate object?" She mumbled to her horse, as she paused to smooth her quivering hand down his mane. "I can't even get grace from our charming physician neighbor."

The horse huffed as she walked him to the paddock beside the barn.

"That's right, Captain. I shouldn't expect anything from anyone. All I wanted was to make some friends, fix up the old house, have a life."

While he drank from the trough, the horse's ears flickered.

Caroline took it he was still listening. "Jedidiah was the one who said he liked me. He was the one who was always taking my hand—as if women like to be led around like that. He was the one who said he wanted to love—"

She stopped herself when her full-volume voice reverberated off the empty trough as she pumped water from the well. The words she almost said shouldn't be shouted, even if only the horse was there to hear her. She lowered her voice to the gentle tone Captain seemed to prefer. "He said he wanted to love me, the real me."

"Who are you talking to?" Noah hollered from the barn door, his grease-covered hands polishing some rusty farm implement.

Caroline made a silly face at him and pointed a thumb at the horse. "Just old Captain here. All the mad spinsters in the Land talk to their horses, don't you know?"

Noah held up whatever he was working on to the light to inspect it. "Well, don't. You aren't a spinster. Besides, it makes you sound like Grandma whenever she couldn't get the TV remote to work."

Instantly, her eyes scanned the yard, the garden, and the house. "Is Lena inside?"

"Of course." He took his attention off the tool long enough to raise an eyebrow at her. "What's got you so edgy?"

He was the one person in Good Springs who knew the whole truth—the truth Jedidiah had begged to hear. But he was also the one person who would lose everything if that truth were revealed. He didn't deserve the position their adoptive parents had put him in, nor did she.

Still, every day they invested their lives in this orchard, keeping their cover story seemed more important, no matter how much her insides felt like bursting open. She forced a casual shrug. "I just don't want anyone to overhear anything and get the wrong idea."

He shook out his shop rag. "How'd your deliveries go?"

"Fine."

"Did you tell everyone we'll have crates of Lena's preserves available for trade at the market tomorrow, and pies next week?"

She closed the paddock gate, giving its latch far more scrutiny than necessary. "I told Connor when I picked up the deliveries at the chapel."

"Cool. He'll get the word out. That guy talks to everyone. And everyone talks to him. He has that kind of relaxed way about him that makes conversation easy."

She hadn't found Connor particularly easy to talk to. It seemed he had a suspicious brow raised at her half the time. "I don't like a gossip."

Noah flapped the work rag at her and walked back into the barn. "He's no gossip, but believe me, that guy knows everybody's business. I can tell."

While Noah disappeared into the barn, his words sank into her mind. Surely Jedidiah didn't talk to everyone too. He was far more introverted than Connor.

He had said he didn't want to hurt her, but what if his suspicions drove him to take the matter to John? He'd already written to his old boss to verify the story. And he'd said Connor was the person who told him she was originally from Stonehill.

Maybe Jedidiah was already in discussions with Connor and John about this, in the same way that Mrs. Owens's complaint made it through the village elders and into the common chatter before Caroline had heard a word if it.

Her heart sank and took her hope along with it.

There would be no jovial autumn harvest party on her back lawn, flowing with throngs of happy villagers and new admirers. Her parlor wouldn't host gaggles of village ladies who marveled at the beautiful decor. She wouldn't have people waving her down along the village roads for rides into town, chatting and laughing and enjoying the autumn breeze while trading her their freshly baked this or intricately stitched that for her services.

She could not fashion a life here that would look anything like Mom's back in America—the old America before whatever happened that had destroyed it and the world.

What could she do? What should she do?

There had to be a bright side to the dark clouds that filled her life.

As she ambled toward the house, she let her gaze follow the trees to the crisp afternoon sky.

The summer had passed and taken its humid air with it. The earth and the orchard had lost the sweetness of flower and budding fruit. All was now spicier with the drying foliage of limb and vine.

Tomorrow was the orchard's biggest offering at the market so far. They needed this village to accept them, not suspect them. She needed friends, allies. Just in case.

She might not be able to count on Jedidiah, even though he had once said he would always be on her side, but she still had one friend here.

Four crates of preserves stood on the back porch. She owed Bette a visit and some compensation for the chicken flock since Sue had mandated the children not be driven to town anymore.

She slipped three jars out of the crate and nestled them into the crook of her arm, then peered through the screen door. "Lena?"

"Yes?"

"Mind if I take three jars of apple jam to Bette?"

"That's a good idea."

"Do you want to come with me?"

Lena's silhouette moved into the doorway between the kitchen and the mudroom. "You mean to visit Bette and the kids?"

"Sure. You made the jam, after all."

"Oh, um. Can't you just tell her for me?"

"Tell her what?"

"How grateful we are for the chickens."

"All right. I'll be home in time to help with dinner."

Lena's figure moved back into the kitchen. "No need. Sandwiches and salads tonight since I've been working on the jars all day."

The delight in her sister's voice brought some hope back to Caroline's heart. "I hope it's all worth it for you."

Lena sang out from deep inside the kitchen. "It certainly is!"

Instead of walking out to the road or cutting straight across from their property to the Owens's, Caroline zigzagged around the garden shed and behind the chicken coop. Her feathery friends were clucking happily. At least she'd gotten one thing right here. And that success was thanks to Bette.

Before coming to the first row of apple trees, she ducked to miss a low branch in the hedges that separated the properties. The jars in her arm clinked lightly. Smoke from the chimney rose in delicate wisps above Bette's darling cottage.

Caroline tapped a knuckle on the door and glanced behind her at the Owens's house and then over toward their fields. No one was in sight.

Bette cracked the door with a frown. It quickly flipped to a smile when she saw it was Caroline. "Oh, come in. I do apologize. I thought the children had returned from their grandparents' house early. I wondered why they would knock."

Her silky auburn locks whirled behind her as she spun into the kitchen, waving a hand for Caroline to follow her in. "Sorry, but I must finish steaming this brim before the straw sets in place."

Caroline scanned the spotless cottage with its snug layout and few possessions. Here she'd fussed over making their big farmhouse a showpiece when a simple dwelling sweetly cared for made one feel at home. Perhaps that was all she'd truly wanted... to feel at home.

She set the jars on the table. "These are a small thank you from us. It hardly makes up for my not being able to give the children rides to the village, but between this and the pies I'll bring you next week, you might find it a fair trade for the chickens."

Bette chuckled lightly and flicked a wrist. "Oh, stop it. You own me nothing. Simon and Josie enjoyed the rides they had with you."

"Very well."

"Yes, it is. All is well."

"So being friends with me didn't damage your relationship with Mrs. Owens?"

Bette scowled. "Sue blames me for Jack's death. Nothing could damage her opinion of me because it is as low as it can get."

"Still, I know she hates me, and I don't want to make matters worse for you by walking through her yard to get here." Caroline peeked out the little four-paned window over Bette's sink. The view was of the orchard and in the distance, Noah's barn. "I don't think I was spotted, though. I sneaked through the bushes."

"Oh, Sue sees everything," Bette mumbled through the straight pins trapped between her lips while her hands expertly steamed and formed a hat brim. She poked all the pins in place. "It tickles me so that you might sneak through bushes to visit me."

"Good." She lifted her chin at the view of the orchard. "Noah loves wearing the hat you made, by the way."

A slight blush reddened Bette's already rosy cheeks. It might have been the steam and the work, but it gave Caroline pause. She checked the window again. "Have you seen all the busy harvesting these past few weeks? Noah has worked so very hard."

Bette nodded but focused her attention on the hat.

Perhaps Caroline had only imagined the blush.

She needn't concern herself with anyone else's love life when hers was such a disaster. She leaned her hands on the back of a dining chair, wishing to pull it out, plunk down, and spend the dinner hour talking to Bette, but she needed to return home before dinner.

Bette set her steamer pot on an iron trivet and gave Caroline a side glance. "Is something wrong?"

"Hm?" Caroline broke her gaze from the hat brim and met Bette's fiercely green eyes. "Do you know Jedidiah Cotter, the new physician?"

Bette shrugged. "I met him at the medical cottage when I took Josie for a checkup last month." Her concerned face brightened with girlish interest. "Are you intrigued with him?"

Caroline suddenly felt silly, as if they were a couple of girls at a slumber party, giggling about a cute boy. How could she say that just when she'd decided it might be safe to enjoy Jedidiah's company, he'd snooped around to check her story and now he was making demands she couldn't meet?

Once again, she'd have to give someone an abbreviated version of a story she really wanted to tell in full. Sadly, she was getting good at it. She slumped into the chair. "Well, I don't know if *intrigued* is the right word."

"But there is something stirring in your heart, to be sure." Bette hurried to the table and slid a chair out. She gripped Caroline's clammy fingers with her warm hands and smiled, her eyes shining with curiosity. "Do tell me everything."

CHAPTER ELEVEN

L ast light came quickly to the Land after the autumn equinox passed. The faint glow left on the western horizon was only visible from the road between the passing houses and barns and tree trunks. The lanterns shone gently from either side of the buggy, lighting Captain's way through the village and south toward the Fosters' sheep farm. Of all the properties Caroline had delivered to in Good Springs, she'd never ventured south of John Colburn's house.

Nor had she ever been to a party in the Land, especially an annual festivity where the whole village was invited for dinner and dancing.

Her tingling stomach vibrated with the excitement. "Bette told me some customs for parties here." She checked Lena in the backseat to make sure she was listening. "When we arrive, we must first speak to the hosts, then we can go into the barn or find a seat at a table in the yard, but only if all the elderly people have taken their seats first. Oh, and everyone must dance at least once to show a good spirit. Isn't that fun?"

Noah held the reins with one hand and pointed ahead with the other. "Look at all the lights from the other buggies."

She glanced ahead at the row of distant lights, faintly piercing the dark like fireflies. "Mostly wagons, don't you think?"

"Probably." She continued giving Lena a lesson on the locals. "Levi Colburn, John's son, lives across the road from the Foster farm. He is married to a Foster."

Lena inched forward. "Is it the pregnant lady that plays the violin before church?"

"Yes, her name is Mandy. Bette said Mandy and her brother, Everett Foster, will both be adding their musical talent to the band for the dance tonight."

Noah lifted a palm. "Maybe not. Connor said Mandy and Levi are expecting their baby anytime now. Bethany and Everett's twins are due this week too."

If there were several births this week on top of Jedidiah's usual work, he might not be at the Fosters' party. Half of Caroline's heart was relieved she wouldn't have to face his accusing eyes. The other half was disappointed. She dearly wanted to speak to him again; just a few moments of conversation and she would prove to herself there could be peace between them. Maybe not romance, but peace.

At this point, she would be satisfied with him simply being a friend. She wouldn't enjoy the thrill of having a boyfriend, but it was better than having another enemy.

The truth was: she didn't know where their relationship stood. She hadn't seen him since he confronted her last week. She had gotten used to not seeing him often, but what kept her on edge was not knowing if he would confront her again, or worse, take the matter to others.

And then his sweet words saying he wanted to love her played in her mind over and over.

Lena's voice was small behind Caroline's ear. "Are there going to be many people at the party?"

"Bette says the whole village is invited every year, and it's impolite not to attend any event you are invited to." She gave Noah a side glance. "Maybe one year we can host a harvest party too."

He returned her glance with a glare.

She almost protested, then remembered what a poor job she'd already done in her social efforts here. "You're right—probably not a good idea, since half the village hates me."

Lena rubbed her shoulder. "No one hates you, Caroline. How could they?"

She patted Lena's gloved hand. "Sweet sister. Some do."

Noah huffed. "Only that cranky bat next door."

Lena sucked in a breath. "Noah!"

A laugh bubbled from Caroline's throat before she could tamp it down. "Bravo, Noah. I needed that." She smiled at her beloved siblings. "I still get to deliver the weekly support baskets, but it seems no one else wants my services now. I bartered to get a few things for the house this summer, but there was so much I didn't get done."

Lena's hand returned to her shoulder. "The house is lovely. Isn't it, Noah?"

"Absolutely. You've done a great job with fixing up the place." His voice was a little too chipper.

"It's not just the buggy business or the home improvements. A lot of things aren't going how I'd hoped."

"Everything is fine, Care—," he stopped short of using Dad's old nickname for her, "Everything is fine.

The house is fine. We all have our own rooms for the first time in ages. And you're getting to know Bette. See, lots of good things have happened here."

She appreciated the well-intentioned encouragement. "Fine, but don't take my job."

"What job?"

"I'm the one who always looks for the good."

Noah let the rattle of the buggy and the clop of Captain's steady gate along the gravelly road take over the conversation for a moment, then he leaned his head toward her a degree, his gentle voice sounding just like Dad's. "So, what is the good in this for you?"

She was on her way to a party—her first ever harvest party in the Land. She should be able to think of a thousand good things, but since she was thinking of her messy relationship with Jedidiah, she could only manage a weak shrug. "I don't know. I have met many people and—according to Mrs. Owens—half of them are against me."

Noah raised a finger. "Stop it. They aren't against you. Our booth at the market was crowded Saturday, and it wouldn't have been if people hated you."

"There, then that is the good in the bad: I haven't ruined our family or our business." When she looked at Noah and Lena and then the stars appearing overhead, her gratitude returned. "You two are truly all I've had for a very long time and maybe all I'll ever have. And I love you both so much. I'm fine with a quiet life at home with you."

Lena squeezed her arm. "We love you too. And I like it when you are at home."

Noah chimed in. "Yeah. We've got each other. You don't have to win over a whole village. And after the harvest trading is over, we can tackle those house projects together."

"Well, if my business isn't going to keep me busy, I will need those projects." She returned Lena's squeeze. "And if I'm home all the time, you will have to put up with my incessant chirping and suggestions and silver linings."

Lena smiled. "We're used to it."

Noah gave her elbow a pinch. "And we wouldn't have it any other way."

* * *

Jedidiah gave Dr. Bradshaw one last look as he turned the knob to Bethany Foster's bedroom door. The doctor nodded, acknowledging it was all right for him to leave. She had gratitude in her eyes and her hours-old niece in her arms. Mandy sat on the other side of Bethany's bed holding the other twin—a boy named Samuel after a grandfather he would never know.

Jedidiah left the ladies to care for the sleeping mother and her tiny, healthy babies. Between Bethany's sister being her doctor and having her very pregnant sister-in-law and her doting mother-in-law present, Jedidiah's help hadn't been necessary.

Dr. Bradshaw had wanted him there in case complications with the delivery arose, and also in case Mandy went into labor. Thankfully, neither fear had materialized.

A flurry of activity flowed from the generous farmhouse's kitchen to the roasting pit outside and to the massive barn while Everett Foster's hired helpers spent the day preparing for the family's harvest party. They had cleared the barn for dancing, set up the yard for dining, and cooked enough food to feed almost three hundred villagers.

It seemed like poor timing for the twins to be born on the day of the Fosters' annual celebration, but Bethany and Everett were both too enraptured with the babies to mind.

Lively chatter and savory aromas streamed from the kitchen as Jedidiah walked through the dining room to the back door.

Roseanna Foster halted her exuberant description of her perfect grandbabies when she saw him. "Wait a moment please, Doctor Cotter."

"I'm still simply *Jedidiah Cotter*, ma'am."

She waved a frantic hand and shuffled over, sweat glistening on her mature brow. "Oh, never mind all that. You'll be Doctor soon enough. I'll speak to John Colburn about it myself if I have to. Everett is on the elder council, don't you know? Oh, I have ears to bend. I'll do it, I will!"

"You're very generous, Mrs. Foster."

She pulled him into a matronly hug, squeezing as if he were her own son. "You're a good boy, Jedidiah. We were all so comforted by your being in there with Lydia. She knows what she's doing too, mind you. And Everett has attended hundreds of births—all sheep, of course." She guffawed at her own joke.

"I'm pleased all went well."

"Stay for the party, won't you? There's still plenty of food. You've never tasted such wonderful roasted lamb as ours. And you'll want to turn one dance at least to celebrate this abundant year. It's tradition. Oh, you must stay."

Though he was pleased with the day's outcome and grateful for God's abundant provision for the village, the last thing he wanted to do was dance—unless it was with Caroline.

He glanced out the back door, but only had a view of the darkened western field from there. Maybe Caroline and her siblings were here. Surely Noah knew the local custom, and Caroline couldn't resist a social gathering. He switched his medical bag to the other hand and pointed at the washroom. "Might I freshen up first?"

She waved him through, then whirled back to the kitchen. "Find John Colburn when you go down and tell him I'll be out momentarily. He and I are going to take over the hosting duties for Everett so he can come back up here with Bethany for the evening."

"Yes, ma'am."

After a careful comb of his hair and a retying of his cravat, he shuffled from the farmhouse to the yard, passing the workers who carried pans of cooked vegetables, baskets of bread rolls, and pots of gravy to the serving line. Other workers carried empty pans back to the kitchen.

Though evening had settled in, the path was lined with hanging lanterns, and oil lamps illuminated the dozen long picnic tables in the yard between the roasting pit and the barn. Even more light flowed with music from the barn, its rolled-open doors exposing the swirling skirts and stomping boots of the villagers who were already dancing.

By the looks of it, most of the villagers had already finished eating. Neither Caroline nor her siblings were at any of the half-full tables outside. They were either in the barn or hadn't come tonight. Hoping for the former,

Jedidiah raised his heals for a better view of the crowd without going inside the barn.

Several of the Fosters' workers were standing behind a high table of food offerings, ladles in hand, ready to serve any late-coming guests or give second helpings to anyone so inclined. One man was receiving a scoop of beans about mid-way through the serving line, and a woman at the end was piling her open napkin with bread rolls.

Neither was one of the Vestal siblings, so Jedidiah turned to move on.

"Grab a plate and get some dinner." Connor commanded from behind the serving table, wearing a kitchen apron over his waistcoat. He grinned as he stabbed a hunk of meat with a carving fork and held it up. "There's still plenty of roast."

After being in the house all day while so much cooking and baking was happening in the kitchen, Jedidiah gave in to his rumbling stomach. He set his medical bag on an empty picnic bench and held a plate out to Connor.

"Oh, yeah! I knew you couldn't resist." The American piled on more meat than Jedidiah normally ate in a week. Then he passed the plate to the next server. "Fill it up, ladies and gents! This is Jedidiah Cotter, our new physician. He helped deliver the twins today."

While the line of cheering ladle-bearers amassed a plate of food that would make a glutton squirm, Jedidiah checked the tables once more for the only person he wanted to see. He accepted the plate but stopped in front of Connor's meat station on his way to the table. "Did Noah Vestal and his family come tonight?"

"Yep."

"Are they still here?"

Connor lifted his chin at the barn. "They're in there."

Jedidiah sat beside his medical bag and ate his dinner alone, watching the people that milled in and out of the barn. Soon, Roseanna Foster glided from the house to her son, relieving him of hosting duty. John Colburn joined her and the pair moved from table to table like a lifelong unit, effortlessly conversing with the elderly guests who had earned the right to be excused from dancing.

Before John and Roseanna worked their way to Jedidiah's seat of solitude, he took his last bite and headed for the barn. Revel intercepted him halfway to the barn, pulling out a letter from his messenger bag. "You got another one from Stonehill."

Jedidiah accepted the letter without looking at it. There was no question of who sent it or what they wanted. He stuffed the envelope into his coat's inside pocket, where it crinkled against another unopened letter. "Thank you, Revel," he said as he continued walking.

Dust and sweat filled the air inside the spacious barn as dozens of villagers stomped and spun across the hay-strewn floor. Jedidiah straightened his cuffs and lapels as he took in the festive scene.

Half the crowd was seated on the splintery benches that lined the cavernous space. Some were watching the dancers; some were watching the musicians who stood upon a raised platform on the far end. Their gray leaf wood instruments filled the barn with a robust melody, keeping time by the thump of the drums.

Most of the children held little gourd shakers that were meant to add rhythm. Instead, they shook them out of time as they ran from one end of the benched perimeter to the other, then to the stairs to the hayloft.

The older children climbed up and the younger ran back to the dance floor where they twirled into the dance.

The hayloft's railing propped up a flock of adolescents who leaned over it, watching the scene below. Others milled from the haystacks to the rail and back, the boys joshing each other, the girls looking bored of the boys.

Jedidiah studied the crowd and the dancers, looking for Caroline, but with so much motion, it wasn't possible to see every face. The teenagers had the best vantage point, and it wouldn't hurt to interrupt them with an adult presence. He climbed the stairs to the hayloft for a better view of the dance area below. Bits of hay floated on the air, catching on his woolen trousers.

He sidled up along the rail, ignoring the what-are-you-doing-here looks of the youngsters. There, in the far corner of the barn, were Noah and Lena. No wonder he hadn't seen them; they were practically hiding in the shadows. But Caroline was not with them.

With his index finger helping him sort through the crowd without losing his place, he checked every head from one bench to the next, one cluster of chatting women to the next, and finally all that was left were the dancers.

Close to the stage, the skirt of a soft green dress swirled in flowing turns, keeping time with the music and keeping close to a man Jedidiah didn't recognize. Caroline's hair was piled in soft curls on top of her head, but due to the motion and the dust and the angle, no other details were visible.

But at the sight of her dancing with another man, fire pulled Jedidiah away from the rail and back down the stairs, leaving the youths to their secrets and their mischief.

He stayed against the wall near the dance area and waited—for a full glimpse of her face, for the song to end, for a chance to claim the next dance.

But the longer the song played, the more the fire inside him cooled. What right did he have to be jealous? She'd never declared her affection for him, besides allowing him close to her. And even when he made advances, she'd left him with more questions than confirmations.

He had told her he enjoyed her company, and she'd responded with silence.

He told her he wanted to love her, and she refused to tell him the truth about her past.

Why was he here at all?

Because he loved her.

He didn't want to love her—he *did* love her.

He didn't simply enjoy her company—it was like the breath his lungs ached for after days of being underwater with work.

He didn't want to dance with her—he wanted to scoop her up, carry her outside to where John Colburn was entertaining the Fosters' guests and demand the overseer officiate their nuptials at once.

The violinist glided his bow across the strings in one long note as the song ended. As Jedidiah, along with the crowd and the dancers, applauded the band, he watched Caroline's glistening face. While she thanked her dance partner, her smile was enough to light the entire barn.

Jedidiah left the wall and walked between the other dancers who were disbursing from the floor. Caroline and her dance partner parted ways. As she craned her neck, presumably in search of her siblings, Jedidiah positioned himself in her path. "Have you time for one more dance?"

Her pretty boots came to a full stop, but her bodice rose and fell with heavy breath. "Jedidiah. When did you arrive?"

"I've been here all day." He continued his advance toward her. "On the property, that is. Bethany's delivery."

The drummer counted off a slow beat, and the violinist joined in with a sweet, ancient melody.

"Yes, I heard about the twins." Her fingers started to tidy her loose curls.

"Leave it. You look beautiful." Jedidiah offered her his hand. "Dance with me."

Hesitation shifted her eyes from him to the direction of her siblings, then back to him. She withdrew a handkerchief from her dress sleeve and dabbed her forehead and cheeks. "I should probably take Lena home or... something."

He didn't retract his hand. "She'll be fine."

"Are you sure you want to... dance?"

"I am."

She pointed a finger rapidly between herself and him. "With me?"

He drew her into an unhurried shuffle, thrilled by her uncertainty, her nervousness.

When he confidently placed one hand in the middle of her warm back, she frowned. "I'm afraid I don't know what to do. Is this a waltz?"

"It's just a slow dance. Let me lead." He watched her eyes as he guided one of her hands to his shoulder and held the other to frame her like a beautiful flower for all to gaze upon. But no one was looking specifically at them. Everyone around them was focused on their own dance, and the crowd was full of people either watching all the dancers at once or milling about, enjoying the social aspect of the event more than the music.

With his hand at her waist, his fingers melted into her dress's fabric, and he forgot anyone else existed but them. The soft melody flowed through the room, as gentle as her wayward curls.

He breathed in her feminine scent and wished he'd never written that inquiry letter to Dr. Ashton.

That didn't matter now; none of it did. Caroline was in his arms, and this was the only moment that mattered.

CHAPTER TWELVE

A violin's mellifluous sound resonated from the band's platform, swirled through the dance floor, and soared out of the barn and up into the starry sky. Dancing with Jedidiah, encircled by dozens of other couples, and watched by the crowd, Caroline imagined this was the first dance, the debutante ball, and the senior prom she never had all rolled into one glorious moment.

So what if bits of hay straw sailed through the stuffy barn? She didn't mind. In Jedidiah's arms she could ignore any discomfort, whether it be the sweaty air, the barn odors, or the near-misses from the other dancers, who were oblivious of the potential for this dance to build or shatter the relationship Caroline yearned for.

He'd asked her to dance, taken command when she hesitated, and now softly guided her in slow steps, gradually moving farther from the band and closer to the outskirts of the dance floor. Once under the shadow of the loft, he pulled her closer and held her hand against his heart but kept dancing.

He'd said to let him lead, so she followed the gentle movement of his sway and rested her cheek against his shoulder. His steps slowed to half-time, still keeping with the rhythm, though in the slowest way possible.

She closed her eyes and breathed in the faint scents of soap and leather and gray leaf medicine that clung to him, and beneath it a masculine tone hinted at a mystery she alone was invited to solve.

The last music note waned, yet his feet continued several more steps as if they were the only couple in the building. When he finally stilled, she pulled away and opened her reluctant eyes.

He was watching her face, searching her every feature, though for what she could not say. His back was to the crowd, hers was not. As much as she wanted to stand there, toe-to-toe with the man she adored, the prying gaze of the two people who loved her unconditionally tugged her attention to the door.

Noah was threading his hat between his fingers. When their eyes met, he slapped it on and gave her a nod to let her know he was done with the crowd for the night.

Lena gripped her shawl closed with both hands. The exhaustion of an evening in public had drawn shadows under her eyes. She mouthed, "Let's go."

Caroline nodded to acknowledge their request, and Jedidiah followed her line of sight. "You need to leave, don't you?"

"I do. Thank you for the dance."

He kept her fingers wrapped with his as he walked her toward her siblings. "I wish we had time for one more."

"Me too." She wished they'd had more time to dance, to talk, even to walk out of the dance together, but they reached the others too quickly.

Noah offered a hand to shake Jedidiah's. "Good evening."

The customary gesture caused Jedidiah to let go of Caroline's hand. She sent her brother a glare to let him know she didn't appreciate it. He didn't acknowledge it, but he would have felt her fiery stare.

While Jedidiah made small talk with Noah, Caroline smoothed the fringe on Lena's woolen shawl. "Thanks for staying as late as you did. I needed this."

Lena briefly laid her cheek against Caroline's shoulder. "I know. You looked like you were having the time of your life."

"I was."

"Is that all right with you, Caroline?" Jedidiah asked.

"Is what all right?"

"Noah offered me a ride home with you all."

Caroline almost whooped and gyrated like she'd just scored a game-winning touchdown. Instead, with more control than she knew she possessed, she smiled demurely. "Absolutely. It's the least we can do for our neighborhood physician."

Noah's faint grin appeared more in his eyes than in his lips. She knew he was doing this for her. And he knew she knew. He offered his arm to Lena and led them through the crowd that milled between the picnic tables and the barn. They all said their good nights, thanked Roseanna Foster for the lovely evening, and with a wave to this person and that, they were trudging across the stomped-down paddock grass to the rows of wagons where the buggy was parked.

Captain chomped a mouthful of clover and huffed at Caroline. She gave him a quick pat and checked his lines while Noah loosened the brake and told Lena to sit up front with him so their guest could have the nicer seat in the back.

Of course, that meant Caroline had to sit in the back beside Jedidiah, which would have been delightfully romantic if her siblings weren't inches away.

No one spoke on the ride home—Lena being too tired, Noah habitually reticent, and Jedidiah probably regretting falling for this juvenile scheme—so it was up to Caroline to keep the conversation rolling. She pointed out every moonlit house they passed and told what she knew or didn't know or wondered about its occupants.

By the time they were through the village and halfway home on the road north, the houses were sparse, and so was her desire to talk.

Jedidiah covertly slid his leg over until it pressed against hers.

She restrained herself from looking at him or speaking or drawing any attention from the front seat. Noah busied himself by clicking at Captain, even though the horse could have driven them home without a single command. Lena's head bobbed as she fought sleep.

Maybe Caroline didn't have the audience she thought she did. Good. She could imagine it was only her and Jedidiah in the entire world.

He must have decided to believe her adoption story or at least to forget about his inquiry for him to have behaved so tenderly tonight. Perhaps he was extending to her the grace they both enjoyed in Good Springs. Or maybe he liked her too much to care where she was born. Or he'd realized he didn't simply want to love her, but already loved her.

And love covers a multitude of sins.

As much as she'd hoped to find someone to love who loved her in return, she hadn't imagined what it would feel like. Every cell in her body confirmed she cared deeply for this man beside her. She could think of a million praiseworthy qualities he possessed. Mom and Dad both would have approved, as would Father and Mother Vestal—so long as their secret was safe. Noah must have approved of him as a suitor already or he wouldn't have arranged for Caroline to be sharing this blissful ride beside him even now.

With no objections to her affection for him, all that was left was to enjoy this new experience and Jedidiah's company and their relationship and to dream of a future together while they prayerfully watched where their love took them, slowly, very slowly.

And to allow herself a little internal swooning.

The buggy approached their properties far too soon. She used the last minutes of the ride to lean into Jedidiah's shoulder. He raised his arm, pulling her close to his side. For every move she made, he welcomed her closer. If only she'd leaned on him from the beginning!

Instead of turning left on Jedidiah's land or stopping on the road to let him off, Noah turned right onto the orchard property. Captain's gait increased as he headed for the barn, ready for his oats and brushing. Nipper barked a merry greeting and chased the buggy wheels.

Noah pulled the reins to halt the buggy where they always parked in front of the barn. He nudged Lena to awaken her. "Lena. Come on. It's time to go in."

While she stirred, he looked back at Caroline with that same glint in his eyes. "Mind taking care of Captain while I get Lena into the house?"

She almost squealed at the prospect of time alone with Jedidiah. "Sure. Yep. Thanks."

"I'll help." Jedidiah jumped down from the buggy and offered Caroline his hand. He flicked a glance at Noah. "Thank you for the ride."

"Anytime." Noah hoisted Lena down and mumbled goodnight to them as he walked her to the house, looking back only once to waggle his eyebrows at Caroline. She dearly hoped Jedidiah didn't see.

Nipper followed Noah and Lena to the house, then returned to the barn to wait to escort Caroline home as well. The self-governing herder stood guard under the barn's eave while she unlatched the door.

Three cats were inside the barn door and scrambled to rub her legs first as she groped along the workbench for the match jar and lit the lantern. Winston triumphed over the other cats and nearly tripped her. "Oh, leave me alone, you silly thing."

"Pardon?" Jedidiah stood in the doorway, amusement in his voice.

A short laugh escaped her throat. "Not you. The cats. They're everywhere. I believe the young toms had too much fun while Uncle Vestal was bedridden. Noah said neutering is the first chore on his winter list." She mock whispered, "Don't tell Winston."

"I must offer to help Noah with that chore, seeing as how I am your neighbor with a litter of kittens living in my stable—most of which are colored exactly like your Winston."

"Oh dear. Sorry about that. Want us to remove the kittens?"

He shook his head, then selected a horse lead from the hooks by the door. "Now, Miss Caroline, since you are dressed so beautifully with your silver hair pins and lace collar, please allow me to tend to your horse."

She almost chuckled until she realized his manners weren't an affectation. Her independent streak had nearly made her ruin his courteous gesture. She lifted the lantern high and followed him out to the buggy. "How kind of you, sir."

While he unbuckled the straps, she swapped Captain's driving bridle for the casual lead, her eyes watching the man more than the horse.

Jedidiah unfastened the last hitch and raised an indignant brow at her. "I thought you were going to let me do this for you."

She offered him a coy smile. "When it comes to untacking my horse, I can't help but get involved."

"Very well." He took the lead rope from her and walked Captain into the barn and toward the row of stalls. "Which one?"

She pointed at Captain's stall and set the lantern on the shelf by its half door. "His water trough is full. Want to brush him or fill his oat bucket?"

A darling smirk curved Jedidiah's usually serious lips. "Which chore does he want you to do?"

"Brush him."

"Then I shall get the oats."

"The scoop is on top of the barrel by the wall just through there. Take the lantern. I can brush him in the dark."

He glanced around the stall with a moment's pause, then followed her instructions.

Seconds later, a metal clank resounded as the scoop fell against something. The milk cow let out a bellowing complaint, and the shadows of two cats darted past the stall door.

She speedily swiped the brush over Captain and called out, "Is everything okay out there?"

The lantern light grew as Jedidiah returned with it in one hand and the full oat bucket in another. His serious expression had returned too. "Yes, everything is *okay*."

As soon as he said the word, she realized what she'd said. The evening was going so well—so perfectly unexpectedly well. How could she have ruined it so carelessly?

She regretfully slowed the brush strokes and rushed a subject change. "How exciting it must have been to help Bethany Foster deliver twins today! Did she have a hard labor?"

"I cannot speak about a patient."

"Oh, sorry. Most women seem eager to tell their birth stories. I should think she wouldn't mind."

He slid the oat bucket under Captain's nose and held it while the horse ate with loud lip smacks and drippy huffs. "I didn't say she would mind. As a physician I am forbidden to speak of any patient's details."

"Any details? You can't say if she had boys or girls or one of each or if the babies are healthy?"

"All information between a patient and a physician is held in the strictest confidence—all details, their condition, their prognosis, treatment, everything."

Her brush stilled as his word sank in. "Even what they say to you?"

"While they are in my care, of course. Why do you ask such questions?"

She gave Captain one last stroke, then returned the brush to its place on the shelf. "It must be a relief for a patient to tell their physician something without fear of anyone else ever finding out." She pointed at a large iron ring by the trough. "Slide the bucket through there. It'll hold in place while he eats."

He did and the horse followed the bucket. She patted Captain's flank and skirted the trough to leave the stall. When Jedidiah didn't follow her out, she looked back at him. "What's wrong?"

He didn't answer, but only lifted the lantern from its shelf and gazed at her. It might have been the scant light or her imagination, but his eyes held pity.

She could take the suspicious looks, the dreamy looks, the amused looks, but pity was the last thing she wanted, from him or from anyone else. She held out a hand for the lantern. "It's late. Thanks for your help. I shouldn't keep you."

He passed the light to her, but his expression didn't change. His lips parted slightly, and her mind grasped to say something, anything to keep him from asking about her past again. "The party was lovely tonight, wasn't it?"

"I suppose."

She walked toward the barn door and the fresher air. "Well, it might not compare to the dances you're used to, but I never went to a dance or party or anything like that in Northcrest. I don't know if the Vestals weren't invited or if such festivities existed there, but tonight was my first."

"Your first?"

"Yes. What were the dances like in Stonehill?"

"Stonehill?"

She looked back at him. "Yes, didn't the village have harvest parties or barn dances or whatever?"

The way he eyed her momentarily made her realize if she came from Stonehill, she wouldn't have asked that question. She'd given him another easy opening for interrogation. Was she a bad liar or simply desperate to break free from the lie?

He brushed the bits of oats from his hands. "My parents held a Christmas party for the mine workers every year. My older brother and I were sent to bed before the villagers started dancing. Our parents didn't want us mingling with anyone and making a match that didn't meet their approval."

"That doesn't sound like fun."

He chuffed. "It wasn't for me. My brother always snuck out to find his own fun and usually caused some village girl harm."

"Nice fellow."

"Not at all." His brows knitted as tightly as his voice. "He followed in my father's footsteps in every possible way."

Now it was she who felt pity. "Your poor mother."

The austere shadow in his eyes darkened. "No, no. She is not to be consoled, for she is more manipulative than all the demons in hell."

"Jedidiah! You don't mean it."

"But I do."

"You must honor your father and mother."

"And I have by not speaking of their sins to anyone... anyone but you. I feel as though I can trust you, Caroline. It's a novel feeling for me."

"Me too."

"Just as you have locked away secrets from your childhood, so I have locked away mine. But we are not to blame and are both trying to escape." He snatched her free hand and held it firmly in his. "For whatever reason, you have buried your past in Stonehill. It makes me wish

I could do the same. Soon, I will be free and able to lock it all away."

"Soon?"

"I'm not safe from their reach until I am titled."

She lifted the lantern, thinning the shadows on his face. "What does your titling have to do with it? You completed your apprenticeship. They even built you a house here."

"Perhaps as a woman you have paid little attention to the inheritance traditions, but if my brother died without an heir, I would be forced to return to Stonehill and learn our father's mining business to inherit it one day. The only professions exempt from that tradition are those of overseer and doctor. Since a second son cannot become an overseer, except by marriage if he is trained to take his father-in-law's position, becoming a titled doctor was my only way to secure a life apart from my family." Worry edged his voice in a way she hadn't heard. "If something should happen to my older brother before I am titled, I would have to go home."

"Do you believe something will happen to him?"

"No, but my mother hasn't stopped writing to me since I left Stonehill."

"Mother's write letters."

"Not like this." He released her hand and withdrew several envelopes from his inside jacket pocket.

Mother Vestal had only written to them once and that letter was addressed to Lena and expressed her and Father's contentment with Eli and their daughter-in-law and the grandchild on the way. Caroline had assumed sentiment wasn't traditional here, but perhaps some mothers missed their grown children. "She probably misses you."

"She is not the loving mother you are imagining. She is woefully vindictive and controlling and her letters are full of attempts to get me to come home, not because she misses me, but because she had plans for me. I'm just another instrument to get what she wants." He fisted the papers. "Answering her letters only encouraged her, so I stopped opening them."

"Everyone has someone in their family that makes life difficult."

"I don't have one person. I have the whole lot of them."

She wanted to reach out and smooth his lapel and his soul, yet the hint of fire behind his anger kept her from touching him—not for fear he would hurt her, but to wait and see what other layers hid beneath his polished surface. "Perhaps since we understand each other's predicaments, we can give each other grace."

His eyes lifted from the letters, and the fire subsided. "Yes. And please don't think that is the only reason I became a physician."

She touched her arm where he'd once put medicine on her after a fall. "I know firsthand how good you are at your job. The work suits you."

"And I enjoy it immensely. I was always different from my family. The elders recognized that. Dr. Ashton did too. He was the one who recommended me for this position. He was the person I learned the most from, about medicine and about life." He straightened the stack of letters in his hand, then squinted at one that caught his eye. His voice leveled. "And he is the one this letter is from."

"I thought they were all from your mother."

"As did I. This must have been stuck beneath hers when Revel delivered it and I didn't notice. I hope it wasn't urgent." He looked at the letter then at her, both knowing the last letter he received from Dr. Ashton uncovered holes in her story. "Should I read it at home?"

Every fear rose in her stomach. "No, open it. Just remember that grace we spoke of."

"Of course." He slipped a finger under the envelope's fold and unsealed it.

She held the lantern closer for him and watched his face as he read the few short lines. "Is everything all right?"

His Adam's apple rose as he swallowed hard. "My mother asked Dr. Ashton to write me since she fears I'm not receiving her letters. She asked him to say my brother has taken to the potato whisky hard and she believes he is unwell and I must return home to join my father in the business." He shook the letter. "You see? This is exactly what I was talking about." He read more. "Thankfully, Dr. Ashton is impervious to her schemes and was kind enough to warn me that…"

"That what?"

He looked up from the letter with his eyes wide enough to reflect the lantern's flame. "That if the Good Springs elders don't title me soon, he believes she will have the Stonehill overseer recall me."

"Can she do that?"

"She can do that just as she does whatever she pleases."

"No, I meant—"

"I know what you meant." He tucked the letter back into his pocket with the others, then straightened his cuffs. "And yes, if the Stonehill overseer believes it is best for the village, he could make a request to John Colburn to have me sent home since I'm not officially titled as Good Springs' doctor yet."

"How would that be best for your village?"

"The mines are the village's main source of work and trade with other villages. Stonehill's economy is based on their management. If she can convince the overseer it is in jeopardy, he would insist I fulfill my family obligation."

"What about your obligation to Dr. Bradshaw and the people of Good Springs?"

"There were other candidates for the physician post here."

"So you would leave Good Springs and go manage a mining operation in a village you hate?"

"If a man disobeys the elders, no one will trade with him. He will end up living in the brush, eating what he can catch. It's an undignified life. It isn't what I want for myself," he stroked a finger along her arm, "or for you."

"Me?" Somehow, he'd gone from telling her his family problems to involving her. She looked down at his hand touching hers. Here she'd spent days thinking he didn't want to date her because she wouldn't tell him where she was born, and now he was planning their life together.

Men in the Land were as different from the men in her real family as life in the Land was from life in America. And since Mother Vestal had kept her apart from society, she had no idea how anything functioned. She slipped her hand away from his. "Listen, Jedidiah, I'm sorry you're going through this, and I think it could be cleared up if you had an honest discussion with John

Colburn. I would miss you tremendously if you had to go back to Stonehill, but if we—"

"No, Caroline, I care for you too much to take you into that firestorm. As much as it pains me, if I am sent back, I must go alone. That's why I cannot ask to court you until I'm titled and this matter is settled. It would be far too cruel for both of us."

She studied him in the lantern light. From the swoop of his dark hair grazing his collar to his broad shoulders and dapper clothes, this brilliant physician would surely be a dream catch for any single lady in the Land. For some reason he liked her. She enjoyed their time together and her time thinking about him when they were apart, but it felt liked they'd missed a few steps.

Maybe that was what the courting process was for. Or maybe it was his serious personality that caused him to leap from enjoying her company to assuming she would be his wife. And maybe she would be someday, but that decision would take time. Lots of time. Time actually spent together, not thinking about each other.

Or maybe this was how matches were made here in the Land.

She had so much to learn, and it wasn't fair to experiment with him. She lifted the lantern toward the door. "It's late. I should go."

"If that is what you wish."

"It is. Thank you for helping me with Captain."

He pressed his lips in a firm line and nodded his head as if he understood, but how could he understand her when she didn't understand herself or what was happening between them?

He took the lantern from her and offered his arm. "Allow me to walk you to your house." His tone made it feel like *goodbye* rather than *goodnight*.

She stepped out into the crisp evening air and latched the door shut behind them.

CHAPTER THIRTEEN

Caroline blew tiny waves across her full cup of coffee and watched Bette through the rising steam. Her dear new friend already knew more about her in three months than anyone in Northcrest did in twenty years. And she was Caroline's only hope for answers.

Mid-morning sunrays popped between the fast-moving puffy clouds outside and shone through the square window over Bette's kitchen sink. The pulsing light brightened the red in her curls as she tilted her sincere chin. "Weren't you allowed to court at eighteen?"

"I don't know if the Vestals would have allowed it or not because it never came up." She wrapped her cold fingers around the hot cup, reabsorbing the warmth a chilly morning of outdoor chores had leached from her hands. "They kept us at home. Mother Vestal taught us from the books in their parlor. We didn't socialize beyond them and their son, Eli. Lena and I helped with the housework, and Noah did the farm chores. They attended church, of course, but if Father needed to stay for elder business, Mother walked us home. Not that Noah or Lena wanted to talk to anyone, and for years I didn't either."

Bette patted her hand. "I didn't want to socialize for months after Jack died. Actually, you're the first person

I've enjoyed talking to in a long while. I suppose it's because you understand how grief changes everything." A hint of hope brought light to her eyes. "And how it feels to make a new friend." She took a sip of her coffee. "Still, Mrs. Vestal shouldn't have kept you locked away, you being as outgoing as you are."

"I was scared of everyone when we first... went to Northcrest." A passing cloud briefly darkened the kitchen while Caroline considered how to talk about that time in her life without lying or revealing too much of the truth. "When the Vestals took us in, we felt obligated to them. We felt like they had rescued us. They said to call them *Mother* and *Father* and gave us clothes and a bed and chores and lessons. And they were kind. I don't mean to sound ungrateful, but after a few years, I ached for friends... and sometimes dreamed of a suitor."

"Better late than never. I saw your dance with the handsome Mr. Cotter at the Fosters' party."

Caroline held up a palm. "I wish I could be swoony about Jedidiah, but after his announcement that our relationship depends on his titling, my head won't let my heart get excited. But no matter what happens there, this all has made me see how much I don't know about courting customs. I might never need to know for myself, but I want to be able to advise Lena when her time comes."

Bette set her cup on its saucer and brushed her hands together. "Let's see... well. It is customary for the man to speak to the woman's father before he asks her to court. Since you are out of your father's house and under Noah's protection, Jedidiah will probably seek his approval."

Caroline remembered the way Noah set her and Jedidiah up to ride beside each other and to be alone in the barn two nights ago. "It's safe to say he already has my brother's approval."

"Very good. Then since you are nearly thirty—"

"Twenty-nine, thank you very much!"

Bette chuckled. "Fine, since you are long past *coming of age*—how's that?"

She laughed too. "Not much better, but do go on."

"Since you are old enough to behave yourself, you might not require a chaperone when he courts you."

"For heaven's sake, he is already my friend, he lives across the road, and it isn't like there are many places we could go on dates. Where would I need to be chaperoned?"

Bette tapped a fingertip on her coffee cup. "There will be more barn parties, and of course the annual Squash Festival is the week after next."

"Squash Festival?"

Light flooded in the window between passing clouds. It warmed the kitchen and Bette's eyes. "Oh, yes! The main road will be lined with gourd lanterns along its cobblestones through the village. The children love the festival. It might even make Simon happy for an hour or two. People craft everything you can think of out of squash, and artisans sell their wares. There will be a baking competition and a choir performance and games."

"Sounds delightful."

"It is."

She checked the little clock on the wall beside Bette's cookstove. She needed to leave soon to pick up her weekly deliveries from the chapel. After a long drink of coffee, she set the cup down and realized what was truly bothering her. "I guess it isn't the actual courting that I'm uncertain of."

"Then what is?"

"It's what the commitment of courting implies, I suppose." She leaned in, even though there was no one in the cottage to overhear her. "I want to get to know him slowly. And as seldom as we get to see each other, that would take time. And if Jedidiah doesn't ask to court me, if I meet someone else, I don't want to feel like I have to marry a man simply because we go to a few dances. My parents dated..." she almost said *all through college*, but stopped herself, "for years before they were married. How long did you and Jack court before he asked you to marry?"

"We didn't."

"Do you mean he asked you to marry without courting or that you were lifelong sweethearts and you knew he was the one?"

"Neither. My father didn't think there were any suitable men my age in Woodland, and Mr. and Mrs. Owens wanted Jack to get married and produce an heir. Parents, in such circumstances, ask their overseers to help find a match. The overseers correspond with each other. Anyway, they decided Jack and I would be a good match, and our parents approved the marriage."

Caroline swallowed her coffee sip too fast. "An arranged marriage?"

Bette turned an unconcerned hand. "Jack traveled to Woodland, and I agreed to meet him only to appease my father. We had dinner at the overseer's house and coffee by the fire. After a long evening of conversation, he walked me home and proposed on my parent's doorstep. I didn't want that night to end. It was love from the beginning."

"It sounds romantic when you say it, but my insides were in knots when Jedidiah mentioned marriage. It felt sudden." And then it was suddenly out-of-reach. Since meeting Jedidiah, her hope had flickered on and off more than the sunlight between the quickly passing clouds outside the window. "Everything feels impossible now."

Bette's eyes filled with sympathy. She pointed to the cherry pie Caroline had brought her. "Should we cut into this? You look like you could use some dessert."

"No, save it for when the children get home from their grandparents' house." She drew a cleansing breath and straightened her spine. "I'm fine, really."

Bette stood from the table. "Well, if you don't want food, I have something else that might cheer you up." She walked over to the cabinet by her hat making station and selected a dark blue felt hat from the top shelf. "I finished it just yesterday." She held the hat out with both hands. "I thought blue would look nice with your dark dress this winter."

"It's for me?" It was the first gift she'd received from a friend since her eighth birthday party. "Oh, Bette, it's beautiful."

The stylish felt hat with its feminine shape and pretty dark blue ribbon above the brim meant more than looking nice and staying warm and dry, it meant she was loved and accepted by someone she wasn't related to. "Thank you, Bette. Truly, thank you." She blinked back happy tears that blurred her vision. "All I brought you was a pie."

Bette stepped forward. "And what a pie! Cherry is my favorite."

"Noah's too."

Bette glanced out the kitchen window. "Is it really?"

"Oh, yes. Especially the way Lena makes it." Whether Noah was visible from where Bette stood, Caroline couldn't tell, but the light in Bette's smile had her intrigued. "You and the children should come over for dinner one day soon."

"Why, we would enjoy that very much! At least, I would and I'm sure Josie would too. I can't promise Simon will be good company, though."

"Not to worry. He will come around in his own time."

Bette's smile faded. "I pray every day that he will." She quickly snapped herself back to the moment and pointed at a circular mirror over the washroom sink. "Would you like to try it on?"

"I would!" She settled the hat onto her head before she was halfway to the mirror and drew a quick breath when she saw her reflection. She twirled back into the kitchen. "It's perfect. Absolutely perfect."

"I'm thrilled you like it."

As Caroline moseyed back to the kitchen table wearing her cozy new hat, something out the front window caught her eye and made her toes curl inside her shoes.

She almost ignored the activity across the yard near the big house and returned to chatting about hats and pies and dating, but if Bette was going to be the soul sister she hoped for, hard questions weren't to be avoided. She pointed a thumb at the scene outside the front window. "Have you any idea why Mrs. Owens detests me so? It can't be simply because I drive a buggy."

Bette moved the pie to the sideboard and picked off an overlapping edge of crust. She popped it into her mouth. The kitchen chair's cane creaked as she sat back down. "She hasn't said a word to me about it. She barely speaks to me at all. My little Josie doesn't know about any of the fuss over the buggy, of course, but children have a way of picking up on things."

The last thing Caroline wanted to do was upset the kids. "Oh, no. Josie doesn't think I stopped driving them to town on my own accord, does she?"

Bette shook her head. "I simply told her that her grandfather wanted to drive her and Simon on the wagon that day. But later she told me she asked him why they never had a covered buggy to drive, and he replied it was wrong for women to ride in buggies or any carriages where the passengers could get too comfortable with each other."

"That's odd."

"I thought so too, until I remembered Jack telling me years ago about something happening to his mother before she was married, something bad that soured her spirit." She whispered, though no one would have heard them. "It was an abuse by a man before she and Ed courted. Jack said she never spoke of it, but a cousin had told him that an aunt said Sue never rode in a buggy again after what happened to her."

Caroline squinted through the windowpane to see the stocky woman with the acerbic expression standing near the big house. "And so now a hundred years later, she thinks I'm a Jezebel for driving a buggy for anyone who'll trade with me?"

She shrugged. "It's all the sense I can make of it."

"Mother Vestal used to say people don't make sense, but it seems to me if I could learn a person's story, their behavior would be understandable. It might be ridiculous or rude or aimed at the wrong person, but it usually makes sense. That's how it seemed in all the books I read growing up anyway. And that's why I want to hear people's stories."

Bette set her empty cup in its flower-printed saucer and sighed. "Well, good luck getting Sue Owens to tell you her story. I've been her daughter-in-law for eight years, and she's never told me anything personal."

Caroline finished her coffee and playfully straightened the brim of her new hat. "Thank you for the lovely conversation and this gorgeous hat. I must be off to make the Friday deliveries."

"My pleasure. And do enjoy your drive."

"I'll check with Noah and Lena on a good night to have you and the kids over for dinner." She hugged her friend and peeked out the cottage's front window to make sure Mrs. Owens was out of sight. "I've sneaked over here so many times I've carved a trail through the brush between your cottage and our orchard."

Bette straightened her posture. "Not me. I'm not hiding from her anymore. Next time I visit you, I will march past her house and directly to your door."

Caroline kept her voice quiet as she ducked outside. "I knew we would be good friends."

Her heart was full and her mind alert when she climbed aboard the buggy and set off for the chapel. She gave her customary wave to her siblings as she left the property, but couldn't see if Lena was at the window or if Noah was even looking.

The wind howled through the trees, sending colorful leaves whirling down the road ahead of her. Tall brown grass bowed beneath the force of the air, rippling over the length of the fields. She gave Jedidiah's property a quick glance. Since the little stable was directly behind his house, she couldn't see if his horse was there. Even if it was, that didn't mean Jedidiah was there. He often walked to the village. He had said the long walk home was invigorating after an all-night shift at the medical cottage. Someday, when he was titled and worked from his own office, he would probably be pleased to simply drop into bed down the hallway.

Captain's gait slowed as the easterly wind pushed against his side, tousling his mane indignantly.

"It's all right, boy. Keep going."

The swift wind filled the sky with shoulder-to-shoulder clouds, leaving less room for the sun to blink through. After each delivery, the afternoon grew darker until the billowing stacks of cloud turned from white to gray.

She made it halfway from the village to Jedidiah's when lightning flashed, noiseless and high, like a bully taunting her to hurry home. After several seconds of eerie silence, the deep cry of thunder shook the earth. Captain shuffled askew and whinnied. Raindrops splooshed against the top of the buggy like bursting water balloons hurled by a cruel cousin at a family picnic.

The only delivery left was the basket for Jedidiah, huddling timidly on the back floorboard. He would understand if she waited until the storm passed to deliver it. He probably wasn't home anyway. He was probably brooding over his family troubles or thinking of more ways to confuse her about their relationship.

That wasn't fair.

He was probably at the medical cottage attending to a birthing mother while stitching up a wounded child and setting a farm worker's broken bone, thinking of nothing but his patients' wellbeing.

Before the buggy cleared a patch of forest, the storm pelted the top and sides and hit poor Captain with more wind than a ship's sails could endure. Under the assault, the horse slowed to a near stop.

"No, no, no, Captain! We must keep going! Ha, boy! Go!"

Captain faithfully obeyed her command and charged down the muddy road with enough force to sway the buggy. "Easy, boy!"

She gripped the wet reins, determined to win the game of tug-of-war the wind played with the buggy. Her soaked dress clung to her legs as she neared the properties—Jedidiah's to the left, her home to the right.

She spread her feet on the floorboard to steady herself as the gale rocked the buggy. She hadn't felt such motion nor heard such a tumult of wind and rain since the storm that caught her family's boat off the coast of the Land.

The wind yanked and crossed the reins, and emotion caught her voice as she yelled to Captain. "Let's go home, not Jedidiah's!"

Captain's ears tilted back at Caroline's words while the wind's tugged on the reins. Without warning he abruptly turned left, sending the front buggy wheel into the ditch. Wood cracked and straps broke as the buggy wobbled. Captain cried a haunting scream and his back legs buckled.

"No!" Caroline sucked in a breath as the reins zipped from her reach. She gripped the brake pole with both hands, then squeezed her eyes shut as the buggy clattered to its side and rolled into the ditch, metal bending and wood hissing and cracking on every side.

All went still, yet everything remained in motion as the seconds slowed to heartbeats.

Rain pounded her face.

Captain flailed out of her sight.

The buggy's top crumpled beneath her, then was above her again, whipping and screeching as the life was wrung from its frame and tethers.

In one last fling of inertia, she was heaved to the mud. Pain shot through her shoulder and she yelped into the wet grass that surrounded her face.

Beneath the din of her cries and the rain and the creaking of the one spinning wheel up in the air, the heavy huff of a frightened horse was the last sound she heard. She couldn't have seen anything for the deluge, even if her eyes would have focused.

"Captain?" her numb lips whispered, to no avail.

* * *

Jedidiah dropped the letters in a disheveled stack by the steaming cup on his desk and rushed to the front door. Squinting into the pouring rain, he scanned the yard for the mama cat Mark's child had named *Patches*, which had taken up residence in his stable with her kittens.

He couldn't see her.

Something had made a ruckus. It had to be the cat. He craned his neck out the door. "Patches?"

Maybe the lightning had frightened her, or the wind had disoriented a wandering kitten and she'd screamed for it to return.

He began to close the door, then stopped. Those sounds had come from more than a cat, unless the cat had taken the log pile down with her.

The wind threw rain into his kitchen and flipped his collar up against his throat. The trees and brush between his yard and the road bent and swayed unnaturally, sending broken sticks and twigs across the yard. That explained the cracking noises.

A horse whinnied across the road. Through the dense rain, the dark figure of Caroline's horse frantically dashed onto their property. It was hard to see with a face full of rain, but it looked like Captain had lines hanging from him.

As his vision pulled back from the running horse, the swaying trees bent far enough to expose an unnatural circle in the air beyond the brush by the ditch. The circle moved like a wheel.

He launched from the doorway, over the stoop, and across the yard without hat or coat, splashing through the grass and mud. He didn't stop until he reached the pile of twisted frame and metal that was once a smart buggy.

"Caroline?" He held onto the axle and leaned in to see if she or her siblings were inside the overturned heap, but it was empty.

He squinted through the pelting rain and scanned the brush along the road. A bushel basket was lying on its side a few feet from the buggy, with apples and packages and a smashed pie scattered around it.

Today was Friday. She must have been the person driving. And she had been trying to deliver his provisions in a raging storm. "Caroline?" he yelled into the rain, searching the road as far as he could see in one direction then the other. "Caroline?"

A mumble softer than the distant thunder but too loud to be mistaken came from the ditch. He stepped over a blue felt hat as he skirted the wreckage and there she was, face down upon the earth, one arm trying to push her body up from the ground, the other drooping beneath her.

"Caroline!"

Her faint voice responded with part of his name before she groaned, "My arm!"

"I've got you. Here, turn this way." He rolled her toward him and scooped her from the mud, her drenched dress hanging as limply as her right arm. "Hold still. You're all right. I have you."

"So dizzy."

He trudged through the wet grass, lifting his face to the rain only enough to aim straight for his open front door. Though her eyes were half shut, her coloring was satisfactory. Blood ran from her right eyebrow to her hairline.

She winced. "My shoulder hurts."

"Almost there."

He turned sideways to carry her through the doorway, then again from the kitchen to the corridor, ensuring her arm moved as little as possible. His thighs burned as he lowered her to the patient cot in his office.

When he stabilized her arm beside her, her eyes lolled back.

"Caroline! Caroline, can you hear me?" He checked the pulse at her wrist and throat. It was strong and steady, as was her respiration. "Caroline?"

"Mm hm?"

"Can you speak to me?"

Her eyelids fluttered halfway open again. "I think my shoulder is broken."

Though more concerned with the possibility of a head injury, he quickly felt along her scapula and clavicle from medial to distal, palpating the muscles and tendons inserted along the way, finally ending at the shoulder joint with one hand and coming up the humerus bone with the other, his fingers analyzing the bone and ligaments. "It's dislocated downward."

"Dislocated?"

"Hold still."

"How can you tell without an X-ray?"

"A what?"

She didn't answer, and it wouldn't have broken his focus if she had. He continued ascertaining his patient's injuries, sensing as best he could through the thick, wet material of her dress. "I detect no broken bones. I must examine you for head trauma. Don't move while I turn the lights up."

Her eyes closed again.

"Caroline?"

"Yes."

"Stay awake."

He hurriedly turned up all the lanterns, then returned to the cot with gauze and a bowl of water to clean and assess her head injury. Much of the blood was already clotting. He wiped the crimson drips from her skin to check the wound. "You won't need stitches."

Her eyes shot fully open. "Stitches!"

"No. I said you won't need stitches."

"I hit my head."

"I see that." He lifted each of her eyelids one at a time to check her pupils.

"Captain! Where's Captain?"

"He ran home." He held his fingers above her face. "How many fingers am I holding up?"

"Two." She blinked hard several times. "And two over there."

It was not the answer he wanted to hear. "Follow my finger here… and here. Now look up. Can you see the ceiling clearly?"

"Forget the ceiling, Jedidiah. My shoulder feels like it's on fire."

"You're going to need a full dose of gray leaf tea before I can perform the closed reduction."

"Before you what?"

"Before I put the bones back into place." He cleaned the rest of the blood from her forehead, then stood. "The kettle is still hot. It won't take long to boil. Remain still, understand?"

She hummed a pained response, and he raced to the kitchen to put the kettle back on the cookstove. Though the rain had slowed, a puddle ran from the door to the table. He closed the front door, then drew one of the two teacups he owned from his kitchen shelf and returned to his patient while the water boiled.

"Caroline?"

She moaned.

"Keep yourself awake. You might have a concussion."

The mortar and pestle Dr. Ashton had gifted him was waiting beside a jar of dried gray leaf flakes for its inaugural use. He ground the leaves in the same fashion Dr. Bradshaw recommended to best release the pain-relieving and healing properties of the tea as quickly as possible for the patient.

While grinding, he sat on the hand-me-down wooden stool by the patient cot. "The gray leaf tea will be ready for you soon. You must drink it all. Then we only have a few minutes to get you out of those wet clothes and into a patient gown, so I can mend your shoulder before the gray leaf takes you under."

"Will it hurt?"

"As soon as your shoulder bones are back in place, the pain will decrease significantly. And nothing will hurt once the gray leaf medicine removes your pain."

He checked her profile, and for a split second she wasn't his patient, but the woman he loved. He could not think that way while he was treating her or he would lose focus. She was his patient, only a patient. He tapped the ground leaves into a tea strainer. "This will rapidly heal your wounds and ensure no infection sets in."

"Noah? Lena?"

"As soon as you are stable, I'll go fetch your brother and sister."

She reached for her shoulder with her good hand. "They must be frantic with worry."

"I would guess they have not seen the wreckage yet, for when they do, they will come here immediately." The kettle whistled in the kitchen. "I'll be right back."

While the gray leaf medicine brewed, he shook open one of the linen patient gowns from his supply cabinet. "It isn't elegant, but you cannot lie there in a wet dress for twelve hours."

"Twelve hours?"

"That's right. You haven't taken gray leaf tea, have you?"

"No. Never."

He knelt beside the cot. "Can you sit up so I can remove your dress, or do you prefer I cut it off?"

Her eyes widened and she looked directly at him for the first time. She reached her good hand for him. "It'll take me long enough to wash the mud out, never you mind cutting it too. Here, help me sit up."

He slipped the patient gown over her neck and let it rest atop her shoulders, then inched it down to protect her modesty while peeling off her muddy dress.

She reminded him of an illustration of an ancient peasant girl he'd once seen in a storybook, sitting there battered with hair unruly, wearing the boxy linen gown. Her good arm held her bad while he tied the closure at her back.

"Stay sitting up so you can drink the tea."

The cup had cooled enough, but he checked the tea with a fingertip to be sure, then proffered the cup. "Sip slowly. You will feel a warming sensation begin in your middle and spread throughout your body. You must drink it all."

She nodded as if an obedient child, then sipped. "Not bad. Sort of minty." And with the second sip. "It tastes how the trees smell, but bitter." She sucked in a short breath after the third sip. "I remember when I first smelled the gray leaf. I didn't know what it was, of course. Oh, my! Oh, I feel it now!"

"Keep drinking slowly."

Her loud swallows proved the throat's greed for the gray leaf had overcome her obedience. She handed him the empty teacup. "Sorry. This is amazing! I feel great!"

He set the cup to the side and quickly began to work on her shoulder. "Take long, deep breaths."

"Why? I'm fine. More than fine."

He felt the socket and gently maneuvered the bones back into place with a pop. She sucked in a fast breath. "Oh, that's why."

"Yes." He cut a length of muslin to create a sling and wrapped her arm. "This will help you hold it in place for a couple of days while it heals."

"Jedidiah?"

He didn't look at her, but kept wrapping and adjusting the sling for the correct tension. "Yes?"

"Am I your patient?"

"Yes."

"Are you my physician?"

"Yes."

"So anything I tell you will be held in the strictest confidence?"

He lowered her to the cot, forcing himself not to look into her eyes, and covered her with a woolen blanket. "Of course."

She giggled. "That gray leaf medicine is miraculous."

He picked up her wet clothes and shoes, needing to busy himself in the last few moments of her consciousness. "I'm glad you are enjoying it. As soon as you're asleep, I'll take these to Lena. She can bring fresh clothes for you to wear home in the morning."

Her eyes were halfway closed again. "Jedidiah?"

"Yes, Caroline?"

"My name isn't Caroline Vestal."

"Go to sleep."

"It's Caroline Engler. I'm not from the Land."

"Pardon?"

"I was born in Boston, in America. I'm not from here. You promised you wouldn't tell anyone anything I said while I was your patient, right?"

The word escaped his lips while his mind stumbled to process what she said. "Right."

"That's my big secret—the truth you wanted to know so badly. I'm not from the Land."

The clothes he held dripped on his boots while he stood there in the doorway of his medical office, mouth agape like an uneducated ninny. He'd suspected the story of her parents dying and her being adopted was false, and she occasionally said things he didn't understand, but he hadn't suspected this. "Do Noah and Lena know?"

As she slipped into the medicinal coma the old physicians called *gray leaf sleep*, her voice became quieter. "Noah does. Not Lena, though. She was only a tiny tot when our parents drowned."

The gray leaf made her giggle. It had to be the medicine, because what she said was in no way funny. "You won't tell them I told you, will you?"

"No. Sleep now. Your secret is safe with me."

Her pretty face rolled to the side and she spoke no more.

CHAPTER FOURTEEN

Rays of golden light danced through Caroline's eyelids. Perhaps the curtain of her mind's stage was about to open to another dream. How lovely were the dreams while she slept beneath the influence of the gray leaf tree's astonishing medicine!

She squeezed her eyes, hoping to open them in a dream to live more wonderful memories: sailing into the harbor with Dad and Mom and Noah after a long summer day on the water; playing dolls in her plush childhood bedroom with baby Lena sitting in a bouncy seat, fascinated by her big sister's every move; jumping on the trampolines in gymnastics class, pretending she could fly; launching herself from the diving board with Mom applauding her from the poolside lounge chairs while Nanny made fruit smoothies in the estate's outdoor kitchen.

Another dream didn't begin. She blinked against the soft morning light, only to find the gray leaf had left her to awaken to reality.

Slowly, she let her eyes open to Jedidiah's medical office.

Her fingers rubbed the sheet beneath her and the stiff patient cot beneath it. A rough fabric like a man's work shirt itched her body. She was still wearing that potato sack of a gown.

She wiggled her fingers again on both hands simultaneously. They felt the same, moved the same, except her right arm was restrained over her body. She rubbed it with the left and remembered the sling. But there was no pain—not in her shoulder or her head—thanks to the miracle of the gray leaf and, of course, Jedidiah's expert care.

All at once her experience of drinking the gray leaf tea came back to her—and what she had said to Jedidiah in those foggy, light-headed moments while the medicine whooshed through her veins, igniting every cell in her body with its healing power.

She glanced around the office. He wasn't in here. Beside his desk was an empty folding cot with a rumpled blanket on it.

Light clinks came from the kitchen. He must be eating breakfast. She shucked off the wool blanket and shifted on the cot to check her dizziness. All gone. Pleased with her recovery, she sat up and planted her bare feet on the floor. Her toes curled at its coldness.

The instant she moved, the fork and plate noises in the kitchen ceased and footsteps hurried through the hallway.

He stood in the doorway, clean clothes and combed hair. Morning sunlight flooded around him as if an angel had arrived. "You're awake."

She rubbed her eye with her free hand. "I'm waking up, at least."

"How do you feel?" He stepped close and gazed down on her the way Dad used to when she had caught a cold at school and slept all day.

"Much better." She pointed at the other cot. "Did you sleep in here?"

He shook his head. "Noah did. Lena stayed with you the rest of the afternoon and evening while Noah and the men cleared the wreckage, then he came back and slept beside you."

Every inch of her heart warmed. "I love them so much."

"And they love you." He pointed a thumb toward the kitchen. "Lena brought breakfast. Actually, more than breakfast. There is a feast fit for a banquet in there."

"It's the least we could do to repay you."

"The food is not for me alone. She said she wanted you to have all your favorite dishes when you awakened, and also she said she couldn't sleep last night, so she cooked the whole time."

"Poor girl. I never want her to worry about me." She caught a scent of the food. "She's an incredible cook."

"Possibly the best food I've ever tasted." He knelt in front of where she sat on the cot. "Has your vision cleared?"

"I think so."

He held up two fingers. "How many?"

"Twenty."

"Very funny."

"Two."

"Good. Any lingering feelings of fogginess or confusion?"

"No."

"Headache? Ringing in the ears? Nausea?"

"No, none."

He set his thumb against her eyebrow and raised her eyelids one at a time, focusing deeply into each eye. "No sign of concussion." He touched her forehead. "And the gray leaf completely healed the scrapes. Allow me to check your shoulder."

As he unwound the sling, she forgot about her shoulder. "I may have said some things after I drank the medicine yesterday."

The sling dropped to the cot, and he straightened her arm, then felt along the joint. "Raise your arm to the side. Good. Now forward."

"What exactly did I tell you?"

"Now make a fist. And release it. Good." He continued examining her shoulder as if they weren't having the most important conversation of her life. "Any pain here?"

"No."

"Excellent."

"Jedidiah?"

He lowered her arm. "The gray leaf dosage was successful. No stiffness or pain anywhere?"

"None. Please, tell me what you heard me say yesterday?"

"Let me finish my job first."

Ever the committed physician. She should be grateful for his care. It was what saved her, after all. And she was grateful. She was also impressed and amazed and more fond of him with every second she watched him work.

Still, her waiting words burned on her tongue.

He went to his desk and wrote something down. "Use the sling to immobilize the joint for the next two days to ensure it heals correctly and completely. You might be prone to future dislocations if you aren't careful."

He shook out the muslin sling. "I'll rewrap your arm after you're dressed."

She smoothed the thin fiber of the ghastly gown. "Do you have a robe or something I could borrow to walk home in?"

He grinned then, amusement replacing the concern in his eyes. "How about something better than a robe?" He opened a palm to the hallway. "Your sister brought clean clothes for you. She hung them in the washroom, along with towels and your favorite soap."

"God bless her."

"Indeed. She even donated a few extra towels and blankets for my future patients."

She stood and stepped across the chilly floorboards, happy to be walking out of his office on her own two feet. "Hopefully, I won't be one of your patients again."

He blew out a breath. "I pray you will not be."

As she passed him to enter the hallway, she sensed the worry and exhaustion that hung in the air around him. "I know that was difficult for you."

"It's my job. I'm trained to handle difficult situations."

"And you did it well. Thank you. But this situation, having to save someone you…" she pointed from him to herself and back again. "This was not what you trained for."

"No, but the Lord saw me through." He lifted his chin at the washroom. "Hot water has already been pumped into the tank."

"How thoughtful!"

Once clean and dry, she smoothed the bodice of her Sunday dress. Lena was sweet to bring her best clothes for her to wear for the first day of another chance at life.

After a quick check in the mirror over the sink, she left the washroom and stepped into the hallway. The house was small enough she could see into both the kitchen and the medical office from there.

Jedidiah waved her into the kitchen with a casual finger. "What would you like to eat?"

The table was covered with a variety of dishes; sticky buns, muffins, egg casserole, and every sort of fruit from the orchard. She selected a muffin and sat down when he pulled out a chair for her.

"Coffee?"

"No, thank you. Is Captain all right?"

"Noah said he is fine."

"Please, tell me what I told you yesterday before I went to sleep."

He picked invisible lint from his waistcoat. "That you were not born in the Land."

She set the muffin down. "It's true."

He didn't respond, but only looked up from his sleeve into her eyes, an unknowable expression glazing his face.

"Jedidiah, I'm sorry if I shocked you. You were right when you said my story was a lie. I'm only keeping my past a secret to protect my family and our adoptive family. The Vestals orchestrated the story and commanded our loyalty to them since they rescued us and gave us a home and a life.

"Mrs. Vestal was convinced the cover story was the only way she could keep us. She desperately wanted more children after Eli, yet none came. She said God sent us children to her to fill her home. We were so young and knew nothing about the culture we had been washed into, orphaned."

He crossed his legs, ankle over knee, and gazed at her intently. "And Lena does not know."

"No. I've wanted to tell her all along. The older we get, the worse it will be if she finds out."

"When."

"Pardon?"

"When she finds out."

"You must understand the secret isn't mine to tell. And you cannot either. It would destroy Noah's inheritance. He didn't take the orchard from anyone else. There were no other heirs, so it isn't hurting anyone for him to own it. But if the elders in Northcrest find out the Vestals lied and never legally adopted us, they and the elders here might deny Noah the property."

His gaze didn't falter. "I won't tell anyone. You told me this in the confidence of being my patient. Since neither you nor anyone else is in danger, I'm sworn to secrecy." He raised a finger. "However, I never condone lying. I will not lie, nor will I perpetuate Mrs. Vestal's lie. If asked about your birthplace, I will simply refer the inquisitor to you. I understand you were raised to say you are originally from Stonehill and such, but, Caroline, you cannot lie and please the Lord."

The disappointment in his eyes matched that in her heart. "I know. I try my best to be honest and to remain loyal to the people who rescued us. I truly thought coming to Good Springs would be a fresh start, that the past wouldn't follow me here."

He nodded slowly. "Then we have both made that mistake."

"And both received grace?"

"Indeed."

Her heart warmed. "Jedidiah, you don't know how desperately I've wanted to tell someone my story. I'm so glad it was you." She reached for his hand. "Please, tell me I haven't been relieved of my burden only to place it on you."

He covered her hand with his. "As long as you are safe—and I saw last night in your siblings' care that you are—your situation is no burden to me. I'm relieved to finally know the truth." Then he withdrew his hands. "But, Caroline, you must understand, if I suspected something was amiss, others might too."

"Connor?"

"Possibly, but if so, he is keeping his suspicion to himself."

"Please, don't tell Noah you know."

"I won't." He poured a glass of fresh milk and set it beside her plate. "Yesterday, you said your real name is Caroline Engler, you were born in America, and your parents drowned. Since I know the Stonehill story isn't true, might you tell me what really happened?"

She took a drink of the milk, still warm from the cow, then set down the cup. "It was my dad's dream to sail around the world with his family. When I was eight, he sold his company to live his dream. He and Mom always wanted to sail to Tristan de Cunah. Something enticing about being that far away from the rest of the world, isolated. We island hopped through the Caribbean, then sailed to Rio.

"After a few days in the South Atlantic, an electrical storm came out of nowhere. All the onboard electronics went out. We lost communications and navigational control. Dad was certain we were close to Tristan, but the waves were so high and rough and the cloud cover so thick, he couldn't get oriented.

"Then it all happened so fast. We were tossed from one side of the boat to the other. Dad and Noah tried to secure the sails while Mom put life jackets on Lena and me. Just as she tossed one to Noah, the boat capsized. It felt to me like we'd hit something first, but Noah says we didn't."

Faint shadows encircled his eyes from too much work, too much worry, yet there was still concern in them for her. "And then you were in the water?"

"Helpless on the waves. The boat broke apart and the currents sucked most of it under. I thought we were all separated, but Noah had one arm in his life jacket and one arm holding Lena. She was screaming so hard half of her little face was an open mouth.

"I could barely see Mom bobbing between waves. She was beside a chunk of the stern and her face was bloody. She didn't have a life jacket. Dad didn't either. He was fighting the waves desperately to get to Mom."

A sour lump rose in her throat as she released the story she'd held inside for two decades. It was supposed to feel good to finally tell it, but it brought up an ache no gray leaf medicine could cure. She swallowed the lump in her throat. "Dad yelled for Noah to take care of us girls. Noah promised he would. Dad dove under to swim to Mom. They both disappeared. Then the air changed over us—like it was full of electric sparks.

"The waves calmed around me and Noah and Lena. My feet tapped something and I stood on it. Noah yelled at Mom and Dad to tell them we found a sandbar, but they were gone. There was nothing behind us. Not our parents or the remnants of the boat or even the storm. We could see calm sea all the way to the horizon.

"As the tide changed, we were swept off the sandbar and carried north by the currents. Noah held Lena, and he and I locked arms. All three of us floated along in our life jackets, at the tide's mercy. It might have been hours later, but it felt like days when we touched land. We didn't know it was *the* Land. How could we? This place isn't on any map or satellite image."

He didn't flinch when she spoke of outside technology. He only rubbed her knuckles with his thumb. "Caroline, I'm so sorry."

"It was a long time ago." A tear stream wet her cheek. She swiped it away. "Twenty years later and here I am crying like it just happened."

He straightened the muslin that was holding her shoulder immobile. "Often long after an injury heals or an illness is cured, a patient will sometimes return to the physician, insisting it's still there. The patient could be completely symptom free and given a dose of gray leaf medicine, which we know removes all pain, yet they insist they still feel the wound." He slid his competent hand from her bandage down to her fingertips and held them. "It's because the body remembers. The ordeal can be long past, but the body does not forget a moment of the battle."

He wasn't speaking of her repaired shoulder joint, but of her shattered mind and broken heart. "The Vestals found us when we floated ashore—Noah, Lena, and me. They saved us, and we were grateful. Mom always lived with gratitude, and I wanted to honor her by living that way too. And because of it, I've had more good days than bad."

"But you were never allowed to tell your story. Why?"

"Mrs. Vestal had lifelong strife with the overseer's wife in Northcrest. She was convinced the woman and her cronies would take us away, so she made up a story.

Even Eli never knew what really happened. He just came home from school one day and we were living in his house. She told the overseer they adopted us when distant relatives died in Stonehill. She picked that village because it was the farthest away and she'd met no one from there. She said it was a place no one ever left."

He released her hand and raked his fingers through his hair. "That is because of my parents. They have most every man in the village believing they are indebted to them."

"How?"

"My father learned a scheme from his father. He keeps control not by outright bullying but by subtle manipulation, finding a way to create a debt for one of his workers, then keeping the man silent and ashamed. This is a land where no man need be indebted to anyone, least of all his employer."

"Should you expose your parents scheme?"

"It is no more my place to expose them than it is your place to expose yours."

It might not be in either of their plans to reveal the sins of the people who had raised them, but there were steps they could take to free themselves and build their own lives. Her first step had been telling someone the truth, and in doing so, much of the weight had been lifted. Now she must encourage him to do the same. "Seeing as how you are still my physician and I am still in your care, you might not want advice from me. However, I must ask... have you spoken to John about your mother's interference in your titling?"

He shook his head. "I intended to."

She took a long drink and as the nutrients sank in, so did the joy of having the confidant she'd always dreamed of finding. The weight of her past floated off her, and a smile tugged at her lips. "Well, you should speak to him soon. No need to keep things inside. I've heard it's unhealthy."

A charming grin lightened his expression. "Well then, I shall deal with the matter today." He lifted his own cup. "Grace be with us both."

* * *

Jedidiah handed Dr. Bradshaw his logically arranged patient chart, complete with thorough notes and a detailed treatment summary. She sat at her desk in the medical cottage and studied it a little too long for his liking. Caroline had been *his* patient, after all.

Finally, the doctor turned her eyes from the page and lifted her brow at him. "In the future, be sure to perform final balance, memory, and reflex tests when concussion has been suspected before you release the patient."

This morning, he had observed Caroline as she walked through his house and ate breakfast at his table, and he had listened to the harrowing story she recalled from twenty years prior. He had charted her recovery, monitored the gray leaf medicine's affect, and ensured her vision and confusion cleared before he allowed her to leave.

He was certain the gray leaf had completely healed her long before she went home mid-morning, but if his exhaustive notes weren't enough to satisfy the doctor, defending himself wouldn't prove his competent care either. He leaned against the wooden slats on his chair beside Dr. Bradshaw's desk. "Thank you for your advice."

She laid the chart on her desktop and squared it with the corners. "I must commend you on your rescuing and tending to Miss Vestal so speedily. I'm sure the situation was traumatic for everyone. My father will call on the Vestal family soon to ensure they are well in spirit after such an ordeal." She tilted her chin. "How about you? Were you able to sleep last night?"

"A little."

She folded her hands like a schoolmarm assessing a naive pupil. "Physicians are often called to help after such emergencies, but it is rare for us to discover the patient ourselves. It does happen, though, and it gets easier with experience. Would you like to talk about it?"

He knew the look she gave him, but it wasn't finding Caroline after the buggy accident that had kept his mind racing all night. It was what she'd confessed to him. Now that he knew Caroline's story and they'd talked about it, he will sleep soundly.

He met Dr. Bradshaw's patronizing gaze. "Dr. Ashton trained me well, and I believe I honored his training yesterday by keeping my nerve and handling the incident with strength and professionalism. I expect a speedy recovery for all involved."

Dr. Bradshaw nodded once and stood. "Well, then go home and rest. Don't worry about your shift tonight. I will be home if anyone needs medical care."

He paused at the door with his hat in his hand. "Any word from the elders on my titling yet?"

She shrugged and went about straightening her desk files. "They tell me nothing. You will probably know before I do."

"Good day, Dr. Bradshaw."

"Good day."

He closed the cottage door and walked the flower-lined path to the kitchen door at the back of the Colburn house. Since it was open, he hoped John would be inside. He tapped on the doorframe and leaned in. "Hello?"

"Jedidiah, come in."

Connor's relaxed speech only made Jedidiah think of Caroline. Neither she nor her siblings spoke that way. Probably Mrs. Vestal's doing. Still, Caroline was more special to him now than she was just twenty-four hours ago. She had always been special to him because she was such a positive light in his life, but now more so because she was truly unlike all other women in the Land.

Connor was standing at the sink, downing a cup of water. Little Andrew was running around the table, holding a winged wooden toy in the air as if it were flying. John wasn't in sight.

Jedidiah crossed the threshold into the wide kitchen, warmed by the gray leaf log burning on the grate in the fireplace. "Is Mr. Colburn at home?"

"Nope." Connor refilled his water cup at the sink. "What's up?"

"Pardon?"

Connor spoke again. This time, he clipped his words like a man of the Land. "Can I do anything for you?"

Andrew ran past them with his toy held high and made the loud, erratic play noises only a three-year-old could make.

It was no time for a serious conversation.

While Connor quaffed a second cup of water, Jedidiah watched Andrew dash around the long table, wishing someday he might have an energetic son of his own. "It's not important. I'll speak to John tomorrow. Enjoy your evening."

"Here." Connor ignored his goodbye and took another cup from the shelf. He pressed the foot pedal beneath the double-basin sink and filled the cup with cold water. "Have a drink before you walk home."

Jedidiah accepted the cup. "Thank you."

"That was some wreck Miss Vestal got herself into yesterday. We were picking pieces of buggy out of the grass on both sides of the road. Noah said she had a dislocated shoulder and hit her head. Is she going to be okay?"

"I expect a full recovery."

Connor grinned. "Spoken like a true physician."

"I'd hoped to be a titled doctor by now."

"I know."

"Dr. Bradshaw has heard no word on my titling." He took a slow sip of the water, hoping accepting the hospitality would help his effort to get information. "Do you know why the elders continue to delay?"

Connor set his cup in the sink. "They are waiting on me."

Jedidiah withheld his surprise. He slowly sipped the cool water, giving Connor a chance to elaborate without him pumping him with questions.

Connor leaned against the kitchen countertop casually, as if they were simply exchanging bread recipes. "Since I was the person who was tasked with finding our new physician and I suggested you, the elders selected me to investigate the matter raised by your family—"

"By my mother."

"Yes, by your mother." Connor straightened his posture. "She wrote to John and asked that the issue of your family's business be brought before the elders here.

She says your father was already in poor health when you left Stonehill, and now your older brother is too."

Jedidiah knew her game too well to wait for someone else to explain it. "And she fears they will both die and our family will lose control of the mines and my grandfather's legacy will be lost, all at the village's demise."

"The elder council believe it to be a valid concern, according to the Land's inheritance traditions."

"Maybe it would be if it were true. This is only her latest ploy." He whipped out the letters stashed in his inside coat pocket. "These are the letters she has written me in the past month, clearly laying out her plan to get me home, and this one," he tapped the top letter, "I received from Dr. Ashton days ago—the only trustworthy man in that village—warning me that my parents requested letters from him stating both my father and brother are ill."

Connor held out an open hand for the letters. The wrinkled envelopes crackled as he took them, but he didn't look away from Jedidiah. "Did your family approve when you left home for your medical apprenticeship with Dr. Ashton?"

"Of course."

"Six years ago, right?"

"Correct."

"Did they approve last year when you told them you were leaving Stonehill permanently and coming here?"

He shook his head. "I had confronted them about their... treatment of their workers." How could he tell the Good Springs leadership his parents lived unrighteous lives without dishonoring them? He took another sip of the water, needing it this time. "Suffice it to say: they knew I wanted nothing to do with their business. They didn't try to stop my leaving."

Connor held up the letters. "But now she wants you to go back?"

"They. She is deceptive at every turn, but she does nothing without his approval and usually her manipulations are at his insistence."

Connor opened the top letter—the one from Dr. Ashton—and leaned against the counter's edge as he read it.

Jedidiah's toes curled inside his boots while he waited. For years he'd tried to reason with them to change their ways—ever since he'd first gone to apprentice with Dr. Ashton and saw how noble men behaved. When reasoning didn't work, he'd decided to separate himself from his family without dishonoring them.

They'd disappointed him time and again in life, and yet he gave them every concession. Even when he'd first read the letter Connor was now holding, he'd told Caroline he couldn't court her until his title was secure, just in case he had to deign to their authority. And why?

Because they might convince the Good Springs leadership to have him sent home. He was a man of twenty-nine years, for heaven's sake! He was doing the work he was born to do. There was no way he would be forced back into those mines like the rest of the spineless creatures his father controlled.

He would not dismiss his love for Caroline to placate a tradition that had never been instated for such a despicable family. No, he was taking control of his life right now.

Connor lowered the letter, but before he said anything, Jedidiah stepped forward. "If the elders of Good Springs decide not to title me and wish to find another physician, I will accept their authority, but I will not return to Stonehill. I will find other work. My family is not following Christ and so I will not follow them. If it leaves me without my profession or even without a village, I will trust God to lead me to where he would have me to go."

He swallowed hard and continued. "And if my father and brother both perish before I am titled and I am made heir, I would only return to Stonehill to dissolve the family holdings and donate the mines to the village for every man to mine and sell his findings as he wills for his own livelihood. I would absolve the workers of the artificial debts that keep them bound to my family. Then I would return to Good Springs and to the work and the people I love."

Connor pursed his lips and nodded. "Not that I want your father or brother to die, but you make that situation sound best—for the people of Stonehill."

"My father and brother are in no danger." He pointed at the letter. "You read what Dr. Ashton said—both men are in fine health, aside from an overuse of potato whisky."

Connor folded the letter and added it to the stack. "Mind if I keep these for a while?"

"You may."

"I'll discuss it with John and we'll present the case at the next elders' meeting. You might not have felt you could trust the leaders in Stonehill, but you can trust us. Good Springs is different with John's leadership of the elders. Let us do our job. We will make the best decision for our village and for you."

Jedidiah still wasn't ready to exhale fully. "Soon, I pray."

Connor nodded. "Soon."

CHAPTER FIFTEEN

Caroline hung the last of the morning's laundry on the clothesline to flap freely in the crisp autumn air, then spread her arms high to stretch her stiff shoulder. The muscles and tendons warmed pleasurably as she moved in all directions—her new routine since the day Jedidiah saved her from the wreck one week ago. She ended her stretching regimen with both hands raised to the heavens in praise.

The azure sky's limitlessness held her gaze. Anything and everything in life seemed possible when she first came to Good Springs four months ago. Unlike the sky here, life was teaching her its limits. Her buggy business was a bust. She hadn't redecorated the farmhouse to perfection like Mom would have. Her social life consisted of more animals than people. And no matter how far she'd traveled, she could not escape her past or its pain because it was part of her.

But the Lord's grace truly was sufficient for her needs.

A cool breeze swirled through the orchard's acres of trees, rustling the remaining foliage in a chorus and sending fallen leaves of golden yellow and vibrant orange and plum red dancing across the property. Winston launched himself from his guard station on the porch and chased the leaves, behaving more like a playful kitten than the sentinel tomcat he was.

Caroline didn't hold back her laughter as she watched her furry friend. She didn't feel as though she was holding anything back anymore. The perfect sky let the sun's warm rays highlight all the colors of the orchard in autumn, and the sweet breeze blowing in from the nearby ocean carried the scents of the sea and the barn and the gray leaf forest and blended them to perfection.

There was nowhere else she wanted to be than right here on her brother's farm in the village of Good Springs on the east coast of a hidden island in the middle of the South Atlantic Ocean.

It wasn't simply fine weather and nature's blessings that brought about this complete sense of contentment. She'd found a confidant in Jedidiah, and her secret was safe with him. And even though she loved him, if his family troubles took him from the village or his work kept him too busy for their relationship to grow, she would be content with their friendship.

Through him, she had found healing for her body and for her soul.

And his care for her was a gift from God. An undeserved gift. Grace upon grace.

The thought brought to mind an ancient hymn, and she hummed it as she carried the empty laundry basket into the mudroom. The screen door clanked shut behind her.

Lena began humming along with her from the kitchen, and just like when they were young, the humming turned to singing, and the singing grew in volume as their voices harmonized from years of practice.

Caroline grabbed her vegetable basket and garden clippers from the shelf in the mudroom, then climbed the two steps to the kitchen and poked her head around the corner to join Lena while they sang the hymn's final lines, now at full volume with full smiles.

"The earth shall soon dissolve like snow,
the sun forbear to shine;
but God, who called me here below,
will be forever mine."

Lena's voice trailed off respectfully with the final note. She returned to her kneading bowl while Caroline added mock stage-like vocal gymnastics to the ending, as if she were a contestant on a televised talent contest. The silliness always made Lena laugh, even though she didn't have a clue what Caroline was imitating.

And Lena's laugh made Caroline even happier. She lifted her garden basket. "What would you like from the veggie patch today? We still have squash, cucumbers, and a few tomatoes. Plenty of carrots and onions. I'll have to check the cabbage. Oh and remember, Bette is coming over for lunch."

Lena brushed at the flour on her cheek, only adding more powder to her face. "Cucumber and tomato, please. Will the children be with her?"

"No, it's their day to go into the village." She turned to leave the kitchen, then paused and looked back when Lena began humming another tune. Her little sister had made herself at home in the kitchen of this old house. She seemed blissfully content, cooking and baking all day, regardless of the old stove's quirks and the faucet's loud pipes. "There was so much I thought I would have improved in this house by now."

Lena pressed her fists through the dough rhythmically. "I like it the way it is."

"I know. You'd never complain if you didn't. Still, I plan to fix things up more now that I have more time and since the harvest gave us plenty of trade."

She pulled her hands from the bowl, dough clinging to her knuckles. "What if…" Color brightened her flour dusted cheeks. "Never mind."

Caroline stepped back into the kitchen. "No, tell me. Whatever you want, I'll make it happen. New baking pans? Fresh wallpaper? A better cookstove?"

Lena shook her head. "It's nothing like that. I was wondering what if…"

"Yes?"

"What if someday I didn't live here anymore? Would you be terribly upset?"

Caroline would have choked on a sob if it hadn't been for the rising blush in her sister's cheeks. "That depends. Would you not live here because you didn't like us or because you liked someone else better? Say, a caring, mature gentleman who lived out at Falls Creek? An articulate overseer with an eager pen, perhaps?"

Lena shrugged, but the light in her dreaming eyes betrayed her nonchalance. "I don't know. Maybe. Someday." She turned back to her kneading bowl. "I wondered if you would be hurt. I mean, you've done so much to make this house lovely for us and you plan to do so much more."

"That doesn't obligate you to live here forever, especially if you desire to be a wife and to have a family of your own."

Lena's innocent gaze shot to her. "Oh, I do. So very much. Don't tell Noah."

"He won't be offended. We know you've grown up. We want whatever you want." Caroline set her garden basket down and squeezed Lena's thin shoulders. "Is your correspondence with Philip getting serious?"

Her voice softened with uncertainty. "Not as such. But I do think about him often and wonder what life might bring."

"Perhaps he is wondering the same things about you."

"He hasn't given any indication of it. Not yet, but I want to know you will be happy for me if he does."

"Of course, I will. And maybe one day life might take me somewhere else and maybe it will bring someone here for Noah. But until that day," she raised the basket, "we have lunch to prepare." She gave Lena a kiss on her floury cheek. "I'll be back shortly with your veggies."

Lena's humming trailed off as Caroline stepped out of the house and back into the glorious day. As she skirted the flowerbed at the front of the house, she clipped a few clusters from a golden flowered rose-type bush at the corner of the front porch. By the girth of the stems, she was sure it had been planted many generations ago. She wished she knew the flower's real name. Mom would have.

She laid the lovely cut flowers in her basket. They would make the table beautiful for lunch. A thrill of glee tickled up her spine at the thought of having Bette over for a meal. Hopefully, she would come for dinner next time and bring the children.

If Noah and Lena could get used to having one family over, Caroline could invite more people and more often. Being content with the present didn't mean plans for growth weren't allowed.

She gave the roses a sniff and hummed in delight. As she made her way between the berry bushes to the vegetable patch on the north side of the property, she spotted Mrs. Owens bent over in her own garden across the way.

She almost ducked back around the house to avoid her cranky neighbor, but this was no day for hiding. In fact, she was done hiding altogether.

Winston ran to meet her at the edge of the vegetable garden, but stepped no farther.

"You got a nose full of pepper last time you tried to scratch around in here, didn't you? That'll keep you from using our garden as your litter box."

The cat snubbed her in response.

As she squatted to check the sprouting winter greens, Mrs. Owens said something. With the distance and the wind, Caroline couldn't make out her words. She looked up, but the older woman was looking in her direction.

Caroline looked at Winston. "Maybe she's talking to her cat too."

She stopped then as the realization hit her: Surely she had something in common with her neighbor. She didn't want anyone to dislike her, especially the person living next door. And she was friends with the woman's daughter-in-law. There might not be anything she could to do make Sue Owens like her, but she could at least let the woman know the feelings were not mutual.

She gave Winston one last glance. "Love your neighbor as yourself."

He chattered a response and ran in the opposite direction.

"Fine, but I will." She stood and carried her basket across the yard.

The grass on the Owens's property had been mowed very short at the end of the growing season, and it crunched under Caroline's shoes.

Mrs. Owens looked up from her gardening, plunked her fists on her hips, and hollered. "What do you want?"

Caroline wasn't close enough to speak without yelling, so she offered a warm smile as she approached. On the outside, her poise and friendliness couldn't be questioned. On the inside, her thoughts were a mix of insults and prayers. Remembering her purpose, she let the prayers prevail.

As she neared Mrs. Owens, she saw the sweat dripping down the older lady's temples, the swelling of her fingers and ankles, the deep troughs of sorrow pulling her face into a permanent frown. It wasn't just the buggy that this woman didn't like. She was sad and angry and mean before Caroline ever came to town, probably decades before.

But they did have one thing in common.

Caroline stepped within arm's reach and collected the cut flowers in her basket. She held the bouquet out to Mrs. Owens. "I thought these might look nice in your kitchen." When the older woman only glared at the flowers, Caroline softened her voice even more. "Or on your son's grave."

The older woman didn't accept the flowers, yet she didn't take her gaze off them.

Caroline inched closer, flowers still proffered. "I too have suffered great loss. My parents died when I was a child."

Mrs. Owens chin began to quiver and her eyes reddened. Without looking directly at Caroline, she took the flowers, nodded her thanks, and walked away.

Caroline wedged the butter dish between the breadbasket and the water pitcher on the beautifully arranged table, then ducked into the washroom to give her hair one last check.

Nipper barked twice outside the back door, announcing a visitor was approaching the house. Before there was a knock, Noah hurriedly finished washing his hands and rushed to open the back door.

Caroline paused in the kitchen to exchange a curious look with Lena. Maybe their brother was becoming more social after all. As encouraging as that was for their future entertaining, Bette was Caroline's invited guest today.

Though Noah had let her in, Caroline was ready to give the official welcome.

Bette climbed the two steps from the mudroom into the kitchen and held out Caroline's blue hat. "All mended."

Caroline pulled her friend into an excited hug. "Oh, thank you! It's just like new."

Bette touched Caroline's once-injured shoulder. "And it looks like you are mended as well."

"Better than I was a week ago."

"You gave us all quite a scare."

Noah chuffed in agreement as he passed them to help Lena carry food to the table.

"Myself included, but I'm well now. Captain is fine. Only the buggy was lost."

"Can it be repaired?"

"Sadly, no." She hung the hat on the rack by the doorway, then took Bette's shawl and hung it as well. "Despite everything, much good came of the situation."

Noah furrowed his brow at her quizzically, but she ignored it. He didn't know she'd found Jedidiah to be an excellent confidant as well as physician.

She opened a hand to direct Bette to the table. "We're so delighted you came. Sit here."

Noah stood back up from his seat and pulled Bette's chair out for her.

Caroline resisted meeting Lena's gaze, for they both might giggle at his exuberance.

Bette watched Noah return to his seat, but she shook out her napkin and faced Caroline as she sat across from her. "This all looks so lovely and smells heavenly too. Cheese curds, fried potatoes wedges, and gravy. Cucumbers and tomatoes, bread and jam. My, oh my!"

Caroline lifted her chin at Lena. "We have my sister to thank."

"And we will as soon as we say grace." Noah bowed his head and said the blessing.

Caroline had to squeeze her eyes shut to keep from looking at the others. She had a friend! They had company! Her brother was participating, and her sister hadn't passed out from the pressure of having a guest in her kitchen!

Her eyes shot open the instant Noah said, "Amen."

While Bette asked Lena about the food and her love of baking and cooking, Noah kept his posture unusually straight and took gentlemanly-sized bites.

When Lena had shyly given more one-word answers than Caroline could bear, she asked Bette. "Will the children be joining us while we get dressed for the festival?"

"No, they are staying in the village all day. I'll collect them before the festival begins."

Caroline wiggled her brows at Lena. "So it'll just be us girls."

Lena's eyes widened briefly. "I don't want to dress up."

Noah pointed with his fork across the table at Lena, then quickly put it down as if remembering his manners. "You can stay home with me if you want to."

"Oh, no she isn't."

"I'm not?"

"No, and neither are you," Caroline nudged Noah, then looked at Bette. "Do you have siblings?"

"Only a sister." She raised her cup to her lips but didn't drink. Her green eyes turned to Noah. "I should think I would have liked having a brother too."

Caroline checked to see if he was looking at Bette, but his gaze was fixed on his plate. "We sure like having a brother, don't we, Lena?"

Lena nodded while she spread a layer of jam on her bread. "Especially if he stays home with me tonight."

Caroline wouldn't hear of it. "No, ma'am. You're going. You both are. And we'll have a wonderful time. There will be a squash baking contest. You might enjoy seeing all the things the ladies make with squash. And there are games and singing and strength contests for the men. That should be fun, right Noah?"

He gave her a side glance.

"And what else, Bette?"

She dabbed her lips with her napkin. "A choir performance and apple bobbing." She looked at Noah. "I do hope you will go."

"All right. I'll go."

While the group chuckled, Caroline watched them all for a moment—her brother and sister and new friend.

When she'd first moved to Good Springs, she had been certain her past and the pain and the lies hadn't followed her here. She'd been wrong, for wherever a person went, they took themselves. But she had been right that anything was possible. She was building a new life here, one filled with hope for the future.

And she was ready for all that future had to offer—the pleasant surprises and even the challenges, because they too always had a bright side.

* * *

Jedidiah turned onto the Colburn property as the sun dipped below the horizon. The few high, puffy clouds remaining from the flawless autumn day blazed with the oranges and reds of a sailor's delight. He switched his leather medical bag to the other hand while he walked between the sandy wheel ruts that led from the road to the stately brick house.

Though nothing had been settled with his titling here in Good Springs and the threat of his influential and idolatrous family back in Stonehill still loomed, his love for an enchanting, intelligent woman born far, far away brightened his spirits more than any glowing sunset.

His eager feet rounded the Colburn house, then slowed as he approached the cottage.

Dr. Bradshaw was posting a note on the medical office door, still wearing her work dress.

He scuffed his steps on the pavestones. "Good evening, Doctor."

"Hello, Jedidiah." She turned to face him, wobbled a bit, and caught the door handle to steady herself.

"Are you quite all right?"

She wiped her glistening forehead with the back of her wrist. "Yes, I'm fine. Thank you. How were your house calls today?"

"They went well." The last light of day illumined her face enough to give him clues to her condition. Rosy cheeks, puffy eyes, a slight flare to her nostrils. Not enough sleep and an unsettled stomach. He pointed at the sign she was posting. "Are you still going to the Squash Festival?"

She tucked a loose strand of light brown hair behind her ear. "I was supposed to meet Connor and Andrew there a half hour ago, but I was... detained."

"By a patient?"

"Um, no." Her hand covered her middle. "Step inside the office for a moment, please."

He followed her into her medical office and closed the door. "How far along are you?"

Her gaze shot to him, but settled quickly. She raised a surrendering hand. "About ten weeks."

"Congratulations."

She gave a pain expression. "Thank you. I'm pleased in spirit—joyous, exuberant even. My stomach, however, finds the first few months disagreeable."

"Might I prescribe ginger and long naps?"

She returned a fraction of his smile.

"Does Connor know yet?"

"Of course." She leaned against the edge of her desk. "We aren't telling anyone, though. I'm sure Father suspects it since I can't keep anything down, but he is gracious to not ask. Between keeping house and caring for Andrew and this unceasing nausea, I fear I must step away from my work for now. Could you take on all the house calls and routine appointments for a while?"

"It would be my honor."

"Excellent." She rubbed her abdomen, already bonding to the baby inside. "You must think me unprofessional."

"Not at all."

"The elders will."

"Quite the contrary. Remember, I was summoned to Good Springs by the council because once you became a mother, they felt you lacked time for your medical practice. Time, not professionalism."

She absentmindedly played with the silver charm bracelet at her wrist. "Very well, then. I will write a list of the patients for you to check on regularly, mostly elderly folks. You already know how to handle everything else here. All the patients you've treated thus far speak highly of you. Doubtless, you will take good care of the village." She stepped to the door and offered a tired grin. "But for tonight, don't think of work. Everyone will be at the festival, including you."

Her faith in him—in his competence—gave him more satisfaction than all the patient compliments combined. He opened the door for her. "Is John still at home?"

"No, he's been setting up the booths and tables all day, and he was going to help Roseanna Foster light the gourd lamps at sundown."

"Then I shall walk you to the festival."

She smoothed her messy hair and looked down at her work dress. "I still haven't changed. I started to, but became ill. You don't have to wait for me."

He opened a hand to the back door of the main house. "Go ahead. Take your time. I will wait in the kitchen."

"Are you sure?"

After he nodded, she hurried through the house, called out for him to get himself a drink if he liked, and charged up the stairs.

Within minutes, she returned wearing a velvety evening dress with a silver turtle-shaped brooch pinned beneath the lace collar. He offered his arm when they stepped outside. "You look lovely, Doctor Bradshaw. Connor is a blessed man."

"How kind of you." She took his arm. "And is there a blessed woman you might be hoping to see at the festival this evening?"

He hadn't mentioned his fondness for Caroline to anyone but Noah. It was probably best to let his intentions be known to Dr. Bradshaw, as he was technically still under her authority.

When they stepped from the Colburn property to the pebbly road, two lines of tiny lights in the distance illuminated the way to the festival. Several villagers were walking the road ahead of them, and a few behind them. He glanced back to make sure no one was close enough to overhear. "I plan to ask Caroline if I may court her."

Dr. Bradshaw snapped her face toward him, her voice sharp. "Caroline Vestal?"

He kept his focus straight ahead and his volume low. "I spoke to her brother, and he gave me his blessing."

"Did this start before she was your patient?"

"Yes, of course. She was my neighbor before being my patient."

Dr. Bradshaw's hand relaxed on his forearm, and she faced forward while they walked together. He wouldn't be breaking any protocol by courting Caroline, so the doctor couldn't harangue him, and she surely wouldn't do so while he escorted her to the festival.

She remained quiet for a moment, then whispered, "Well, how wonderful!"

"The gourd lamps?"

"No, no." She chuckled once. "The prospect of you and Miss Vestal courting. You are both new to the village and about the same age. I was thinking it must be wonderful for you to start your new lives here being neighbors, and now possibly becoming more." The aristocratic air of authority returned to her voice. "I wish you the best in your endeavor."

He couldn't stop himself from jesting when a woman took that tone. "Do you think she might reject me?"

"I don't know Miss Vestal well personally, nor what she might do. I simply wish you the best." A smile added warmth to her voice. "She'd be a fool to turn you down."

The lively music playing in the center of the village grew clearer as they approached the festival. The two rows of little lanterns spread wider, one line ending at the chapel, the other on the opposite side of the cobblestone street where the booths began.

Light flowed out of the chapel where John Colburn stood on the steps, greeting villagers as they passed by. Jedidiah was eager to say hello, but a couple approached John from the other direction and held his attention with news of expecting their first baby.

Dr. Bradshaw pointed at a long table bountiful with food dishes and a banner above announcing a baked goods competition. Connor stood in front of the table, talking to someone, while Andrew pulled at his leg, begging for more treats.

The doctor smiled. "There is my husband. It looks like my son is already sampling the squash breads." She let go of Jedidiah's arm. "Thank you for walking me here."

"Are you feeling better?"

"Yes, much. Enjoy your evening, Jedidiah."

"You as well, Doctor."

He straightened his cuffs and strolled past the squash carving booth, the gourd shaker competition, and the squash soup selections, but didn't see Caroline or her siblings. With such a bustling crowd, he needed a better vantage point. As he circled back to go stand on the chapel steps with John, a familiar laugh danced on the breeze.

He turned to see Caroline smiling at some fortunate baker. Every person near her was smiling too. Of course they were. Her presence was like the sweetness of a quiet dawn after a night spent in battle.

And to him, that battle was finally over.

At long last, he was in command of his life—maybe not of the matters ordained by the Lord, but certainly the matters within his own power. He was no longer handing that power over to the godless, nor leaving sacred opportunities unfulfilled.

He parted the crowd and caught Caroline's attention, then stopped to allow her the decision to come to him. She enjoyed the freedom to make her own choices too.

When the laughter around her died down, she spotted him, excused herself, and met him outside the booth. "Jedidiah, you made it."

He kissed her gloved hand. "Only in hopes of seeing you."

Her noble chin tilted. "Aren't you charming."

"How is your shoulder?"

"As good as new."

"Excellent. Walk with me." He threaded her hand through the bend of his elbow and meandered to the edge of the crowd. "There is a matter I wish to discuss."

She checked the crowd behind her. "Now?"

"It will only take a moment." They weren't far enough from everyone for privacy, so he led her toward the library's vacant doorway. Once near the ancient arched door, he held her fingertips in his hand just as he had that night in her family's barn and whispered, "Miss Engler—"

"Shhh." She glanced around them. "What if someone hears you?"

"They won't. You're safe with me." He smoothed her delicate fingers and wanted to remove her glove, but didn't. More people shifted the crowd in their direction, so he kept his voice quiet. "I know who you truly are, Caroline, and it makes me want to know you more."

Her lips parted slightly and her eyes widened. The surprise in her aspect encouraged him. Before she could speak and break the sincerity of the moment with a nervous giggle or change the subject, he rushed to the point. "Would you allow me the honor of courting you?"

She stared at him, unblinking.

Perhaps she didn't hear the question. Or didn't understand it.

Or wasn't as fond of him as he was of her.

"Caroline?"

She withdrew her hand from his. "What about your problem in Stonehill? You said you might have to move back there. Is that situation over?"

He wished he could offer her the certainty she deserved. "Not yet. In truth, I don't know what the elders will decide, but I have made my decision. If they don't approve my title, I will not return to Stonehill. It might take me a while to find other work and to build a home here and to win the approval of the community so that I'm free to trade and earn a living, but I won't leave."

She nodded slowly, her face relaxing. "Good for you."

"Then will you accept my request?"

A family walked past with eight children in tow—including two sets of twins—all dancing and singing and skipping circles around each other.

Caroline remained silent.

Jedidiah gave the children's father a cordial nod, then returned his attention to Caroline. "This might not seem like the best time to ask you, but it is the only time I have. If you aren't prepared to answer, I understand."

"It's just that," her voice softened to a near whisper as she leaned close, "with my upbringing, I'm not sure what you would expect of me."

He drew his face back to look into her eyes. "Expect of you?"

She shrugged and rumpled her pretty brows beneath her blue hat. "What if we aren't well suited?"

Her words pricked his pride. How could they not be better suited? He straightened his lapels. "Caroline, if you aren't interested, simply decline my request and—"

She chuckled and gently gripped his forearm. "No. Of course, I'm interested. And flattered. And very happy you are asking me and even more happy that you are staying in Good Springs. I also want to be honest with you: Mother Vestal didn't teach me anything about courting. I don't know all the customs and rules and, yes, the expectations. You once stopped me from bartering for a mattress because I didn't know all the facts. You certainly wouldn't want me to agree to court if I didn't know what it meant. Does courting mean are we obligated to marry?"

Now it was he who chuckled, remembering the first day he spoke to her at the market not far from where they now stood. She had looked so regal and so lost all at the same time that fine summer day. And even now, she carried the same air of total confidence paired with complete innocence. It made him want to guide her and to protect her even more. "Courting simply means I will call on you and we'll spend time together for the purpose of seeing if we are compatible. And if you feel we aren't, you're free to walk away at any time. And if I'm denied my profession and must find other work and build my own home, it may be a long time before our courting can lead to marriage." He stepped closer. "But if you aren't afraid of the unknown, I would be honored to court you."

"The unknown? That's the story of my life." She cast her gaze to the starry sky above. A satisfied smile graced her lips and she looked back at him. "And it seems I rather enjoy my life that way. So, yes."

A group of adolescent boys ran past, hollering as they chased each other. The band's drummer counted off a beat for a lively tune, and the laughter and chatter at the booths grew in volume. He had to be sure he heard her answer correctly. "Yes? Yes, I may court you?"

An elderly couple hobbled by, both talking to each other at the same time, voices raised to combat their own lack of hearing.

Caroline laughed. "Yes."

He resisted the urge to whoop with joy and run a triumphant circle through the festival. Instead, he took her hand in his. Before he could say more, the elderly gentlemen greeted them, then another family strolled by.

Jedidiah gently squeezed Caroline's hand, and she squeezed back. This wasn't the place for privacy, but it had been the time to ask her. Her acceptance was the only proof he needed that the path he'd chosen was the right one.

Mark Cotter and his family approached as they crossed from one booth to the next. Mark caught Jedidiah's attention and pointed toward the chapel. "John Colburn is asking for you."

"Thanks." Jedidiah released Caroline's hand. "If I am allowed to keep my profession, there might always be interruptions."

She smiled. "I know."

He kissed her cheek before walking away. Mark gave him an acknowledging look as he passed, and he returned it with a quick brow raise. Such an exchange was all men needed to ask and answer an unspoken question.

John was standing at the top of the church steps. As Jedidiah climbed the stairs to join him, he turned back and saw Caroline meeting Lena near the baking contest booth. It bolstered his pride to think the ladies might talk about him, but gratitude quickly replaced the feeling, for if he couldn't give Caroline all the attention she deserved, he was grateful she had her siblings for company, and no doubt in a short time she would make many new friends in Good Springs.

He met John on the top step. "Good evening, sir."

"Evening, Jedidiah." He thrust out his hand.

Jedidiah shook it. "Mark said you were looking for me."

"Yes, I have some news about your situation."

A lump lodged in Jedidiah's throat, so he simply nodded.

"Connor presented your case to the elder council, and we voted unanimously to award your title. The ceremony will be after the church service this Sunday."

Jedidiah released the breath he'd held for six years. He shook John's hand again. "Thank you, sir."

"Congratulations, Doctor Cotter." John's gray beard spread as he grinned. "I am glad you are pleased."

"Very pleased, indeed."

The older man held up a commanding finger as his smile dissolved. "Understand our vote was not against your family, but for you."

"Yes, sir."

"Your obligation to the inheritance traditions are nullified by your titling, however, your new position comes with greater responsibility. As our doctor you will be expected to practice medicine in this village so long as you are physically able to work."

"Yes, sir."

"When you correspond with your parents, exhibit the grace you have been shown."

"I will." He looked away long enough to scan the crowd for Caroline. She had moved to another booth with Lena, and the young widow who lived in the cottage next door to them had joined them.

"You appear to be eager to tell someone this news." John folded his hands the way he did when he was behind the lectern on Sundays. "Would that someone be Miss Vestal?"

Jedidiah would forever keep her secret, but he wished he could call her by her real name in public. "I have asked to court Caroline, and she has accepted me."

John's countenance lightened again. "Then I congratulate you on two counts."

"Thank you, sir. I have her brother's approval."

"And mine as well." The overseer leaned back on his heels. "She will be pleased to hear of your titling, no doubt. Go and tell her."

Jedidiah watched her chat with the ladies around her, then she glanced in his direction and smiled. She had accepted him, not knowing what would come of his profession. He hadn't thought a woman like her existed.

And if it hadn't been for a storm at sea twenty years ago, she wouldn't exist in his world. But her past hadn't stolen the light from her heart, nor her joy for life—the small things as well as the grand and all the unexpected in between. She found the good in everything—even him, and he would make it his mission to show her what the bright side of a life with him would be like.

He looked back up at the overseer, certain of his path and his plan and his choices in both his life's profession and his perfect companion. "No, sir. I'll wait and let her see the ceremony for herself on Sunday. She greatly enjoys life's pleasant surprises."

EPILOGUE

Lena shuffled to the varnished church pew, second from the back, and followed Noah down the row far enough to leave room for Caroline, but not too close to the next family. With the chapel's tall doors being propped open, a fresh morning breeze susurrated through the long building and flickered the overhead lanterns' wicks within their glassy globes.

Lena sat in her usual place and hid her chilly hands beneath the thick woolen shawl Mother had knitted for her two Christmases ago.

Noah sat beside Lena and gazed at the wooden cross affixed to the wall behind the violinist, who filled the sanctuary with her meditative melody.

Lena's loquacious sister had strolled confidently up the chapel steps a pace ahead of them, then disappeared in the crowd that gathered in the entryway. Caroline must have found someone to chat with before entering the hushed chapel. She'd better hurry if she was going to be seated before the service started.

It was always dizzying to walk into a public place without Caroline close, but at least Lena had Noah beside her. He didn't enjoy crowds any more that she did. She pressed against her brother's warm shoulder and whispered, "Where did Caroline go?"

He upturned an unknowing palm.

She wanted to turn around, spot Caroline, and give her a stare to urge her to come sit down, but that might draw attention. Instead, she joined her brother in focusing frontward and listened to the violinist's sweet hymn.

A shadow stopped in the periphery of her vision. She didn't break her forward stare to look directly at whomever was in the aisle. Noah would acknowledge them first if the person intended to speak to them.

An outstretched arm held something close to her. "For you, Miss Vestal."

Her heart doubled its beat and she slipped the envelope from the messenger's hand. "Thank you, Revel. Thank you ever so much."

She quickly hid the letter under her Bible's cover and handed him a letter she'd tucked therein after writing it by lantern light in her bedroom last night.

The lean man wearing faded suspenders accepted her letter with a polite nod and walked away.

During the exchange, Noah had turned his face to her.

She glanced at him and shouldn't have. Her cheeks flushed with heat.

He graciously returned his gaze to the front of the chapel. Surely he wondered who the sender was. She'd only received two letters from Mother since moving to Good Springs, and she'd shared them both with him and Caroline. He had to know someone else was writing to her, someone special to her.

Very special, indeed.

The chapel doors closed, and Caroline sauntered into the pew. "Scoot down more."

Lena obeyed but gave Caroline a quizzical glance. Her question was soon answered as Jedidiah Cotter stepped into their row too and sat beside Caroline. He folded his hands respectfully, but by mid-way through John Colburn's sermon, the dapper physician was holding Caroline's hand.

Lena tried not to look. Her sister had promised to tell her all she learned about courting, but she hadn't mentioned that the suitor might sit by her and touch her sweetly during the service.

Philip wouldn't behave thus. Not that she knew what tender gestures he might make, but if he did, it wouldn't be during church since he would be the man standing at the lectern, teaching. He was the overseer at Falls Creek, after all.

What it must be like to be admired publicly by a respected man! Oh, it would surely be too much attention to endure. Not for Caroline, of course, but for her.

Admiration in private would be a different matter, and how she longed for it. She'd read about it in all the darling novels left in the farmhouse by its original owner, several of which were written by that Founder's daughter. In those ancient stories, the maiden was usually admired from afar and wooed in private gardens.

Perhaps Philip was admiring her from afar. He must, or why would he write to her weekly, sometimes twice?

The overseer ended the sermon with a prayer. Lena's eyes closed and her head bowed out of habit, even though her thoughts were not here with the church in Good Springs but miles away in the tiny village of Falls Creek where she had once spent a glorious Sunday listening to the eloquent teaching of the only man ever to capture her heart.

After John prayed, an elder stood to announce upcoming village events, none of which Lena cared to attend. This village was so big and the church was attended by so many people. She just wanted to go home and serve her siblings lunch and spend the afternoon baking, then slip into her bed, pull her blanket up to her ears, and read Philip's letter, again and again.

John returned to the lectern and said something that made Caroline draw in a quick breath. Before Lena could look at her sister, Jedidiah stood, straightened his cuffs, and walked to the front of the chapel.

She leaned close to Caroline. "What is happening?"

Caroline's hand was pressed proudly to her heart. "Oh, my! He must be going to take the oath."

"What oath?"

"Just watch." Caroline craned her neck to see Jedidiah kneel before the elders.

He repeated a promise about treating medical patients and doing harm to none, then he stood to face the congregation as John gave him a certificate and declared him to be *Doctor Jedidiah Cotter*.

When everyone applauded, Caroline clapped doubly fast, her face beaming, a single tear sparkling in the corner of her eye. After John dismissed the congregation, she looked to Noah and then to Lena. Both answered her pride by mirroring her eternal smile.

"He must've known this was happening today, but he let it be a surprise for me."

Lena didn't enjoy surprises the way her gregarious sister did, but she loved seeing her sister excited. "How thrilling for you!"

"Oh, it is! I wish I could tell you how happy this makes me for him." She dabbed the tear with the edge of her handkerchief.

"And for yourself?"

"I was already happy, but yes. I hope you will know this feeling one day—loving someone who can be trusted with… everything." Caroline gave her a quick hug. "I'm going to congratulate him and invite him to lunch. Don't wait for me. I'll walk with him."

Lena picked up her Bible and touched the letter beneath the cover to make sure it was still there. She looked up at Noah.

He was watching her with his deep, big-brotherly eyes. "Are you ready?"

She hugged the beloved book and its hidden letter against her chest. "Ready for what?"

"To go home."

"Oh." Her face warmed as if she had opened a hot oven. "Home. Of course. Let's go home."

She ignored his puzzled squint and cast her gaze to the front of the chapel, where Jedidiah held his certificate in one hand and Caroline's hand in the other.

Lena gave Caroline a little wave and paused, struck by the thought of someday being the woman at the front of the chapel, fingers laced with the man she loved.

Caroline must have seen the apprehension in her eyes because she flashed her a half-grin and brow wiggle—their secret smile that meant everything would be all right.

Thank you for reading my book. I'm so glad you went on this journey with me. More Uncharted stories await you! Are you ready for the adventure?

I know it's important for you to enjoy these wholesome, inspirational stories in your favorite format, so I've made sure all of my books are available in ebook, paperback, and large print versions.

Below is a quick description of each story so that you can determine which books to order next...

The Uncharted Series
A hidden land settled by peaceful people ~ The first outsider in 160 years

The Land Uncharted (#1)
Lydia's secluded society is at risk when an injured fighter pilot's parachute carries him to her hidden land.

Uncharted Redemption (#2)
When vivacious Mandy is forced to depend on strong, silent Levi, she must learn to accept tender love from the one man who truly knows her.

Uncharted Inheritance (#3)
Bethany and Everett belong together, but when a mysterious man arrives in the Land, everything changes.

Christmas with the Colburns (#4)
When Lydia faces a gloomy holiday in the Colburn house, an unexpected gift brightens her favorite season.

Uncharted Hope (#5)
While Sophia and Nicholas wrestle with love and faith, a stunning discovery outside the Land changes everything.

Uncharted Journey (#6)
When horse trainer Solo moves to Falls Creek, widow Eva gets a second chance at love. Meanwhile, Bailey's quest to reach the Land costs her everything.

Uncharted Destiny (#7)
The Uncharted story continues when Bailey and Revel face an impossible rescue mission in the Land's treacherous mountains.

Uncharted Promises (#8)
When Sybil and Isaac get snowed in, it takes more than warm meals and cozy fireplaces to help them find love at the Inn at Falls Creek.

Uncharted Freedom (#9)
When Naomi takes the housekeeping job at The Inn at Falls Creek to hide from one past, another finds her.

Uncharted Courage (#10)
With the survival of the Land at stake and their hearts on the line, Bailey and Revel must find the courage to love.

Uncharted Christmas (#11)
While Lydia juggles her medical practice and her family obligations this Christmas, she is torn between the home life she craves and the career that defines her.

Uncharted Grace (#12)
Caroline and Jedidiah must overcome their shattered pasts and buried secrets to find love in the village of Good Springs.

The Uncharted Beginnings Series
Embark on an unforgettable 1860s journey with the Founders as they discover the Land.

Aboard Providence (#1)
When Marian and Jonah's ship gets marooned on a mysterious uncharted island, they must build a settlement to survive. Love and adventure await!

Above Rubies (#2)
When schoolteacher Olivia needs the settlement elders' approval, she must hide her dyslexia from everyone, even charming carpenter Gabe.

All Things Beautiful (#3)
Henry is the last person Hannah wants reading her story… and the first person to awaken her heart.

Find out more on my website keelybrookekeith.com or feel free to email me at keely@keelykeith.com where I answer every message personally.

See you in the Land!
Keely

P.S. If you enjoyed this story, please consider leaving a review at your favorite online retailer.

ABOUT THE AUTHOR

Keely Brooke Keith is the author of the beloved Uncharted series. Her books are best described as inspirational frontier-style fiction with a futuristic twist.

Born in St. Joseph, Missouri, Keely was a tree-climbing, baseball-loving 80s kid. She grew up in a family who moved often, which fueled her dreams of faraway lands.

When she isn't writing, Keely enjoys gardening and is slowly learning how to not kill plants. Keely, her husband, and their daughter live on a hilltop south of Nashville, Tennessee. She is a member of ACFW.

Join Keely's email list at keelykeith.com/sign-up so you will always know when the next Uncharted book is available.

Made in the USA
Middletown, DE
05 October 2023

40234247R00163